The Shapewalker's Song

JH Tomen

ISBN: 978-0-578-66620-4
ISBN-13:

Dedication

To you, Dear Reader, for taking this journey with me. I'm so honored by your interest. Stories have always brought me solace and joy in life's struggles. I hope this book can give you even a fraction of what's been given to me. And if you ever feel called to write, please don't hesitate to share what's in your heart. All any of us can do is live in joy and see what shape we take.

To all my friends who gave me untold support; your interest and listening ears kept me going thousands of times. Thank you to Joe & Karl, you've cared about Sumi as long and as dearly as I have, and she wouldn't exist without you. You understand her heart and helped me keep my vision true. To Austin & Buddy, for being my valiant beta readers, I'm so humbled by the time you spent.

Life without friendship has no shape.

Cover & Map of Berill by Karl Nilsson (@sigvardnilsson)
Map of Wellonai by Jeremy DeBor (@jeremydeerboar)
Editing by A.K. Edits (@AdotKEdits)

et tui amóris in eis ignem accénde
renovábis fáciem terræ

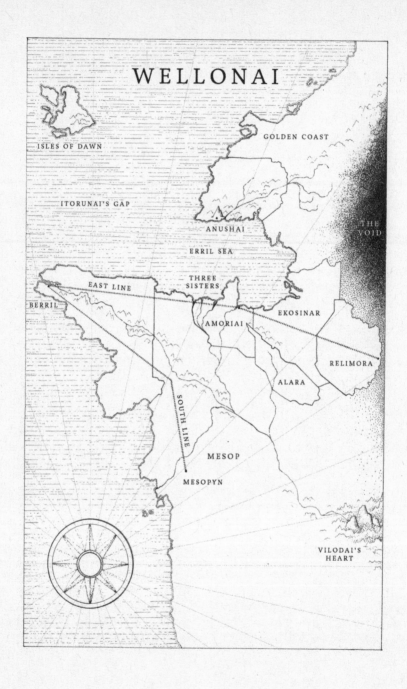

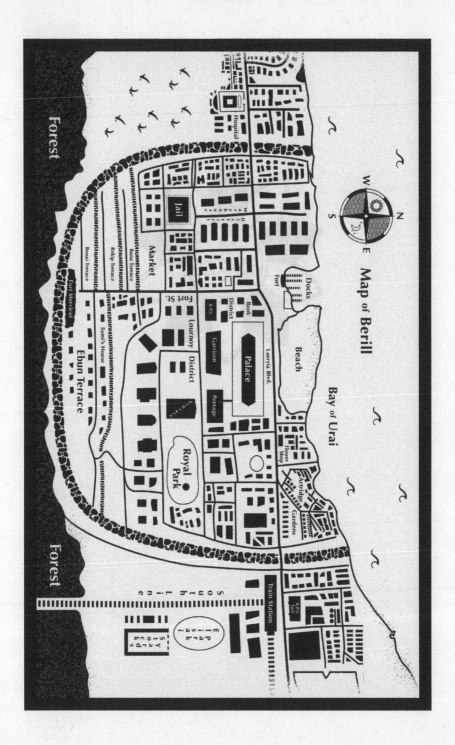

Prologue

Thirty-nine Years Ago

Essolurei stood on the bow of her ship, watching as it sailed into the bay. She could just make out Berill through the fog. The city seemed so much bigger than she could have ever imagined, its buildings sprawling along the coast and covering its steep hills. She closed her eyes, taking a deep breath. There was no turning back now.

She looked down at her necklace one last time, its sparkling green gem catching the light. She thought of her mother, who had given it to her, of everything they had lost. And her dear father… She took it by the chain and hid it under her blouse. That was the past now, and she had to stay focused on her future. She had already spent enough of her voyage obsessing over events long past. Though, that was probably natural enough, moving to an enemy kingdom as she was… The Battle of Strussfaran, the Treaty of Trilathdrei — all of that history already written; though if luck was on her side, none of it in stone.

She looked back at the horizon and smiled. It was time to seize the future she had chosen for herself. She was going to marry a wonderful man, and she would have a family of her own again. She would fight every day for the life she wanted, to build something no-one could take from her. It wasn't just her new home rising up on the horizon but that future itself, shining with promise and hers for the taking. Anushai was behind her now, and Berill was ahead, with nothing but memory and water between them.

1

If all hope was lost, then why did she still feel this yearning for a different life?

-Excerpt from The Borimol Plains

—:—

The clock struck six, the low chime ringing out like a dirge, finally signaling the long-overdue death of the work day. Sumi straightened in her seat, looking around and blushing as she realized she'd been daydreaming again. There was no-one to blush for, though; the flower shop was completely empty. The golden light of the evening sun had just started coming through the windows, lighting up dust motes that floated listlessly through the air.

She jumped up and smoothed her dress, shaking her head as she got ready to close up for the night. Even with no-one there, she shouldn't get sloppy. What if a customer had come in for a last-minute bunch of roses and caught her leaning on the counter in a daze? Mr. Furttenhur, the shop's owner, had done her enough kindnesses lately, and letting him down now would only make her feel worse. He'd let her have a whole week off when her grandmother died, splitting up her shifts with his daughters.

Her *grandmother*. Her shoulders slumped a little again at the thought. Her grandmother — Nela, as they'd called her, since she was from Anushai — had been like some giant sun, the unifying force around which her whole life had revolved. Without her, there was just a blank, an empty sky devoid of light. Sumi pulled a tiny notebook out of her dress pocket and scanned her to-do list for the day. She frowned — basically everything was crossed off; all she had left to do was some shopping on her way home.

She had been checking her list pathologically since Nela died, constantly feeling as if she'd forgotten something. Before, she'd always had a dozen things to do, all of it in service of the women's group. Her grandmother had started the charity early in her married life, and over time, it had taken on the role of feeding and nursing hundreds of people throughout the city — all done by their small brigade of volunteers.

It had always left her feeling like a tiny boat on Nela's ocean, dragged along since she was little, carrying parcels bigger than her body as they shuttled on and off the trolley. The woman had been equal parts inspiring and terrifying, barging her way into homes and kitchens across Berill to secure supplies for the less fortunate. Still, it was all she knew. After being orphaned at an early age — her mother to sickness, her father to the sea — her grandparents had been the only family left.

Of course, she'd found it all horribly frustrating when she was younger, never understanding why she couldn't play like the other girls. But with time, it had come to give her great solace. She'd been able to help so many girls that were just like her; orphans, sick and dirty, with no one to look out for them. And now that she was in her twenties, Nela's passion for helping seemed seared onto her heart. The only problem was, now that she was alone, her to-do list had shriveled to nothing...

She'd been ready to take over Nela's work, eager for some tiny way to carry on her legacy, however poorly. But at the funeral home, she had been cornered by the other women in the group. They'd surrounded her by the tea tray, coming in with their brooches and heavy perfume. They cooed in soft voices, patting her arms and consoling her as they dismantled her role in the organization.

"Leave it to us," they'd whispered, "we have everything in hand. Don't worry about a thing."

Then they'd picked apart the remnants of her grandmother's routes. Surely they'd thought they were helping her, unburdening her in her grief. But now, all she had was a void, an eager heart with none of Nela's ability, and an obsession with checking a to-do list that had nothing on it.

It made her feel helpless, torn between this yearning to help people and her complete lack of ability. Where Nela had been like a typhoon, blowing over opposition and inspiring everyone around her, she was just a mousy girl, more likely to run and hide than charge ahead. Before, Sumi could pretend it wasn't so. She could hand food to the widows and feel a connection to them, even if she'd never have the courage to forge it on her own. After all, it took a special kind of bravery to burst into someone's home and shower them with love they hadn't asked for, especially when they really needed it.

Sumi shook her head; if she kept losing herself in thought every five minutes, she'd never make it home! She began busying herself around the shop, removing the most valuable flowers from their tin buckets and placing them in the icebox in the back room. The ice block was getting small, though, so she made a mental note to order another for Mr. Furttenhur. Then she went back to the front of the store and began pulling down the window shades, the smooth tarpaulins pulling down from their rolls like maps in a schoolhouse.

Finally, after sweeping under each and every flower stand, she locked the cash register and slipped the key around her neck. She ducked into the employee room and put on her coat and hat, stopping for just a moment to look at herself in the tiny mirror. Turning her head, she poked at her bun, where it stuck out from behind the hat. She frowned; without Nela's fierce brushing, her hair was really becoming a mess. Tiny brown strands flew out in all directions as if keen on escaping her head altogether. She shrugged; there was really no sense in wasting time over a lost cause. She smoothed her dress again and nodded, heading out of the shop.

She locked the door, twisting the handle twice to make sure it held. The flower shop was on the second story above a bakery, and they had a small veranda outside. It was covered in flowers to draw in customers and had a wide iron staircase that lead down to the street. As she did every night, Sumi walked up to the railing of the veranda and looked out at the city, breathing in the sweet salt air from the harbor as the evening sun hit her face.

She opened her eyes, looking down at the bustling street below. The deathly quiet of the shop in the evening was completely out of step with the throng of people outside. Her city, Berill, was a commercial hub, always full of merchants and sailors coming and going. Even in bad times, it seemed the port kept them busy, easily the deepest on the western side of the Continent.

Her flower shop was on the northern edge of the city, nearer to the residential neighborhoods. So, every night, as the city's shops and warehouses closed down, thousands of people made their way down Laeryia Boulevard to their dinners and their beds. She watched the crowds as they passed, people of every age and class hurrying by. Some carried parcels under their arms, while others jogged to catch the trolley as it rumbled past. Even if she rarely spoke to anyone, she still thrived on the energy of all those people. The possibility of it all seemed so…infinite.

She looked up at the evening sky above her, where the light bounced off all the buildings. She took in all the glowing rooftops, losing herself in the bouquet of styles — copper, and tile, and everything in between. In some areas, as certain parts of the city had begun to electrify, there were tangled webs of wires running between the buildings. And beyond all the rooftops, she could just make out one shining spire of the palace sticking up over the neighborhood. The beauty of it all burrowed into the sadness of her heart, lifting her spirits and bringing a smile back to her lips.

Maybe it was strange that she could still find room to notice beautiful things in all this grief. The heroines in the novels she'd read growing up would wander the house like ghosts when their lovers left them, their whole world dulling to monochrome. For her, though, the pain and grief of losing Nela had somehow sharpened the colors of the world. Her grandparents had baked into her this relentless positivity, this constant yearning to look at something beautiful and notice the single star that was shining in an otherwise black sky. And even now, that beauty pulled at her.

Sometimes it hurt, of course, that voice in her head that told her to notice good things even when everything seemed bad. But after a lifetime of thinking that way, it felt like she needed that voice, too. She was desperate to believe that the world was good, even when it felt like it wasn't. And if she wasn't fighting to find joy in her life now, she was afraid that she would just…give up.

There was this tiny well of grief in her heart, dense and dark, and it took every ounce of her strength to keep it from becoming a flood that would sweep her away. So whether she felt like it or not, she still noticed the beautiful sky and the endless sea. It was the only thing she really had left of her grandparents, and at least, for a moment, it allowed her to leave her troubles behind.

As she continued staring at the rooftops, she caught sight of a clock across the street, her eyes popping open as she realized she'd already let a quarter of an hour pass. She had a long climb to the market, and if she didn't make it by seven, she might have nothing to eat. There was the garden behind the cottage, of course, but none of the fall plants would be ready yet. She threw her bag over her arm and scrambled down the stairs, slipping into the current of people rushing over the cobblestone streets.

The shop's little mercantile district was just off the coast, a stone's throw from the bay, and as Sumi dodged between the vendors and pedestrians, a strong breeze picked up. She took in another deep breath of sea air,

9

sighing it out in satisfaction. There were almost certainly worse-smelling jobs than sitting in a room with roses and tulips all day, but there was still nothing like the smell of the ocean after her shift.

As she turned onto the main road, she caught sight of the palace gates in the distance. Made of wrought iron, they soared above the street, their spikes glinting in the sun. Each length of fence had its own flag pole, the dark navy flags flapping in the constant breeze from the bay. Even from down the street, she could make out the imposing crest, the silver sea snake roiling through the center like a wave.

The Berillai had always been a seafaring people, their ancestors coming from the Isles of Dawn far off the western coast of the Continent. The histories always made them out to be fierce pirates, raiding the coast of Wellonai with a vengeance, but apparently, one day, they'd simply found the harbor in Berill and decided to stay. Why continue to steal the riches of the Continent when they could set up shop and call them their own? The Berillai didn't seem particularly fierce now, but even eight hundred years later, the royal house still maintained its connection to the sea.

Rather than being insulated inland like other palaces must be — not that she'd ever traveled — the Berillai rulers seemed most comfortable near the water, where the royal navy was always at hand. There was nothing between the palace and the beach but Laeryia Boulevard, and just west of that were the docks, lined with cannons and full of ships. The largest troop garrison in the city was actually south of the palace, as if the real danger would come from the forests and hills beyond the city.

Sumi waited for a trolley car to pass before dashing across the street. She always tried to walk along the south side of the boulevard on her way home, staring up at the shining marble palace through the gates. It wasn't like she coveted royal life — she wasn't one for ball gowns, after all — but she loved her city's landmarks, and this one was the crown. Its bronze turrets lit up like gemstones in the evening light, and the windows were so clean that it looked as if the beach had somehow crossed the street with her. Her spiritual practice of staring at buildings may have nothing to do with the gods, but when she really connected with her city, it felt as though even an orphan like her could belong.

After the palace, she finally reached Fort Street. While Laeryia Boulevard continued to trace the coast towards the old city wall, Fort Street went straight up the hill towards the market and the terrace districts where her cottage was. As she approached the intersection, she saw a trolley waiting at the station. If she could catch it, she might just make the grocer's in time!

She quickened her step, but as she reached the curb, the trolley dinged its bell. She ran, her boots clacking against the cobblestones. But before she reached the other side, the trolley pulled away. She thought about yelling after it, but the words wouldn't rise in her throat. If the trolley had to stop just for her...well, it was too mortifying to even consider. She stopped, leaning against a lamppost for a moment to catch her breath. If only Nela were there. *She* would have gotten the trolley to stop without thinking twice. *Of course*, Sumi thought, chuckling in spite of herself, *Nela also wouldn't have been running late in the first place.*

Sumi shrugged her bag back onto her shoulder and headed up the hill. It was just as well; she was probably out of trolley tokens. Money was getting tighter with her grandmother gone, and if the cost of a trolley ride could cover her vegetables, she might as well walk. She started the climb towards the market, breathing harder as she went. Fort Hill was the steepest in Berill, and the land rose up at an almost forty-degree angle. After fifteen minutes of climbing, she almost jumped for joy when she found the market's gates still open.

Despite the hour, Wembly Market seemed just as busy as it always was, teeming with people of all ages, the haggling of customers and the hawking of vendors rising in a constant hum. It was a chaotic mess, but she loved it more than any other place in the city. There were hundreds of strange things for sale from every kingdom on the Continent, and it was the kind of place where it didn't matter who you were, with rich and poor browsing the stalls together.

More importantly, the loneliness that always trailed her seemed to dissipate at the market. On a good day, she would say she was fairly good at talking to people, even if she was always terrified she'd say the wrong thing. Still, she seemed to be getting worse with age rather than better, and her life was shrinking around her without Nela to goad her into making friends. This place, however, gave her the perfect venue to interact without fear, smiling at the vendors and nodding along as they explained their produce.

She went through the gates, looking up at the building as she went west around the ring. Wembly was such an odd, lovely little place! It had originally been built as a bazaar for Berillai sheepherders, and it was still open to the air, its stone foundation built in an enormous oval shape with a skylight in the middle. The roof just covered the vendors, with each stall set up in what had originally been the sheep pens. They'd removed the paddocks long ago, but it still provided every shop with its own little cubby.

As she worked her way through the building, her eyes scanned for Mr.

Tellemuir. Tellemuir had been selling vegetables and bread here for some thirty years — and serving her family nearly as long. One winter, when his children were young, his oldest, Alip, had gotten terribly sick. Without the women's group, they might have gone bankrupt from the nursing bills alone. But Alip had recovered, and ever since, her family had always done their shopping with Mr. Tellemuir. They paid a fair price, of course, but they could at least avoid that horrible haggling that everyone seemed to insist on at Wembly.

As she approached Tellemuir's usual spot, she stopped dead in her tracks, realizing that Alip was manning the stall. That was the only downside of their connection with the Tellemuirs... As long as she'd known Alip, Nela had been trying to set the two of them up. Alip had adored her grandmother, of course — she'd nursed him herself as a boy, after all — but how could he ever do more than humor her? Sumi had always known exactly who he was dating, and she was leagues beneath him. He *was* fun to talk to, true, but none of that was enough to outweigh how embarrassing it was. It was just her luck that he'd be working on the day she ran out of food!

She took a deep breath, setting her jaw. If she ran away now, she wouldn't have anything to eat. And knowing herself, if she ran away from one social encounter, she'd likely never stop... She tried to ignore the fires that had lit in her cheeks and marched herself up to his stand. He was handing a squash to an older woman, but winked at her as he caught her out of the corner of his eye.

"Ho, Sumi!" he said, holding up a finger to another customer as he turned towards her. "Summer produce is almost over. You want the usual?"

"Yes, please," she said in an overly perky voice that hopefully sounded like someone who most definitely *wasn't* terrified of her grocer.

He nodded, taking her canvas bag. He helped the other woman quickly before moving around the stand and filling her order without needing to be reminded. When he was done, he handed it back and told her the price in a low voice — seven coppers.

Sumi furrowed her brow. "Seven coppers?" she whispered. "That's way too low! What about it being a quarter silver last week?"

"Bumper crop," he said, a sly smile gracing his lips, "huge haul right at the end of summer, just like always. Don't sweat it. You'll get the family discount with me, same as your grandmother, rest her soul."

She thought to refuse again, but simply nodded in thanks. She wouldn't deny him the chance to honor Nela.

"Thanks, Alip," she said, "you were always her favorite. Just make sure you come by the flower shop next time Erial has a birthday, so I can return the favor."

It was his turn to blush that time. He straightened up and scratched his head, trying to look anywhere but back at Sumi.

"I rightly appreciate that," he said, chuckling. "Maybe just don't tell my mom that I've switched from Perai to Erial; she's having a hard enough time getting me settled down as it is."

Sumi crossed her heart. "Your secret's safe with me," she said, flashing him a knowing smile. "Just remember, a dozen roses for three coppers, family discount." She put the bag over her shoulder and disappeared into the crowd before he could respond.

She left the market and started back up the hill. Before her eyes, the terrace districts rose out of the ground. Even knowing them as well as she did, they were imposing, the first retaining wall some fifteen feet high. Her grandfather had always said that the Berillai were more shepherd than pirate, and apparently, once they'd left the Isles of Dawn, sheep had quickly covered the lush Berillai coast. The only problem was, the farmers had needed somewhere to grow crops free of the hungry herds, so the terraces had been born — sprawling farms carved from the hills themselves.

The terraces were more garden than farm these days, though. After a few generations of expansion, there had finally been enough land for everyone, and now the terraces were covered with hundreds of little cottages just like theirs. The plots had grown smaller, but each one still had plenty of space for gardening. Their terrace, Ebun, was the highest, but they were all more or less the same. Even so, she'd actually heard a bunch of old men at last year's rose competition arguing over which terrace had the strongest foundation! She chuckled. She couldn't blame them, of course; it was impossible not to love your terrace, even if the others were just as lovely.

She absentmindedly took out one of the cucumbers she'd bought and crunched on the end of it as she walked. She climbed at a leisurely pace, stopping every block or two to glance in a shop window. As she moved higher, the cobblestone streets continued, but the shops ended, giving way to gardens with ash and oak trees that reached over the garden fences to shade the sidewalk.

She finally reached the first terrace, and as she passed under an especially low-hanging tree branch, a loud sound erupted overhead.

Mrowwwww.

She stopped and looked up, finding her cat Amis staring down at her, his yellow eyes glowing from where he hid amongst the leaves. He was fat and grey with a large splash of white on his chest, but he'd somehow wedged himself into the canopy.

"Amis!" Sumi called out. "We've talked about this. You shouldn't wait for me down here by the street, stay on the terrace where it's safe!"

Of course, that conversation had been typically one sided… The cat simply stood on his branch, stretched his back, and jumped down, landing on her shoulder. She braced for the impact, huffing out a lungful of air as she tried to hold onto her shopping.

"You're growing fatter by the day," she groaned. The cat had gorged alongside her on the food Nela's friends had sent after the funeral. It had been far too much for her to eat on her own, of course, but the extra she gave to Amis was clearly a double-edged sword… He meowed again, at the same volume but this time directly in her ear.

"Here, have this," she said offering him the end of her cucumber, which he began to gnaw on dutifully as she began walking again. "At least you're eating your vegetables. We just have to get you to not eat everything else in sight once you've had them…"

Sumi reached the last part of the hill, where the incline was the steepest, and she began to feel the strain of her burdens. She eyed the cat but let him keep his perch, marching on until she finally made it onto the flat ground of the terrace in front of Fort Merricut. She nodded at the fort — the old place waiting for her, as it did every night, it's dark, lichen-covered stone as old as Berill itself. Just like those pirate ancestors of theirs, the fort had been central to the war effort when Berill was founded, but all of that was hard to imagine now, surrounded by quaint cottages as it was.

She turned left at the top of the hill, following the long stretch of the old city wall into the terrace proper. Everywhere around her was the smell of flowers, with tidy fences running from one cottage to the next. The neighbors who were in their front gardens waved when they saw her, and a few of the local girls laughed, calling out to Amis when they saw him riding on her shoulder.

Finally, after a quarter-mile or so, Sumi reached her cottage gate and turned into the front garden. As soon as they crossed the threshold, Amis jumped off her shoulder and disappeared into the plants — off to hunt mice or whatever it was he did in his spare time. She wound her way along a brick path that cut through the thick mass of plants, breathing in deeply as the scent of flowers greeted her.

There were scores of hydrangeas, rows of foxglove, and sprays of lilies poking their elegant necks out above the rest. Almost all the cottages had heaps of flowers in the front, the tradition supposedly from the farming days, when they'd formed a fortress against the smell of manure. Now, though, as lovely as the gardens were, their main purpose seemed to be allowing the cut-throat grannies to enter the annual flower competition. Nela had been fairly adept herself, somehow using her usual typhoon-level force with something as delicate as plants, going so far as to win for her roses once or twice.

As Sumi passed, she ran her fingers gently across the leaves until she came across a few hydrangea heads that were starting to brown.

"I'm sorry," she said to them, frowning, "you should be in better hands."

Nela had spent a good part of her evenings tending the flowers, while she was barely managing with the vegetables in the back. The front garden likely wouldn't make it through another winter with her in charge, and she couldn't help but feel Nela's loss all the greater as her garden began to fade.

Sumi pulled out her key ring and unlocked the front door. It was a single piece of oak that had been installed by her great-grandfather, its face weathered from three generations of winters and terrace winds. Her grandfather had claimed that he and his father had cut the tree themselves in the forests beyond the city wall. With the tall tales he'd liked to tell, it was impossible to tell if it was true, but she still loved to picture him making the door when she touched the worn wood each evening.

The door opened up into a long breezeway that ran all the way from the front porch to the back garden. The walls of the hall were a clean whitewashed timber and were covered in memorabilia from generations of Elerairs: portraits, mirrors, and even one or two photographs hanging from every inch of flat surface. To her right, stairs lead up to a small landing that had two adjoining bedrooms. To her left was a sitting room, and in the back of the house was a kitchen that overlooked the garden. It wasn't a large cottage by any means, but it had been home for nearly all her life.

Sumi put down her bags on a table by the door. She needed to start dinner, but she found herself drawn to a photograph of her grandmother in the middle of the wall. Since they'd only just built the picture studio in Eastport, it was fairly recent, and Nela looked exactly as Sumi remembered her. Despite the urgings of the photographer to look more stoic, she had been intent on smiling in the photo, and she had a wide, toothy grin. Her white hair was a thick mop of curls, and she was wearing her favorite black dress with the pearls from her wedding day.

"Nela," she whispered, sighing as she reached out to the photograph, running her finger along the outline of her grandmother's face. She stared into those eyes for so long that it almost felt like Nela was right there with her.

Sumi stood there for a long time, until the sun cut right through the breezeway, lighting up the walls and mirrors in golden light. She shielded her eyes with her hand, blinking in the glow. Sunset already?! With nighttime coming so early, it wouldn't be long until winter. She left the photo and drifted towards the back of the house, eager to catch the sun setting on the bay. Once winter came, it would be dark well before her shift was over, and she wouldn't catch another until spring.

She went quickly through the kitchen and out the back door. There was about forty feet of soil and grass before the yard ended in a wooden fence just at the edge of the terrace cliff. Sumi stepped over a short rabbit fence and into the garden, weaving between rows of budding squash and kale until she reached the edge, leaning against the waist-high fence as she stared out at the city beyond.

From Ebun, there was nothing blocking her view of the water, only rooftops, trees, and finally, the bay. She would never tire of this view! Even with the commute, being at the top of the city felt like flying. She could see the curve of the land as it wrapped around the Bay of Urai, the water glistening in the evening sun before giving way to land on the other side. The mountains there stretched towards the sky, the dark patches of forest blending with the slate grey of the water below.

She sighed out, leaning her full weight onto the fence. Looking out at her city felt like staring at the face of a lifelong spouse: each nook and cranny no longer a mystery but still brimming with the love and affection that could only be earned through time spent. As she finally settled her eyes on the water to wait for sunset, her memories returned to Nela. Determined to end the day with a happy memory, her mind wandered over all the moments they had spent in the garden together. She smiled, suddenly remembering her first birthday in the cottage.

Sumi had been turning six. Nela had wished her a happy birthday when she woke up, but nothing else from their normal schedule had changed. They packed up a dozen different parcels and walked out into the city, making delivery after delivery to the families on their route. Disappointment had swirled inside her like a storm, though even at six years old, she was too scared to throw an outright tantrum. As soon as she had moved into her grandparents' house, she'd become as quiet as a mouse, convinced that if she wasn't the perfect child, she'd be out on the street like so many other orphans. Still, she was too let down to hide her feelings entirely. They hadn't been well off, but her mother had always made her birthdays into something special.

So she had dragged her feet across the city. She dropped packages repeatedly, sighing loudly every chance she got. Nela had said nothing, simply keeping on her route, leaving Sumi to run behind her to catch up each time she realized her disruptions went unnoticed. Her birthday was in the middle of winter, and by the time they returned home that day, her cheeks were red from the cold and the tears that had started to streak down her face.

When they finally turned into the garden, Nela had handed her one last parcel, asking her to take it to the back garden. Sumi had wandered around the side of the house, looking down, kicking the frozen stubs of plants as she barely kept hold of the package. But as she reached the garden, a roar of voices erupted, and she looked up to find a dozen of their neighborhood friends circled around a giant bonfire. Kids from the terrace ran around the garden, and Nela was just emerging from the cottage with a giant cake in her arms. Even now, she didn't know when Nela had found the time to bake it.

All of the details came rushing back: the taste of the cake, the laughter of her friends, the crackle of the bonfire. But more than anything, she would always remember Nela's face that day, her cheeks red and smiling as she stood across the garden table and told her to make a wish. As Sumi stood there, awash in memories, the sun touched down onto the bay. There was a loud pop and suddenly, a bright flash filled her eyes with light.

Sumi stood there, blinking, the sun spilling out across the water. Sometimes there was a green flash when the sun hit the horizon, but that had been brighter than any she'd ever seen. And what was that popping noise? Did a trolley engine misfire on its way up the hill? She leaned against the fence, peering below, but Fort Street was quiet. She shook her head, turning towards the house to start dinner.

On her way back across the garden, Amis emerged from behind some bushes and ran up to her, nuzzling her legs and meowing. He would probably be wanting his dinner as well. She reached the rabbit fence, but it seemed...taller than it had on her way out.

"That's strange," she muttered to herself, struggling to step over it.

As she entered the house, she remembered the shopping and started down the corridor to get it. As she passed the mirror, she glanced into it and saw Nela's face looking back out at her. Sumi screamed, jumping backwards. She tripped on her skirt and fell back, hitting her head on the staircase as everything went black.

Sumi groaned, coming to on the floor. She squeezed her eyelids closed and reached up, rubbing the back of her head. She felt Amis brush up against her, meowing and licking her face. She opened her eyes and looked up at the ceiling, the last bit of sunlight filtering through the back door.

"What had that been?" she asked herself. "I must be so sick with missing Nela that I'm…what, seeing things?"

She rolled over with another groan, struggling to sit up. She planted one hand on the floor and pushed herself upright. But as she did so, she caught sight of her hand. It was gnarled and wrinkled and covered in liver spots. She squeaked again in fear, jerking her hand up and away from that ghostly claw. But the hand was hers, and as she snatched it off the floor, she fell back down with a thud.

Sumi rolled into a ball, closing her eyes and grabbing her knees as she rocked back and forth, her heart racing.

"This is a bad dream," she said, "it's nothing but a bad dream."

Eventually, she stopped rocking, carefully cracking an eye open. Nothing had changed in the hallway, and she was still on the floor. Amis sat a few feet away from her, eyeing her with his head tilted. Afraid to look again, she reached her right hand over her left and gave herself a hard pinch. Still, nothing changed. If this was a dream, she was having a hard time waking up…

She clamped her eyes shut again and began muttering to herself. "I want to be myself. I just want to be myself."

There was another loud pop and a bright flash of light lit up her eyelids. She opened her eyes and sat up quickly, looking for the source of the sound, but there was nothing there. She looked down at her hands and found them normal again.

She breathed a sigh of relief. "I'm just tired," she said without much conviction.

She peered at the hallway around her, the light quickly disappearing from the darkened cottage. Had she seen a ghost? Nela would be a good ghost, wouldn't she?

"Nela…" she whispered to the empty hallway. "If that is you…I miss you."

She sat there for a while, listening and looking, but everything was still. She put one hand in front of her face and stared at it in the dying light. If it had only been an image in the mirror, then maybe it could be a ghost, but what about that hand? Had that really been her hand looking like an old woman's?

She thought of the bedtime stories Nela had told her growing up. Her favorites had been about the Shapewalkers, beings that could transform into anything they wanted. Other children made them out to be terrifying creatures that would slip out on dark nights to terrorize the kingdom, but in Nela's stories, they had always seemed thrilling and heroic. Especially when she was young, she'd always daydreamed about their magic, eager to change out of her own skin for once.

"Foolish," she muttered to herself. Those were childhood fancies. Shapewalkers were no realer than ghosts and certainly not a power that would belong to some mousy girl like her.

Sumi smacked herself lightly on the cheek, trying to snap herself out of it. She stood and picked up the bag of vegetables before moving to the kitchen, lighting the oil lamp by the stove. Focusing on busying her hands helped: chopping, boiling, stirring. The familiar rhythm of the kitchen began to soothe her weary mind. Finally, as it grew completely dark outside, the warm glow of the oil lamp began to make it all feel like some strange dream.

That sense of calm helped her get through the cooking. She even started to hum as she filled Amis' bowl with food. But as she slid her own meal onto a plate, her calm evaporated. She mindlessly spooned food into her mouth, the flavor lost to her as she thought. She relived her whole day, trying to find the break in the thread, the moment when she could have possibly fallen asleep and started dreaming. Or even more terrifying, the part of the day where she had lost her grip enough to start seeing things…

She hoped that doing the dishes would provide another brief refuge, but she could hardly focus. At one point, she even dropped Amis' bowl, wincing as the dish hit the stone sink. Thankfully, it didn't break, and she breathed a sigh of relief, squeezing her temples as she leaned on the counter.

Busy. She had to stay busy. She started cleaning the sitting room — something she only did once a month if that. She brushed Amis, getting a few angry meows from him. She even poked her head out the back door to do some gardening but realized it was too dark to do much good. Finally, she settled on knitting, something her grandmother had taught her. She wasn't great at looping the yarn, but Nela had always sworn it could calm you. Sure enough, she finally lost herself in the counting of threads and the clicking of needles.

Eventually, her eyes grew tired, and she had to blink longer between each row in her knitting. Reluctantly, she took the oil lamp back to the kitchen and swapped it out for her bedside candle. She slowly climbed the creaking old stairs, avoiding the dark cavern of Nela's abandoned bedroom as she tiptoed to her own. She climbed into bed, wanting to keep the candle lit all night but knowing she couldn't afford the wax. So she blew it out and lay there in the dark, listening to the silence of the house. The wind from the bay gently passing by caressed the cottage and all the little plants around it. She waited for sleep to come for a long time. She kept thinking of Nela, trying to think of happy memories, ignoring the creeping thoughts of the mirror below.

2

Who but the Berillai can read the wind or hear the stones? We are of the gods, and may all men tremble at our passing!
                    -Excerpt from the Poems of Boran Stonekeeper
                          —:—

Erso banged hard on the door with the butt of his fist. After a minute, there was no answer, so he knocked again as hard as he could. He looked over his shoulder. The street was quiet and dark, but it wouldn't be for long. The police couldn't be far behind him; he'd only just made it from their headquarters himself. He was trying to warn these bloody fools, but if they didn't open the damned door there wouldn't be much of a warning to give.

He lifted his hand to knock again when the door opened just a crack. No light emitted from inside but he could just make out an eye peering out at him.

"What?" a gruff voice asked.

"Here to see the boss," Erso said, leaning with one hand on his cane and trying to act like he wasn't in a hurry. "He didn't tell you to expect me?"

"Who's me?" the voice asked. "Boss said to snap the neck of whoever's bangin' on the door and get back."

Erso chuckled. "No, no, he'll want to see me, trust me. We're old friends — the name's Erso." He reached into his pocket and held out a card. The unexpected usually had a way of disarming men who wanted to punch you, and offering name cards outside of dingy thieving dens was decidedly…unorthodox. Nothing happened for a moment, but finally, a beefy arm covered in tattoos reached out and snatched the card. The man slammed the door behind him, leaving Erso standing in the alley again.

"Come on, come on, come on," he whispered to himself while he waited, looking over his shoulder at the street. He craned his neck, angling his ear to the sky, but he still didn't hear anyone approaching.

Finally, he heard footsteps again before the door wrenched all the way open. This time, the man held a lantern, and Erso was forced to tilt his head to take in the man's size. He was easily two heads taller than Erso, and his neck was weirdly similar in diameter to his chest. His head was shaved bald and he had another tattoo that ran from his forehead up the center of his skull. At least Aelibis hadn't had any trouble hiring the right men for the job... Erso smiled, giving the man a wink.

"Told you he'd want to see me," he said.

The man grunted, cocking his head towards the hallway behind him. "Just be quick," he said, standing aside so Erso could enter. The man slammed the door shut again and put a thick board onto a rack, sealing it shut.

That'll never hold, Erso thought as he followed the man down the hallway.

The building was squat and dark, the small circle of light from the lantern revealing plaster walls covered in dirt and mold. The sagging floorboards creaked under the thug's weight as they continued down the corridor. He probably hadn't been hired for his witty repartee, but Erso tried him anyway.

"So," Erso said to the back of the man's head, "you know my name now, what's yours?"

"Kit," the man said with a grunt, not bothering to look behind him.

"Nice name," Erso said, "you got a surname, Kit?"

"Don't need one," Kit said.

"No, I suppose you wouldn't in your line of work..." Erso said absentmindedly as he stepped over a dead rat. "This is a lovely hideout, though. Did your boss pick it or did you all vote?"

Kit said nothing. Erso shrugged. Maybe it was time to change his tactics. He must have had dozens of chats just like this with tough men in tough surroundings. They seldom if ever responded. If he didn't know any better, he was going to start blaming himself... These little talks weren't strictly necessary for his work, of course, but it hurt a man's pride to have so many one-sided conversations. Did it violate the universal tough man code to gab during criminal proceedings? Still, Erso had to entertain himself somehow. The first time you stepped into a thieving den it scared you a bit. The hundredth time, they all started to look the same.

They rounded a corner, revealing a set of stairs that led deeper into the darkness. Kit started down without hesitation, so Erso followed. The stairs were steep, running down some twenty feet before ending at another thick wooden door. There was light filtering from beneath the frame along with the steady hum of voices. Kit knocked in a pattern, two light knocks close together with a louder knock at the end.

The door opened immediately, and Erso followed Kit into a small storage room filled with wooden crates. Most of the crates were covered with thick burlap cloths, but some were open, revealing an assortment of valuables nestled in hay. There were ten men in the room, all more or less the same shape and size of Kit, with the exception of one man in the center of the group. He had a thick black beard and a coif of unkempt hair that was in direct contrast with his bald associates. That had to be Aelibis. Erso hadn't gotten to see his real face the first time they met, but he felt an invisible energy coming from him, marking the man as a Shapewalker. Aelibis spoke first, his hands on his hips and a glare in his eye.

"I told you already, I'm not interested," he said, turning to his men. "This clown thought to give us lessons at our own game, can you believe that?"

The men all roared with laughter, slapping their knees and drumming on the wooden boxes.

One of the men wiped tears from his eyes. "He looks like a proper dandy boss, was he gonna give you tap-dance lessons or something?"

The men thought that bit was pretty good too, another burst of laughter bouncing off the walls of the confined space.

Erso smiled, walking closer to the group. He was a good sport; he could take a joke. He stopped about five feet away from Aelibis, leaning casually against one of the crates. A nice casual lean was essential to appearing like a easygoing bloke. If people didn't find you threatening, they either thought you congenial or underestimated you. He could work with either, so he made sure to adjust his posture whenever he could.

"Listen gents," Erso said, "first thing's first. Tap dancing is a lot harder than it looks, and I, for one, am offended that you don't find that kind of thing valuable." He stood and tapped out a few steps that his mother had taught him growing up, his shoes clicking on the brick floor. The men just stood there staring at him.

"Well," he continued, "I'll get right to it then. I offered your boss my help with your little scam here cause I'm a nice guy. I didn't want you all to get caught, but now the police are on their way over here. And I am back, *again*, despite my better judgment as a show of good will to suggest to you all that you run. Now."

"I told you," Aelibis said, "we're fine just as we are. I don't know what your game is, but we aren't cutting you in on our loot just because you keep nosing around. Now tap your way back up those stairs before my friends get blood on your pretty coat."

The men laughed again and Erso shook his head, rubbing his temples. Why were other Shapewalkers always so bloody hard to convince? The police certainly didn't refuse backup when they came with three dozen men to kill their kind. You'd think that criminals would be more amenable to sound advice, doing dangerous work and all that.

"Here's the thing," Erso said, "you *do* need my help. If you were doing things properly, like I suggested two weeks ago, the police wouldn't even know about you." He looked around at the crowd of thugs behind Aelibis. "Maybe you all should be asking more questions about this scam you're running. I take it he hasn't told you how he gets into those warehouses you're robbing?"

The laughter died, and more than a few knuckles cracked in the silence. One man stepped off the box he was sitting on and spat on the ground at Erso's feet.

"Unless you're a copper yourself," the man asked, "how would you know the coppers is coming?"

Erso pulled out his pocket watch and looked at the time with a grimace. He had done enough talking — it was time for a demonstration. He generally tried to avoid showing off his powers in front of witnesses, but these fools clearly needed a push.

He looked up at the looming thug, holding the mans gaze. "I happen to know what the police are doing, because just like your boss, I happen to be fairly good at sneaking around. You see, I can look like anybody — a copper if I need to, or even someone you lot would know."

Erso stood up tall and closed his eyes. A quiet hum filled his ears as he began to glow. Even in the stuffy basement, it felt like there was a shift in the air. When he opened his eyes, he had been transformed into Aelibis, complete with black beard and dingy wool trousers. Whispers flew around the group, and the man who had spat on the ground was backing into the closest crate as if he meant to merge with it. Erso made out the word 'Shapewalker' moving around the group at a whisper.

Erso smiled with Aelibis' face. When he spoke, he found his voice was deeper, a perfect match for their boss.

"Good, gents," Erso said, "glad I got your attention. As you may or may not know, in this fine city, being a Shapewalker is more illegal than the rest of your activities combined. I'm not here to spoil the fun, but the police are on their way over here with a squad big enough to swallow your crew whole. I'm not an expert in thieving or anything, but I would suggest you get ready to leave."

No one moved. Aelibis narrowed his eyes, staring at his own face. Erso looked back calmly. He'd done all he could to convince them, it was their choice now to live or die. Finally, the real Aelibis nodded.

"Start packing boys," he said.

Just then, there was a loud bang upstairs.

"Time's up friends," Erso said. "Better hope there's a back door here."

There was another loud bang followed by the sharp cracking of wood. That would be the front door gone. Police whistles started to sound as a stampede of feet stomped on the floor above. The thugs flew into action, some grabbing clubs and running towards the stairs while others grabbed crowbars and ran to the boxes on the edge of the room, hoping to make off with the best of the loot.

Erso took a bow, though no-one was watching.

"That'll be my cue then," he said. "Can't say I didn't try." He began to glow again, and as the basement door flew open under the force of a battering ram, Erso appeared on the floor in the shape of a rat. He ran towards the corner of the room as chaos poured down the stairs. Policemen just as beefy as the thugs began to do battle with nightsticks. There were legs and feet everywhere, threatening to step on the rat that no-one noticed. Erso dodged to and fro, scampering as quickly as he could. He had spotted a hole in one of the walls on his way in, and with luck, that would be his way out.

Above him, a nightstick collided against a skull with a sickening crack. Erso scurried, his tiny heart beating furiously as he slid out from under a collapsing body. He swerved, dodging a policeman's boot, finally making it to the edge of the room. He took one last look back, but Aelibis was nowhere to be found. Hopefully he had escaped for now, though his freedom would be short-lived if Erso couldn't talk some sense into him. He shook his head, disappearing into the hole in the wall.

Just as he'd hoped, there was a two-inch gap between the walls with a knot of rusty pipes that worked their way upwards. He jumped on the lowest one, scrambling along it with his paws. He climbed for a time, the pipe seeming more like a mountain at the scale of a rat. Finally, he reached the ceiling and squeezed through another hole, emerging onto the roof.

He pricked his ears and listened. There was a tumult on the street down below now, police wagons pulling up along every curb, the shouts of men still sounding out in the night. Erso scurried to the other side of the roof, crossing to another building on a broken gutter. There, he found some electric wires, and scrambled up, following them like train tracks away from the crime scene.

Once he was a safe distance away, he climbed down onto another rooftop and paused to catch his breath, his tiny rat lungs struggling to fill with the cold night air. When his heart finally slowed, he closed his eyes and glowed again, returning to his original form.

He patted himself down, lifting his hat and running a hand through his hair. Then he smoothed his mustache, making sure it was straight. But of course it was. Transforming back into your original form was better than a bath. You could start from scratch and put everything back the way you liked it, no fuss. He walked up to the edge of the rooftop and looked out across Berill.

"Beautiful city," he said, "but it'll be the death of me."

He ought to leave. Aelibis was probably a lost cause at this point. With zero training, it wouldn't be long before the police were on him again. Even worse, Aelibis would probably grow desperate and use his powers to survive, giving the police exactly what they needed to be on his trail. Erso shook his head, pressing at his temples. It was madness to stay in a place this dangerous, but still didn't sit right.

On his way to the hideout, he could have sworn he'd sensed another transformation. Was it another Shapewalker or just the echo of Aelibis in his mind? It was rare enough to find any novices still alive in a place like this, but two in one trip? That was certainly tempting, even in a nightmare of a kingdom like Berill. He nodded to himself. Even if he was dancing in the serpent's jaws, saving just one life from the Berillai would be worth it. He would wait for now, and he would watch, and then, with any luck, he could be done with this kingdom forever.

3

Huge thunderclouds gathered in the distance, their dark shadows rising up like castles in the air. Vorseyai idly fingered her moonstone necklace, sighing as she thought of her mother. It still shocked her that her mother had died. She hadn't thought that anyone on her mother's side of the family was even capable of an act as frivolous as dying.

-*Excerpt from **The Borimol Plains***

—:—

As soon as the first ray of sunlight crept over the mountains, roosters all along the terrace began to crow, jerking Sumi out of her shallow sleep. She woke in a heap, twisted like a pretzel, with one arm over her face and drool covering her cheek. She groaned; it felt like she had only just drifted off. She remembered vaguely dreaming of Nela, but the dreams were already fading. Like so many mornings since the funeral, in that moment between sleeping and waking, she could feel Nela's presence, like she was just in the other room. If only she could hold onto that dream a little longer…

She lay there like that for a time, hoping that if she didn't move, the world wouldn't notice her in her hiding place. Still, she'd be kidding herself if she thought she could go back to sleep. Too many years with her grandparents had trained her to distrust the comfort of bed after dawn. Grandpa had been the worst one to catch you sleeping. After his stint in the navy, he could never let go of the virtues of rising early, and even worse, his sense of humor meant that his 'wake ups' were most often pranks. Like the time he'd poured water on her head… Not a lot of water, of course, but enough to scare her straight.

Sumi finally rolled onto her back and blinked her eyes open. At least she didn't feel afraid anymore. Every shadow that held a boogeyman just hours earlier had dissipated in the blue glow of morning. The house was just a house again.

"You just got too tired," she said to herself. "Today is a new day."

She took a deep breath and stretched before pushing herself to a seated position. There wouldn't be much time to waste getting ready. If she wanted to be at the bank by noon for Nela's will reading, that would mean getting to work early. She had avoided that dreaded place as long as she could, but after that letter they'd sent the week before, she clearly couldn't put it off any longer. If only she could get a single smile from those wretched bankers! They seemed to consist entirely of judgmental sighs and fancy spectacles. Even passing by the building made her break out into a sweat, and their meager savings only filled her with more shame when she did have to go there.

Mr. Furttenhur wouldn't mind her taking an hour off, of course — on more than one occasion, he'd even told her she was like one of his daughters. After ten years working together, his trust made sense, but it was precisely that kind of trust that filled her with dread, making her want to work twice as hard. There was nothing more terrifying than the thought that she would eventually slip, letting him down and revealing that she hadn't been worthy of it after all.

Sumi walked quickly across the floor, her mind already focused on the day ahead. But as she reached the bedroom door, she froze, her thoughts suddenly back on the night before. She undid the lock and slowly turned the handle, wincing as the hinges creaked. When it was open just a crack, she peered out at the landing, breathing a sigh of relief. In the dark, Nela's room had been a terrifying cavern, but in the light of day, it too was just a normal room again.

She tiptoed across the landing and stood in Nela's doorway. Everything was just as she had left it after the funeral: the bed made, the lace wedding shawl draped across the quilt, and the window unshaded and glowing with morning light. It smelled of her still, even after several weeks, though less strongly than before. She reached for Nela's perfume on the table by the door, spritzing the air twice and nodding in satisfaction as she breathed in the mature spice. She was tempted to buy another bottle, anything to keep up the charade, but it was imported from Anushai, and she'd almost certainly regret it. Still, for now, at least, she had two-thirds of a bottle, and plenty of time to pretend.

Sumi walked to the water table between the two bedrooms and splashed some water onto her face. The nights were starting to grow colder and the water was cool to the touch, but there just wasn't time to heat the stove downstairs. She smoothed her hair and carefully began applying her makeup — not that it would make a dent in the rock-hard shell of the bankers. She'd tried it all with them, every type of fashion and hairstyle, and they still looked at her like a bug worth squashing. Sometimes, it even seemed to make things worse. She winced, thinking of the time she'd worn that rouge from a magazine… It was just as well, really; a girl like her did better by hiding behind her makeup anyway.

On her way down to the kitchen, Sumi caught a glimpse of the clock and sped her steps. It didn't even matter that she was almost never late, the ticking of the clock always filled her with dread. Just like waking up early, growing up with a navy man would do that to you. Grandpa had always sworn that the measure of a man was the measure of minutes and seconds.

"Let the clock slip at sea," he'd always say, "and it's not just missed dinner — it's death on a rocky shore!"

And so, even when she had all the time in the world, she hurried. Or at least…she used to, before Nela died. More often than not lately, she seemed to drift through her mornings as if she hadn't woken up in the first place. But she refused to get sucked into her daydreams today! She whirled into the kitchen like a storm off the bay, flinging open the door to the root cellar with a bang, waking a sleeping Amis from his perch on the windowsill. She heard his meow from above as she stepped down into the dark stairwell. She didn't waste time with a candle, instead reaching out from memory as she grabbed a hunk of cheese and a jar of apples. As she came back up, Amis was already at her ankles, looking for his own breakfast.

"I know, I know," Sumi said, clucking at him with her tongue, "if anybody gets to eat on a morning like this, it's you."

She walked quickly to the front door and opened it, finding two bottles of milk. She slapped her forehead. That was the third week in a row she'd forgotten to write to the milk company. If she kept ordering for three, Amis would have to start bathing in the stuff! She leaned her head against the doorframe and closed her eyes, calculating how much she'd lose on milk that week alone. It was becoming a struggle to match the mounting costs with her pay from the flower shop.

"I don't have time for this!" she blurted out, throwing her hands up. As she walked back to the kitchen, she gave Amis a wink. "Extra milk for you, at least."

She filled Amis' saucer to the brim and placed it outside before scooting him through the door. Then she turned back to the butcher's block, dropping some of the cheese and apples onto a hunk of stale bread. She stood in the kitchen as she chewed the meager breakfast, eyeing the tea pot with pointless longing.

When she was only halfway through her bread, the clock in the hallway chimed. She threw the rest in wax cloth before stuffing it in her bag and bolting towards the door. It hadn't made a great breakfast, and a few more hours wouldn't make it a better lunch, but like the saying went, shepherds didn't ask why they had wool sheets.

She threw on her shawl and burst out of the cottage, almost running down the terrace. But as she reached Fort Street, she still forced herself to stop, taking a deep breath and nodding to the fort before turning away. Just another strange tradition of hers, of course — who nodded to a fort? — but with her family gone, it felt...vital. Since her people didn't believe in graves, those old stones were all she had. If they remembered the generations of Elerairs that had passed, maybe they'd remember her too when she was finally snatched away.

She laughed as she walked down the hill, suddenly remembering another one of Grandpa's sayings. Could she even make it ten feet in this city without thinking of one?! Whenever they'd walk past Fort Merricut together, he'd always say the same thing—

"You know, Sumi, we're lucky we live by the fort, makes us tough! You know what they say — 'arrowheads in the garden means steel in the gut.'"

If having a million sayings made you tough, then her family would win first place. Though that particular saying did always make her wonder — were the terraces really that dangerous back then? The fort *had* been essential to the kingdom's founding, but that was more than eight hundred years ago! The way the histories talked about those early battles, though, it must have been harrowing.

They'd been fighting the Mesop then, which was hard enough to picture in its own right. She'd seen the pictures of Terrai — the capital they had in the south — and it seemed almost quaint now, with beautiful fields stretching out in every direction. But back then, they'd been traveling herdsmen or something, hadn't they? According to the histories, their tribes had covered the entire southern half of the Continent. They'd fought the Berillai in skirmishes when they took the port, but it had taken a full year for the word to spread as the rest of the Mesop assembled for years of brutal war, the Berillai building the fort as they clung to the land.

She shook her head, chuckling. The war sounded awful, of course, but it would be just like Grandpa to try and insert their family into that story. Supposedly, only poor farmers had moved to the terraces then, facing storms of arrows for a deal on the land. Still, if that was what it took to make their family tough — to make the whole kingdom strong — she'd take it. Steel in the gut or not, she'd be facing her own army of bankers today, and she'd need every ounce of strength she could get.

When she finally reached the shop, Sumi was out of breath, the cold of the morning long since banished by the flush of her cheeks. She took the stairs two at a time, stopping for just a moment to smooth her dress. The little chimes above the door tinkled as she opened the door, slipping inside. Mr. Furttenhur was at the desk, his half-moon glasses low over his nose as he inspected the books. He didn't look up as she entered, frowning at the accounting.

"Good morning, Mr. Furttenhur," she said with a smile as she took off her coat. He didn't look up, and she was left standing there, wringing her hands. She needed to get into the break room to change, but after last time... Well, suffice it to say, Mr. Furttenhur might not survive being startled again. Finally, she reached behind her and shook the door knob.

As the chimes rang again, he looked up, taking off his glasses and wiping his brow with his handkerchief.

"Ah, good morning Sumi," he said. He stood, but stopped, narrowing his eyes at her. "A yellow cat only drinks its mother's milk—"

"—every other Queen's Day," she replied, adding her part.

At that, he finally relaxed, smiling as he came around the desk. She'd never met anyone as proper as Mr. Furttenhur. Sometimes, when they were busy, he'd skip the formal greeting, but when he did, he never really seemed to relax.

"Well," he said, "lot's to do; I'm glad you're here. Put down your coat and I'll show you what needs arranging."

Sumi nodded and slipped into the back room, hanging up her coat before tying on her apron. As she fixed her hair in the mirror, she thought about Mr. Furttenhur's phrase. It was such an odd one! Plenty of people had the secret phrases, of course — it was one of Berill's oldest traditions — but why the yellow cat and the milk? It was an odd choice for such a straight-laced man. Most people just used some inside joke — if they bothered at all — but Mr. Furttenhur's was more like a riddle.

Sumi chuckled; Nela would have chided her for thinking about Mr. Furttenhur's phrase for so many years without bothering to ask. "My granddaughter the otter," she always liked to say, "never asking nothing." Her metaphors were admittedly...abstract, translated haphazardly into Berillai, but that had to be the oddest one. Still, it took years of Nela calling her an otter before she finally took her advice and asked what it meant.

31

"You're all underwater," she'd answered, "head...stick out, only climb out to eat." Then she had poked Sumi on the side of her head. "It means your thoughts all *inside*."

At least otters were cute... She stepped out of the back room with a smile on her face. She hurried over to the window, and Mr. Furttenhur started walking her through what he wanted with the extra daffodils. She got to work quickly after that, trying to find the impossible balance between speed and perfection. She still didn't ask him about his passphrase, but at least she had another memory to keep her company.

———

Three hours later, Sumi ran back down the stairs, already late for her appointment at the bank. Even with one eye on the clock, she'd still worked on the displays well past when she should have left. But as Grandpa always said, "a mast half-hung will only spin the ship." Still, as she walked past the shop, she couldn't help but look up at the window and smile at how good the flowers looked. Even if she hadn't been thinking of Mr. Furttenhur, those daffodils were a better use of her time than those miserable bankers! At least this way someone might smile for her efforts...

She hurried west down Laeryia Boulevard. The bank, Naval Maritime, was just past the palace on the north side of the Royal Police. It was far too prime a location for her measly account, even if Grandpa's service had given them the right to bank there. It was arguably even a little too nice for the sailors, but if anything, it was a throne for the bankers. As Grandpa always said, "a woman in the palace wears a crown, but the bankers are the real kings."

As she passed the palace, there was a changing of the guard happening. She really didn't have time to stop, but her feet slowed of their own accord. She'd loved watching the ceremony as a girl, but it never lined up with work. She couldn't miss this one! What were the bankers going to do anyway, give the cottage to the cat? She turned, leaning against the fence. One of the guards eyed her, but a few others had paused too, staring at the ceremony.

The guards, some hundred in all, stood in two long rows across from each other in front of the palace. The guards whose shift was ending stepped forward, removing their swords and holding them up in the air. The new guards raised their right arms, pulling down their sleeves to reveal their tattoos. Their mouths moved inaudibly, each man whispering a phrase that only their counterpart would know. As they finished, the soldiers with the swords knelt, raising the weapons above

32

their heads for the other men to take.

As the ceremony ended and the guards marched back to the garrison, Sumi finally tore herself away at a jog with a wide smile on her face. Angry bankers or not, stolen time like this was precious. She ran until she reached the steps of the bank, pausing for one last moment to look up at the building. It took up an entire corner of Fort Street, its limestone walls running all the way around and three stories up. At the top was a giant statue of the Angel of the Sea, her radiant staff held high and her gaze towards the water.

A man with a briefcase pushed past her, grumbling to himself. Perhaps she'd pushed her luck a little far... She shook her head, chuckling as she scurried behind him into the bank. As the heavy door closed behind her, it was like she'd stepped into another world. The thick glazed windows kept the bank in a permanent dusk, and the bankers were huddled in small pockets of desks lit by gold-plated electric lamps. Secretaries dashed about delivering paperwork, and a line of navy officers stood by the main counter, waiting to deposit at-sea pay.

Sumi sucked in a deep breath, standing as tall as she could before walking down onto the main floor. She quickly scanned the rows of desks, counting in her head until she had the right one. She marched across the lobby, stopping where the nameplate read 'Alveinus Luthaine'. Luthaine was there, the gaunt man sitting properly as he raked a finger through his ledger, his glasses low over his nose. Nela had always said that if the dead had any money, the man would have been an undertaker.

Sumi stood there for a minute, but Luthaine didn't seem to notice. She looked around, self-conscious from loitering in the middle of the bank floor. Finally, she raised a fist to her mouth and coughed, making him glance in her direction. If she hadn't been so nervous, she probably would have laughed, the man somehow managing to look down on her from a seated position.

"Ah, Ms. Elerair," he said, closing his ledger as he stood, towering over her even more. "I thought we said noon."

"Er...yes, sorry," Sumi stammered. "Things were...uh...busy at the shop, and er... yes..." she trailed off, realizing he wasn't listening.

"Very well," he said, nodding absently, already looking at his paperwork again. "Please have a seat. I'd very much like to wrap up this piece of business."

As Luthaine dug through his papers, Sumi looked at his emerald-glass lamp, her eyes traveling from the ceiling to the floor. How had they laid the wires without tearing up all that marble? It seemed like just a few years ago that the palace got electric lights, but now with the trolley lines finished, they were installing the cables everywhere. The light looked cold up close, though she did love the way they twinkled from the terrace at night, like another set of stars.

"Well then," Luthaine said, tapping a stack of papers against his desk, "let's begin." He took the top sheet and laid it out in front of Sumi. "I took the liberty of speaking with your grandmother's barrister, a Mr. Perlais. Everything in the will has been set up for a direct transfer of assets to you. This includes the cottage and the account here at Naval Maritime. If you'll kindly sign at the bottom here."

Sumi scanned the paper, squinting in the dim light to make out the thick lines of text. She saw Nela's name along with hers, and *transfer of assets* in a bold hand at the top. It appeared to be what he said, though it was hard to feel good about signing anything with the skeletal man watching her, his fingers tapping impatiently. He finally cleared his throat and she reached for the pen, signing her name on the form.

"Very well," Luthaine said, "that's one piece out of the way." He took the next three pieces of paper off of the stack and handed them to her. "I took the liberty of having one of our scribes draw up a personal ledger of family assets. Not a terrible amount left, of course, though your grandfather's pension will continue to be deposited here at the reduced rate. Beyond the 50% pension due to his wife, his rank provided for 25% payments to one next of kin. He named you, and so I set up the paperwork to continue its deposit at the bank in your name. Simply sign here on the second sheet."

Sumi briefly scanned the next page and signed again. She gulped, the math of making ends meet from this morning would only be getting harder on the reduced pension.

"Finally," he continued, "I have some items in my possession of a…sentimental value." It was doubtful that Luthaine had ever been sentimental in his life, so the word must have been a foreign one to him. "The first came by way of the barrister, a letter he was instructed to deliver to you at your grandmother's death. In addition, it is bank policy to close safety deposit boxes upon the death of the owner. Given the state of your…accounts, I presume you will not be opening a new one. Therefore, I would like to deliver these items to you today."

Sumi perked up, a letter for her? Nela had been so sick at the end, she'd simply…faded away. No goodbye, no last words of wisdom. For a moment her shame at slinking into the bank faded, the possibility of the letter shining brightly.

"There's a letter for me?" she asked.

"Hmm, yes," Luthaine said, no longer looking at her. He was looking across the bank floor and waving. "I thought I might have a secretary provide you a private conference room for the materials, in case you should become…emotional."

A secretary quickly walked over, never raising his pace above the propriety of a walk, but seeming to glide across the floor like a runner all the same. He was a young man with slicked back hair and a full, closely cropped beard. He didn't wear a full suit like Luthaine, but had a nice wool vest and a collared shirt.

The man smiled at Sumi as he approached. "Yes, Mr. Luthaine?" he asked.

"Please take Ms. Elerair to Room Three," Luthaine said without standing up from his chair. "Ms. Tuttle has some personal effects from Box 702 for her. Thank you, Darren"

"Of course," Darren said, nodding. He turned back to Sumi. "If you'd follow me miss, we'll get you set up in a private room."

Sumi stood, awkwardly turning back towards Luthaine and nodding her head in gratitude.

"Thank you," she said.

"Yes, of course," Luthaine murmured, but he was already back in his ledger.

As they walked quickly across the marble floor, Darren turned and smiled at her again, speaking in a low voice.

"Sorry about old Luthaine," he said. "He doesn't bite, but he may as well."

Sumi grinned. "Thank you, Mr. Darren," she said. "It's just good to know he doesn't have some kind of grudge against me personally."

"No, miss," he said, chuckling quietly. Unfortunately, his grudge is with all of mankind."

They turned into a corridor that led deeper into the bank. After several doors they came to one with a glazed window and a large *3* embossed on it.

"Here we are," he said, pulling out a key on a brass chain and unlocking the door. It opened onto a room that was far cozier than the bank floor. There was a dark wooden table in the center surrounded by leather chairs and a hearth with a fire crackling in the grate. Darren stepped in and pulled out one of the chairs, offering it to her.

"Please, make yourself comfortable while I grab your things." He turned to go, but paused by the door. "Could I bring you a cup of tea as well, Ms. Elerair?"

Sumi nodded, her head still swimming from the abrupt contrast between the two men. It felt like she'd gone from rolling in the snow to soaking in a hot bath. He asked for her preference on cream and sugar and then disappeared back into the hallway. She eased into the chair and closed her eyes, sighing out in relief. The worst of it was over now. She really ought to switch banks someday, though there was probably another Luthaine at every bank in the city… Besides, it wasn't like anyone would leap for joy when they saw how tiny her account was.

She must have drifted off, because some time later, she jerked awake as the door to the conference room clicked behind her. Darren came around the back of her chair with the safety deposit box in one hand and a cup of steaming tea in the other.

"There you are, Ms. Elerair," he said, placing the tea in front of her. Then, he set the lock box down in the middle of the table and emptied it, lining up a satin pouch and a letter in a thick envelope. When that was done, he stood back and folded his hands. "That should be everything. I'll leave you to it, but if there's anything you need, just ask for me at the front desk."

He nodded and turned to go, but Sumi put up a hand, stopping him.

"Thank you, Mr. Darren," she said, "for being so kind."

"It's my pleasure, miss," he said. "A customer's a customer, after all. Luthaine would do well to remember that." He winked at her and left the room.

She eyed the letter for a moment but grabbed the teacup instead. As much as it galled her to prove Luthaine right, she probably *would* get emotional, and as the saying went, 'if you're plan on crying salt, you'd better take your tea with honey.' She took a quick sip, humming with delight. It was thick and sweet, the heavy cream tasting like luxury. Even though the tea was steaming, she still gulped down a few mouthfuls in quick succession. Then, taking a deep breath, she turned back to Nela's things.

She started with the black satin pouch, pulling open the drawstring as she carefully reached inside. She felt cold metal and pulled her hand out, revealing a long gold chain with a pendant on the end. It was the size of a large coin and shaped like a flower with onyx and pearl petals that wove together. In the center was a large emerald shaped like a star. She held it up, the necklace spinning on its chain as it glowed in the firelight.

"Wow," she whispered, "where did this come from?" She had never seen Nela wear anything like it. She held it for a moment but then slipped it over her head, hiding the pendant under her blouse. She couldn't risk leaving something so valuable on the outside of her clothes, but knowing it was Nela's, she couldn't resist wearing it either.

She patted the necklace once beneath her blouse before taking up the letter. She turned it over, her breath coming up short as she saw her name written in Nela's handwriting. She ran her finger over it, tracing the familiar looping script. Even though the ink was long dry, it felt like it could have just been written, as if Nela had just written it in the other room. She closed her eyes and broke the seal, pulling out a thick sheet of folded parchment. As she started reading, Nela's voice seemed to echo in her mind:

Dear Sumi,

It pains me to write this letter to you, my sweet girl, but I'd rather do it now while my faculties are still present. I've had this letter in my mind ever since you came to live with us — such a beautiful and tragic day all at once. Losing your mother broke my heart to pieces, but you, my second daughter, have helped me put it back together again.

Sumi laughed, wiping tears from her eyes. It was such a joy to hear Nela's voice as she must have sounded in her own mind. She had known Berillai well, of course, living in the kingdom as long as she had, but she'd always complained that the language was too fast to speak properly. It hadn't stopped her from speaking circles around everyone, even in her second language, but this letter hinted at how powerful her mind had really been. It was like when they'd spoken in Anushai, Nela's sentences coming out like songs, the words weaving together into perfect chords. Sumi read on:

You are such a wonderful young woman. I'm sorry if I've been too harsh in raising you. I hope you can forgive an old woman her failings. Let us chalk it up to the hand that fate dealt us. Grandmothers are better at serving cookies than they are at starting over at sixty. I have loved you every minute, and I love the woman you've become. But I see the fear in you, too. Stop being an otter, sweet girl. Please let the world know you, because you are a gift.

There is so much I never told you, about my family, about my home. They all feel like another lifetime now, and from the day I met your grandfather, I put my past aside and chose love. I chose this land, and this people. I truly never knew how much of myself would remain. The Berillai are rough and strong, like stone, and we Anushai are softer things. Your mother always took after her father: his eyes, his jaw, his sailor's way of seeing the world. I see more of myself in you, Sumi, but if I leave you nothing else, I hope I leave my love in your heart.

In Anushai, my family's motto is this: Myeol et myeol, reolan guyang lessem guyang. Dyeol sheng et myeol, bulgyeong shaldeom elshim. It means: "Let the earth be the earth, and the light be the light. The soil is a secret, but the grass always shows." This necklace was my mother's. It is a symbol of all that we are. Keep it hidden, but always let your heart show. Never let the shadows of the world stop the light from getting in.

Sumi felt the pendant beneath her blouse. The hard stone seemed to ground her, pushing the letter deeper into her heart.

I never told you much of my past because if you didn't take after me, I wanted to leave you in peace. But I leave you this letter in case you ever have need of it. I can't promise the secrets of our family will stay where they are hidden, and if anything <u>strange</u> should happen to you, remember this letter. No matter what, I know you will do great things just as you are. Keep your heart on happy memories, and I promise, the light will guide you.

Sumi flipped over the parchment, eager for more, but there was only a sign off:

I love you always sweet girl,
Your Nela

Thick raindrop tears fell from her eyes and onto the paper. She squeaked, frantically dabbing at them with her skirt. She flipped the letter over, but thankfully, the ink hadn't run. She let out a breath, putting down the pages as she stared into the fire. If anything *strange* should happen — Nela had underlined the word as if she had something in mind. Her thoughts suddenly flashed back to what she'd seen the night before. In her rush through the morning, she'd finally stopped thinking about that ghostly hand. A shiver went up her spine. If that was what Nela meant…she may have to admit that it was no dream. But where would that leave her?

Outside in the hall, a clock chimed one long, slow gong, signaling the end of the lunch hour. Sumi jumped from her seat, scrambling out of the chair. She had to get back to the shop! She carefully put the letter in her bag before reaching for the necklace beneath her blouse again, making sure it was secure. Once her hat was on, she ran out of the bank, ignoring the frowns of the bankers as she hurried towards the light.

As she jogged back through the streets of Berill, it was easy to pretend that it was all just a dream again. A dim room and a crackling fire made foolish things seem too real, like the veil of night had slipped back down. She shook her head and pushed ahead, ignoring the letter for the moment. Back at the shop, she bowed in apology to Mr. Furttenhur, rambling nervously until he left. He didn't seemed angry, though. He acted like he hadn't even realized she was gone, which very well could have been the case… On his way out, he simply smiled at her, tipping his hat.

As soon as she was alone, however, the frantic energy fell away. Dim afternoon light filtered into the shop, and everything from the bank came rushing back. She felt like she could feel the presence of the letter in her bag in the back room, beating like a drum, calling her attention to its contents. Memories began to flood her mind, and she scoured them looking for clues. How was it all connected? Was there something she'd been missing all these years?

It was true that Nela had never talked much about Anushai. All of her stories had seemed to begin with Grandpa, focusing on the day she met him, his crisp uniform, their whirlwind romance. After months of letters back and forth, she'd just bought a ticket and sailed for Berill to get married. There was nothing before. She didn't even know her great grandmother's name, but now, somehow, the woman's necklace was pressing against her heart.

Besides, Nela had never really seemed to like telling stories about herself anyway. She had far preferred fairytales, fanciful stories from across the Continent that were full of things like…Shapewalkers. Why did her mind keep circling back to those creatures? They had never seemed like anything that could be even remotely real. Could she really be silly enough to think otherwise because of one strange vision and a vague letter? And even if they were real, what would they have to do with a mousy girl who worked in a flower shop?

As her mind crowded with thoughts, Sumi started busying herself around the shop. She dug out the old feather duster from the back room and got to work on the windowsills, something she hadn't done in ages. Mr. Furttenhur wouldn't mind a clean shop, of course, but like the night before, movement suddenly seemed essential. As she pushed through chore after chore, her worries finally faded into daydreams, the dark hallway from the night before giving way to fairytales. With her arms elbow deep in floor polish, she pictured herself as a pirate, a knight, an angel — all of the things the Shapewalkers had become in the stories.

Was the letter from Nela a doorway into a world of dreams, or was it just the last goodbye of the woman who had loved her best? What she needed most now was to know more. Nela, Umilai rest her soul, had loved to speak in riddles and sayings. But she needed something concrete, something that could give her some direction. As she lay on her back, wiping down the bottoms of the flower racks, it finally came to her — the library! If she had any chance of finding answers in Berill, it would be there.

An hour later, Sumi was ready to go, hat in hand and her shawl draped over her shoulders. She stood by the door, every conceivable task in the shop done and done well. She heard the clock before it chimed, the old gears grinding over the ticking of the pendulum. As the hour rang out, her hand was already turning the knob, her pulse suddenly quick as she stepped through the door.

4

Hear the echoes of the true voice! The one that gave us the courage to leap into the sea, to come along the winds so we could become kings. Twice, thrice, infinite times have I heard its ringing tones, the vessel of the blue divine.

-Excerpt from the Poems of Boran Stonekeeper

—:—

Sumi turned the key in the lock and took off, nearly skipping down the stairs. She turned left instead of right, heading south towards the Royal Library. Everything she knew of Shapewalkers had come from children's stories only half remembered. There must be something formally studied and written that she could look to. If such a thing really existed, some scholar would have written about them by now, wouldn't they?

As she crossed Laeryia Boulevard, she looked longingly at the palace, but it wasn't as if the library wasn't a gem in its own right. It was opposite the Peerage, guarding the lawmakers like another fortress, only one filled with books. She'd never seen a Peer roaming the shelves, though… Perhaps it had simply been built to remind them that they weren't pirates or knights anymore, the laws they passed to the Queen far more important than their swords.

Luckily, the Peers had built the library to be larger than its original catalog, and there was far more stored in its endless shelves than stuffy old laws. Once, they'd even found copies of Nela's favorite love saga from Anushai, both original and translated. Only peers could check the books out, but that hardly seemed to matter. It felt like every moment they weren't with the women's group, they were at the library, sometimes passing entire afternoons in some abandoned nook, devouring stories until it was time for dinner. How had she let herself forget those days? Everything had felt possible then, a thousand different lives lived in each book that were far grander than her own.

At the top of the first hill, the street turned past the Royal Park before continuing on to the library. She decided to cut through it, crossing onto the wide gravel path. It was a beautiful stretch of greenery, cut out of the bustle of the city in a long oval shape. And that view! Just one hill up from the beach, and she could already see the water. The sea was paling to its usual winter grey, and the trees had just started to change their leaves, oranges and yellows peeking out from behind the disappearing green.

As she passed the middle of the park, she paused, looking up at the monument there. Built on a large stone square, it had a huge block of marble in the center surrounded by five pillars. Each pillar held a bronze statue of an angel with a sword, and in the center, twice as large as the others, was King Rummon, the founder of Berill. She'd always fancied that strong chin of his, though the royal sculptors could be rather generous. Not that he'd had much say in the matter... He'd been assassinated during the Mesop Wars, hadn't he? His sword was unsheathed, its point facing down, and his eyes were pointed towards the Isles.

As she watched, a large gull flew up and landed right on the king's head, letting out a shrill cry. Proving that the sword was no threat, another half dozen birds flew up and joined him, perching on the king's shoulders. Of course, there were no kings in the eyes of seagulls...just another place to poop. She chuckled, continuing on towards the other side of the park, where another gate let her out right in front of the library.

Despite their historic connection, the library and the Peerage really couldn't look more different. The Peerage was built like a keep, made of rough stone with ramparts and arrow slits lining the facade. Even the doorway, which was slightly more modern, was reached by crossing a trench on an ancient-looking drawbridge. This was a home of necessity, built by knights who were still used to fighting when they'd formed their government.

The library, on the other hand, was like some kind of temple where men worshipped books. It had balustrades soaring into the air before ending in star bursts of turrets. Berillai flags lined the roof, and the walls were filled with multi-story stained glass windows, shining in every conceivable color as they told the story of the Royal House. This was what you built when you had won, something that would rival the great buildings of the Continent in a place you meant to endure.

As she climbed the steps to the library, Sumi stared up at the windows, the reds and golds of the glass lighting up like wildfire in the evening light. Her favorite window was just to the left of the entrance — King Rummon storming the beaches of Berill, his sword held high in the air. He wore a blood red tunic, and his sword was a gleaming silver. The surf jumped in whites and blues, and his face was turned up towards the heavens.

She was so engrossed in the window that she almost ran into a barrister on his way out. She squeaked out an apology as she narrowly avoided a collision, the man's court robes swirling as he clutched to his papers. He merely grumbled and kept moving, probably late for a meeting with a peer. She grinned sheepishly, shaking her head. That made the second time that she'd almost run into someone on the same day, a personal record. Still, this *was* a special day. She had a mystery to solve, and hope for once that she might get some answers.

_____

Sumi stepped inside the library, the heavy doors sealing her in stillness. The entryway had a beautiful ethereal glow from the stained glass before the library proper disappeared into the shadow of the thick stone walls. Squinting, she could make out the narrow hall of information desks and the cavernous body that held the stacks. There were dozens of stairways running up and down in a central column, each one stretching off into a darkness that hid the books beyond.

As she ventured further, the light of the stained glass gave way to a soothing blue glow that radiated from a series of lanterns. Candles were banned to protect the books, and aside from the windows, the lanterns were the only light. It felt like something out of a dream, like she'd wandered into a cave, which wasn't all that far from the truth… The lanterns were lit by large luminescent rocks that were mined in the mountains outside the city. They were called 'speaking stones', though she'd never heard anyone say why.

Sumi slipped up to the first desk on her right where an old man sat. He wore thick glasses and had a long, wispy white beard that reached down to his waist. He was categorizing cards in a metal box, and despite his glasses, he was still squinting, muttering to himself as he put them in order.

"Excuse me, sir?" Sumi asked hesitantly, leaning against the desk. The old man forced one last card into order before he pulled his eyes away from the box. He blinked at her for a moment before raising a finger, pulling off his glasses and exchanging them for another pair in his shirt pocket.

"There we are," he said, smiling, his voice low and gravelly. "Welcome to the Royal Library, dear. What can we do for you?"

Her mind raced for a moment. It had seemed so natural to run to the library with her question, but she couldn't very well ask him if Shapewalkers were real!

"Well…" she said slowly, "I wanted to do some research on the legends behind popular children's stories. So, maybe history?" That didn't sound too bad. Luckily, the old man started nodding vigorously.

"I think I have just the thing," he said, trading his glasses back out. He poked through the box in front of him with an ancient, knobby finger, muttering to himself again. "Aha!" he finally exclaimed, removing one of the long manila cards. He held it up in front of his face before nodding again and sliding it to her. There was a large four-digit code printed on the top and a long list of book titles.

"It's a good topic for research," he said. "Most of what we brought from the Isles were legends anyway. There are plenty of scholars who've used those legends as the basis for historical analysis, and plenty of compilations too. There's tremendous value in the stories of common folk." He chuckled. "If only we could get the peers to remember that, eh?"

Sumi scanned the list of names as he spoke: *The Founding of Berill, The Myths of Dawn, Creatures of the Continent.* Her eyes lit up as she moved down the page.

"This looks like just the thing," she said, "thank you!"

"It's my pleasure, young lady," he said, smiling at her again. "There's nothing more important than the curiosity of youth." He lowered his voice to a not-so-quiet stage whisper. "You see, not many of our leaders come through these doors anymore. Whenever I see a scholar your age, it gives me hope."

Sumi chuckled, shaking her head.

"I'm flattered," she said, "but I'm no scholar."

He seemed content to ignore her denial, turning his focus to the desk, where he clutched the wood, hauling himself up with a groan.

"Shall I take you to the section in question, miss?" he asked.

"Oh, no," Sumi said, waving her hands. "I wouldn't want to trouble you."

"It's no trouble," he said. "Besides, it's slow tonight. I need to move around before I become part of the desk."

He picked up a cane from beside his chair and took one of the blue lanterns, shuffling towards the nearest stairwell. She caught up easily, though it took a bit of practice to match his pace. She eventually found her rhythm, taking one step for every four of his shuffles. As they reached the stairs, he handed her the lantern, grabbing the railing in a vice grip as he dragged himself up.

"I started working here when I was no older than you," he said, huffing with the effort of climbing the stairs. He looked like he could use the air for breathing, but he still had a smile on his face. "King Talmun was on the throne then, rest his soul, and Queen Welaya wasn't even born yet." He began to laugh. "When kings and queens start to look like children, you'll know you've gotten old."

When they reached the next landing, the librarian rested on his cane for a moment, looking up at the staircase as it disappeared into the darkness. She lifted her hand to steady him, but he caught her eye and waved her off.

"Just one more floor, miss," he said chuckling. "If it was Amoriai poetry you needed I might admit defeat, but I think I can still make it to history."

He started up the next staircase and Sumi followed, the blue light bobbing gently as they climbed. At the top he held up a finger, asking her to wait as he huffed in and out. He reached his hands out behind him, cracking his back with a deep pop.

"Oof," he said, letting out a sigh, "that's much better." He nodded to her, shuffling off into the shadowy stacks. They were a maze, twisting like trees in a forest, the dark wood of the shelves swallowing the soft light of their lantern. The librarian may have risked his life on those stairs, but she was glad he'd come now. Somehow, he was able to find his way, turning back and forth without once checking the row numbers.

"Aha!" he finally shouted as they made one final turn between two shelves. '*Row 166*' gleamed in brass numbers nailed onto the end of the stack.

"The light please, miss?" he asked. Sumi handed him the lantern, and he moved into the shelves, lifting the light as high as he could as he leaned his face into the books, his nose almost touching the dusty spines. He began to pull thick volumes off the shelf, passing them to her. Soon there was a large pile in her arms, her muscles aching as each new one was dropped on the others. She was about to suggest finding a table to place them down when he turned towards her.

"That should do it!" he said, wiping one hand off on his coat and smiling. She nodded, biting her lip in a nervous smile as she looked at him over the stack.

"Would you be able to show me to a study room by chance?" she asked.

45

"Ah, yes!" he said. "I suspect you'll need some time to dig through these. We don't close until the eleventh bell, so you should have plenty of time."

He turned off to the right, leading her out of the stacks and along the smooth interior wall of the building. They walked past a few windows, the last glow of sunset filtering through the colored glass. They moved along the corridor until they came to a series of doors cut into the stone. The librarian opened one, revealing a cozy alcove with a table and a fireplace that was filled with speaking stones. He beckoned for her to enter, and she stepped through, dropping her stack of books with a thump.

"I'll send a porter over to bring you a lantern of your own," he said, "and when you're done for the night, go ahead and leave the books here. I'll have them re-shelved for you."

"Thank you very much, sir," she said, giving him a quick bow.

"No trouble at all," he said, waving off the formality. "I hope we'll see you again. May I ask your name for when you return?"

She told him and his smile broadened. "A lovely name," he said. "It sounds a bit like Anushai no?" He opened his mouth to comment further, but a bell tolled somewhere deep in the library. It must have been the giant central clock, the gongs seeming to shake the stone even on the third floor. "Ah, the dinner bell," he said. "You haven't eaten yet, have you, Miss Elerair?"

She shook her head, blushing. She hadn't even thought of food in her rush to get to the library. Her stomach rumbled on cue, seeming to just realize she'd neglected it.

"Well," the librarian said, "best not try and learn on an empty stomach. I'll tell you what…this service is meant for peers, but I'll have the porter bring some meat and cheese when he brings the lantern. No reason for it to go to waste. Keep it between us, but the porters don't have to know you're not the daughter of a peer, pretty as you are."

"Are you sure?" she asked. "I wouldn't want to get you in trouble on my account."

He winked at her, stepping towards the door.

"Wouldn't be much point in being the Queen's Librarian if I couldn't feed a young scholar now and then." With that, he shuffled out of the room and into the darkness.

The Queen's Librarian! But that would mean he ran the entire library. She never would have approached his desk if she had known his rank. He was basically a peer himself… But he had been so kind! She shook her head. Her luck seemed to be holding up for once; first with Darren at the bank, and now with the librarian. She just had to be careful before she used it all up. She looked up at the ceiling, the stone glowing in the blue light.

"Thanks for keeping an eye on me, Nela," she whispered.

She hung her shawl on a hook by the door and eased down into one of the stuffed chairs by the table. It was too dark to read until the lantern came, but she didn't have to wait long. She heard the sharp squeak of a wheel just before a porter in white livery rolled a cart into the room and bowed.

"Your dinner service, madam," the porter said, placing a covered silver tray on the table along with a large blue-light lantern. She was no madam, but at least the light was dim. Hopefully it would hide her dingy clothes.

"Thank you," she managed to squeeze out, but the porter didn't seem to notice. He simply nodded, bowing once more as he left the room.

She went back around the table and sat down. Her chair was in the center, placed evenly between the silver platter and the row of books. She looked back and forth between the two, torn between the simple needs of hunger and the deeper, but no less pressing need for answers. She glanced at the books — they could offer her the truth! But then she looked back at the platter — it could offer her…sausage. Her stomach grumbled.

"Fine!" she said, lifting the cover off the platter. She gasped, her mouth watering. There was a huge spread with four types of cheese, two different sausages, bread slices, and a tiny bowl of honey. She hesitantly poked her finger through the yellows and oranges of the cheese — she didn't even know the names of most of them. The rinds were stamped with the royal seal, and one of the sausages looked like venison, which the market only had on holidays. The Master Librarian really had done too much!

She glanced towards the hallway before sneaking one sausage and one cheese into her handkerchief, stuffing them both in her bag. It was embarrassing to pilfer from a bounty she already didn't deserve, but with money so tight, she might never see a spread like this again. If she ever made it out of her present circumstances, she'd have to do something good for the library, or at least some other poor soul looking for answers.

She cut a chunk from an orange wedge of cheese and put it on one of the slices of bread before drizzling it with honey. She took a bite, squeezing her eyes shut in pleasure. Her moral dilemma wasn't completely forgotten, though its edges were certainly softened… Besides, like the librarian had said, it would be horrible to let it all go to waste, wouldn't it? She rapidly inhaled the remainder of that slice of bread before eating another, topping it with a different cheese and a slice of the venison. She had to catch her breath after that, and she wiped her mouth, turning towards the books.

The pile in front of her was like a basket full of foraged mushrooms, all different colors and sizes spilling out onto the table. She took up the oldest looking of the books, one of the first titles she'd noticed on the filing card: *The Founding of Berill*. She may as well start with some history; even if she was fooling herself, at least she could learn something in the process.

She cracked the spine of the book, the leather creaking with age as the scent of dust lifted off the parchment. The first page was taken up by a large ink etching. It showed King Rummon with his famous sword again, standing on the cliffs over Berill, his blade pointing towards the sea. Sumi stuck her finger into the middle of the book and let the pages flip by, opening one at random. She started reading at the top, trying to figure out how far back in history she had landed.

King Rummon, eager to civilize the Berillai in the ways of the Continent, chose to parley with the Mesop chieftains in the custom of these lands. He brought them to his keep and ensured their safe passage. However, they proved recalcitrant, refusing all offers of peaceful exchange. So war it was going to be.

The opposite page had another print of King Rummon in a feast hall, his arms spread wide as the Mesop chieftains looked on, their plates brimming with pheasant and potatoes. Sumi flipped through the next few pages, recognizing some of the names of key battles from statues around the city. The drawings became more violent as she went, with grisly aerial tableaus full of the dead and wounded.

She kept scanning quickly as she turned through the book, looking for anything that mentioned creatures or shapeshifting. Eventually, she stumbled onto a section called *King Rummon's Death*. He had been assassinated, of course, though the details were hazy in her mind. She stopped and read again:

The Isles of Dawn had very different magics from those of the Continent, and when King Rummon began to carve out the beachhead, he was ill prepared for the threats he would face. In the early days, the Mesop number had been small and easily routed. Yet after only one winter in the harbor, the Mesop returned in greater numbers, and the war began in earnest.

As described in the previous chapter, King Rummon had summoned his brother, Prince Laeryia, to come from the Isles of Dawn after him, and with Umilai's blessing, he arrived in time to increase their numbers against the Mesop attacks. Although the royals were victorious in every outright battle, raids continued regularly along the coast, harrying the farmers in their homesteads.

To stop the raids, the King began a concerted offensive campaign against the Mesop, taking his greatest knights into the southern forest. The Mesop hated King Rummon with a passion, and had learned to see his silver armor from afar. Their King placed a bounty on his head, promising massive tracts of land to whichever warrior slew him. Yet, after months on campaign, no Mesop could even pierce his armor, let alone deliver a killing blow. So the clans turned to the magics that run deep within the Continent, trying to conjure a disaster for the Berillai.

First, they tried to poison him, cursing the wild boars of the forest that the Berillai hunted between battles. However, the loyal warriors always tasted the King's food, and when one tried the meat that night, he fell to the ground, dying as his mouth foamed with blood and bile. Realizing that the forest was tainted, Rummon sent instead for a great number of herdsmen to follow the army and provide sustenance.

The Mesop then used a curse that summoned a thousand deadly snakes. They drove them into the Berillai camp, but this too failed. The knights fought valiantly, as if on the field of battle, the King's honor guard ensuring that no snake could sink its teeth beyond his helm. Finally, in their desperation, the Mesop turned to the darkest magic of the Continent — that of the Shapewalkers.

Sumi leaned closer to the book, her hearth thumping as she read on as quickly as she could:

The Berillai had no concept of such a demon, though the hideous creatures have roamed this land since time immemorial. The Mesop sent their best warriors back to Berill, crossing the enemy lines in search of the royal family. Attacking in the night, they captured Queen Kesselia, bringing her back to the forest. There, they set the vile Shapewalkers upon her, allowing them to steal her face as they slew her.

Before word of the attack could reach King Rummon, the Mesop Shapewalkers came to the Berillai camp. They wore the royal colors and arrived in splendor, looking like the Queen and her attendants. Rummon was surprised to see his bride, but having been in the field for three seasons, he was eager for their reunion and welcomed her with open arms.

The King demanded a celebration, roasting a dozen lambs in honor of his queen. They feasted until the fires burned low, the sounds of their singing filling the forest. Back in his tent that night, as the King leaned in to kiss his betrothed, the Shapewalker struck. The creature slit his throat, cackling as it watched him bleed out, finally revealing its true form. The Shapewalkers were slain to the last, but the damage had been done. The King was dead.

Sumi flipped the page to find another ink etching, gasping as she stared at the horrible picture. A woman stood next to the King, a knife in her outstretched hand. He had shock in his eyes, his hands around his neck as he tried to keep the blood in. And the woman... She had two faces. One, the perfect face of a Queen, had been pulled up like a porcelain mask, and the other was the face of a monster. It cackled in victory, its open mouth full of razor sharp teeth and a snake-like tongue, its eyes as black as midnight. Sumi slammed the book closed.

"They can't be like that!" she cried, slapping a hand over her mouth as she remembered that she was in the library. She slowly lowered it, though her breath still seemed far too loud in the silent building. She squeezed her forehead, her mind racing. That had to be some kind of exaggeration, right? All the old stories looked to magic when they couldn't understand something, and there were few shocks for a kingdom worse than losing their king. But then, why mention the Shapewalkers specifically? Everyone knew they had strange gods in the Continent, but this seemed too specific.

She closed the book without looking at the picture again and pulled out her bag, reaching for Nela's letter. She flipped it over, scanning quickly for the last line. *Think of happy memories,* it said. If this was real and Nela meant for her to become a Shapewalker, she would never let Sumi become a monster. She closed her eyes, taking a deep breath. There had to be another answer, something more than a grisly medieval legend.

"I need a different book," she said to herself, turning back to her stack. She took one off the top, its cover done in thick green cloth. *Creatures of the Continent by Sir Arteir Pallinayum.* She held it loosely, like it might burn her. She gently lifted the cover, peeking at the introduction.

Our forefathers, when they built this great kingdom, found themselves in a land far different from the Isles of Dawn. Many tales survive from those days, though they are little more than legends, the nightmares of a seafaring people in a strange land. Nowhere is this more true than in their depictions of the fauna of this great Continent — monsters and beasts the likes of which had never been seen. In this volume, I hope to present a scholarly study of these creatures, to illuminate that which our forefathers could hardly bear to imagine.

Sumi nodded to herself. Scholarly... That felt safer than what she'd just read.

She turned the next page, finding an index of magical creatures listed alphabetically. Many of them were familiar from childhood stories. Listed near the top were the arnisoles, dandelion fluff-shaped creatures that were supposed to travel the seas and grant sailors good luck. What a strange book! Listing the creatures like that... It made it seem like you could just wander out into the woods and stumble upon one.

"Oh!" she squeaked, reaching the D's where she found the durnijorie. Nela had told her about those! She'd always pictured them like elk but with human faces. She furrowed her brow, trying to remember the story. Young warriors from Anushai would go into the mountains to try and trap them. And once you captured one... it would spit a stone out at you. White or black to tell your fate.

So many interesting things! If only she could take the book home and read it all night. She turned to the second page, finally finding the Shapewalker two-thirds of the way down. She thumbed quickly through the pages, slowing just before the end. She closed her eyes, turning the last one. As she peeked one eye open, she breathed a sigh of relief. There was no gruesome drawing there, no evil, snake-like face. There was only the text. Oddly, it read more like some rich man's travel journal than heady scholarship:

This was a thorny section to write. Every nation seems to have stories of the Shapewalkers, though they often seem like little more than phantoms. Even the most elusive creatures in this volume can eventually be found if you're only willing to climb the tallest mountain or search the darkest forest. The Shapewalkers, however, hide among us, tied to the oldest blood of the Continent.

In many kingdoms, the people contend that Shapewalkers are just humans of a different sort. The Anushai even went so far as to claim that their royal houses were all descended from magical stock. Other cultures seem to view them more like angels, sent from the gods in times of great need. I was never able to meet one for myself, though whether that was because of my Berillai heritage or bad luck, I'll never know.

Unfortunately, I fear the sun is setting on these great and storied creatures. We Berillai, many of who view them as little more than demons, are spreading our beliefs throughout the land, carried by the weight of our coin. The Three Sisters in the east are already mimicking many of our ways, and perhaps it is only time before the other kingdoms of Wellonai abandon their traditions along with their embrace of the Shapewalkers.

I was never granted an audience at the palace in Anushai, though I found many useful records in their libraries. Unlike our legends, their stories of Shapewalkers often carried dates and were attached to famous events that could at least be verified in the historical record. I also found this symbol, seen frequently in the capital city, which some claimed to be the symbol of the Shapewalkers:

Sumi gasped, clutching her chest. There in the book was a sketch that looked exactly like Nela's pendant. The two swirls, one dark and one light, ending in a bright center. Her eyes darted towards the hall again, still finding it empty. Thank Umilai she'd slipped it under her blouse at the bank! Nela had said to keep it secret, but she could have warned her it was some kind of demonic symbol! Still, it wasn't like anyone in Berill would recognize it…right? It was her own grandmother's necklace, and she'd never once seen that symbol in her life. She took a deep breath, reading on:

Despite the records I recovered, the source of the Shapewalkers' power remains a mystery to me. While our people worship the old gods, we have no stories with this sort of magic. The Anushai and Amoriai have the most similarities, claiming that the creatures' power comes from a divine presence (called Mu'lalat in Amoriai and Essomuai in Anushai). Still, I had a difficult time determining whether or not they could truly be called 'gods.'

Essomuai features heavily in the creation myth of the Anushai, known as one of the three daughters of Wellonai. Nowadays, however, they seem to speak of her more like a force, like the air around us. While the Anushai are reticent to explain their religion to an outsider, one scholar told me that Essomuai was 'the blood of the soil and the light of all creatures.' This is an important topic for further research, and one I hope to write about in my next volume.

Sumi turned the page and found that the section was over, ending in an index of events and dates that were supposed to have involved Shapewalkers. She blinked heavily, her eyes strained from reading. Still, she wasn't tired. In fact, her heart was pounding. Pallinayum's book was no fairy tale — it was research, history, facts. And if that meant Shapewalkers could be real… She suddenly felt an urgent need to get home, to the cottage where all of this had started. If it *was* real, then maybe she could get it to happen again.

She gathered up her things and walked quickly down the stairs. As she passed the front desk, she looked for the Royal Librarian to thank him properly, but he was nowhere to be found. She hurried towards Fort Street, thinking of Nela as she watched the stars emerge on the horizon. No matter what was happening, she would find a way forward. She just had to keep her heart on happy memories.

5

How was it that the glorious love of Essomuai's light withered so in her representatives? She supposed something must be lost when her golden spirit was melted into coins, though she couldn't blame the goddess. As the Grass House saying went, 'light makes the harvest, but locked doors the rot.'

-Excerpt from The Borimol Plains

—:—

Thirteen Years Ago

Sumi came out of her room, wincing as she heard the sound of the phonograph blaring from the sitting room. It was playing Nela's old record from Anushai. It was some kind of orchestral collection that she had ordered in the mail, and the main instrument, the sellomaera, sounded like a dying bird. If the music was on, it meant Nela was writing her letters to Anushai.

Whoever the letters were to, Nela was tight-lipped about it, though she insisted on listening to her record while she wrote them. Unfortunately, the phonograph would only fit in the sitting room, so it had to be cranked hard and played loud to reach the kitchen where Nela preferred to write. Since they were so expensive, they only owned two records, though Grandpa's wasn't much better. As soon as she graduated and got a job, the first gift she'd buy her family would be some decent music!

She thought about hiding in her room, but she still had homework to do, and she'd catch an earful if she used ink on the bed. She took a deep breath, heading down the stairs. She'd just have to weather the storm; the phonograph couldn't play forever. As she rounded the staircase into the front hall, her grandfather was passing by.

"Nela's slaughtering her chickens," he said, winking at her.

Sumi giggled. He loved giving Nela a hard time about her music — along with just about everything else. But she had realized long ago that he only did it to please her. Nela would act mad and sometimes hit him with a dish rag, but when he turned away she would always smile. Nela always said that she hadn't had enough truth growing up. She wasn't sure what that meant, but for whatever reason, Nela preferred being badgered over sweet nothings.

Sumi walked into the kitchen and caught the smell of stew on the stove, her mouth watering as she breathed in deeply.

"When's dinner, Nela?" Sumi asked as she picked up her school bag and set it across from her grandmother on the kitchen table.

"When you finish your sums," Nela said.

"Not when the stew is done cooking?" Sumi asked.

Her grandmother tsk-tsked. "This is why I cook stew child; stew is always done and never done. When we ready, stew ready."

Sumi smiled; only Nela could make stew philosophical. She set out her notebook and sat down. She sighed, tapping her pen against the page. Luckily, she heard Amis tapping at the back door, giving her an excuse to delay just one more moment. No doubt looking for some stew, he rushed through the door as soon as it was open. But as he crossed the threshold, he froze, his ears going back.

"Amis doesn't like the music either, Nela," Sumi said, giggling. She picked him up and took him back to the table. Hopefully having him on her lap would make the math easier to bear. She always got good marks, but she just couldn't get excited about it like she did with history class…

"Why do you have to listen to this while you write your letters again?" she asked, sitting down.

"Only way to drown out nonsense Berillai in my head," Nela said. She didn't look up, but smiled as she spoke in a lower voice. "Plus, it drives your grandpa crazy."

"Essie!" her grandfather called from the front hall. "I'm leaving, want me to post any of those letters?"

He came into the kitchen with his coat on. He had found Nela's name, Essolurei, hard to pronounce when they met, so he always called her Essie. He leaned over and kissed Sumi on the head.

"You know I hate missing dinner with you," he said, "but I have to meet an old friend by the docks."

"That's okay!" Sumi said brightly. "Bring me back the cork if you drink wine." She'd been collecting his corks for about a year now. She wasn't sure what she would do with them, but she liked how they looked.

He crossed to the other side of the table, looking over Nela's shoulder. She continued writing for a moment, but Sumi could tell she was starting to sign her name as her hand moved in a wide flourish. Nela folded up the top sheet of parchment and stuffed it into an envelope that she'd already addressed. She lifted up the letter, but as Grandpa reached for it and turned to go, she gripped the envelope tighter.

"What you forgetting?" she asked, turning her face up.

Her grandfather grunted and leaned down to kiss her. Their kiss was long, and Sumi focused hard on her math book as she tried to ignore them. Grandpa finally broke free, grumbling as he wiped red lipstick from his mouth, though she caught a wide smile on his face as he left the kitchen.

Nela smoothed out another piece of parchment and started to write again.

"Forty years and that man still need training," Nela said, scratching her pen across the fresh sheet.

Sumi giggled. "I think you'd have an easier time training Amis," she said.

"This is true," Nela said with a contented sigh.

She continued doing her homework, finally falling into a rhythm despite the wailing of the sellomaera. Just as she hit her stride, though, the phonograph slid onto a new song that grabbed her attention. Like all the tracks on the record, she had heard it a thousand times. This one, though, was the only choral arrangement. Nela had said that it was called *Salshean.* Sumi's Anushai wasn't the best, but she still liked to try and make out the lyrics. Aside from the occasional lesson with Nela and a few books of poetry they had in the house, it was her best chance to practice.

The song began with the rhythmic boom of timpani, woodwinds slowly rising in the background. Sumi tapped her pen against her notebook in time with the music as the choir started to sing. The women hit a whirl of high notes like birdsong, the men's voices ringing out in a deep bass. Sumi sang along under her breath, trying to puzzle out the words as she fumbled over them.

"*Saldan siom salshean dal jeom,*" Sumi sang. She recognized the word grass and mountain, and something about…the *heart* of the mountain? It was some kind of country scene, and she guessed that the women were meant to sound like birds as they flew over the hard stone of the mountain.

"What is this song about, Nela?" she asked, looking up from her notebook.

Nela looked up over her glasses, smiling. She seemed genuinely happy when Sumi asked about Anushai, even though she was always incredibly vague in her answers.

"It is about life," Nela said, "so is about everything."

"Then why sing about a mountain specifically?" Sumi asked.

"All living things are same, child. So mountain is grass, is you, is me." Nela looked back down, continuing with her writing. "Plus, is very big mountain next to Anushai, so is also about that."

Sumi chewed on her pen. She was deciphering the next line when Nela pushed out her chair. She crossed the table and patted Sumi on the head before shuffling into the kitchen.

"Stew time!" Nela announced.

Sumi turned in her seat. "But what about my homework?" she asked.

"You remembered Anushai for mountain," her grandmother said. "I am proud, so you get stew early."

Sumi laughed, jumping out of her chair. She made a mental note to get another book on Anushai from the school library. Maybe she'd finally found a way to butter Nela up… As she stood, she shot a glance at the kitchen, finding Nela busy at the stove. She leaned over the table, sneaking a look at the letter.

"Jiyel Yeolsemm Heoraiyal Meolsemai," the letter started. The first word meant *'Dear'* like the start of a letter in Berillai, and the second meant *'Doctor'*. Did Nela still know enough people in Anushai to be writing letters to doctors? Just then, her grandmother coughed, and Sumi jerked upright, afraid to get caught snooping. She tried to walk nonchalantly towards the cabinet to take out some bowls for dinner.

"Nela," Sumi asked, "who do you write your letters to?"

Sumi looked over out of the corner of her eye and caught Nela tense up as she stirred the stew, but she didn't turn around.

"Well," her grandmother said slowly, finally turning to take a bowl from Sumi's outstretched hand. "I live in Anushai more than twenty years, I know some people. Friends, Sumi, are more rare than gold snails. If you have one write you letter, always write back."

Sumi knitted her brow. Did Anushai really have golden snails? That had to be the strangest saying yet. Although, it was also possible that Nela had started making them up to toy with her… She wanted to ask who the doctor was, but she couldn't reveal that she'd looked at the letter. Sometimes it just felt like these people who she should know better than anyone in the world were still strangers to her.

Nela turned around and handed Sumi a bowl of steaming stew. She patted Sumi on the head and walked back towards the kitchen table with her own stew in hand. Sumi breathed in deeply, taking in the fragrant steam. That smell stopped the questions buzzing around her head. While Nela's past was a mystery, the stew was familiar and grounding. She must have her own reasons for not wanting to talk about her past. The stew told her she was home, and just like Nela herself, Sumi could at least count on that to never change.

6

How could you know the truth without the voices of the gods? Where would you find water without the wisdom of the stone, or passage without the secrets of the wind? Woe to you who forgets these things! For this is the birthright of our people.

-*Excerpt from the Poems of Boran Stonekeeper*

—:—

Sumi banged open the front door of the cottage. The hallway looked a bit ominous again with the sun gone, but she pushed forward, sweeping through the darkness to the kitchen. She fumbled her way to the stove, where she lit the lamp. As she moved towards the table, Amis was there, scratching at the back door. As soon as it was open an inch, he pushed his way in, somehow squeezing through with his giant, fluffy exterior. He rushed to her, meowing over and over as he nuzzled her legs.

"Wanna know why I'm late, eh?" she asked, chuckling as she leaned over to pet him. "I don't think you'd believe me if I told you."

She brought in his empty saucer before hurrying to the table, eager to start whatever this strange experiment was going to be. She emptied her bag, taking out the letter along with the cheese. She also lifted the gold chain from around her neck, holding the pendant in her hand. She leaned forward, her chin in her hands, her mind churning through everything from the library.

There were so many fragments jumbled together — magic, assassins, gods and goddesses. But she had been reading histories and travel journals, not story books… It felt silly, but at this point, it seemed the only logical thing left to do was explore the absurd possibility that Shapewalking was *real*.

"I guess there's nothing left to do but try," she said to herself. She sat up straight, gripping the edge of the table and closing her eyes.

Become Nela, she thought. *Become Nela.*

She cracked one eye open and looked at her hand on the table — still the hand of a young woman. She chewed on her lip. If it really had happened the night before, it had been an accident. So how could she make it happen on purpose? For a moment, panic started to set in. Suppose she had been seeing things? What if…she'd lost her mind the moment Nela died and made up the whole thing?

No, she thought quickly, *it has to be real!* The insignia in the book matched her pendant. That was too strange of a coincidence to ignore. And those histories… Exaggerated or not, even a hint of Shapewalkers in an official record had to mean something. Combining that with Nela's letter and the things she saw the night before, there was simply too much evidence to deny.

She picked up the letter and rubbed the parchment. Like Pallinayum's book said, there was old blood on the Continent, magical blood. Nela had that blood, and even if it was watered down, that meant the magic would be in her veins, too. All she had to do was draw it out… As she kept thinking, Amis jumped up on the table, sniffing at her cheese.

"No luck hunting today?" she asked, stroking his chin. She pulled off a small chunk, tossing it to him. "Just don't tell your friends about this, alright? We can't feed the whole neighborhood."

He gobbled it down before moving back in to nuzzle her, purring loudly. She picked up the letter and scanned it again.

"Think happy memories," she read to herself. That must be it! She had changed right at sunset the night before, when she was remembering the birthday party. She closed her eyes, trying to take herself back to that moment. She pictured herself in the garden, the sunset before her. She tried to pull back that feeling, the *warmth* of it. Still, after a minute or two, nothing happened. She opened her eyes and looked at Amis, scratching the spot between his shoulders that he loved so much.

"Maybe they have to be fresh memories?" she asked him, as if he would know. She nodded. "I'm just rehashing the memories from last night…that's like memories *of* memories. I need to try something new."

What memory could she use, though? She stared into the cat's eyes, the amber surface glowing in the lamplight. What about the day they brought Amis home? That had been one of the happiest days of her life.

"Come with me," she said, groaning as she lifted the cat. He squirmed but didn't escape. She put him on the floor, throwing another piece of cheese in front of him to keep him from running away. She slid down on her stomach until she was at eye level with him, petting him as she tried to recall everything from the day they brought him home: the light, the weather, the feeling of holding him for the first time.

She had been eleven or so. She couldn't recall exactly, but Grandpa had still been alive, so she wasn't thirteen yet. It was Umidiar, the summer sea festival, and she had been so disappointed they wouldn't be going to the beach like the rest of the city to watch the King's parade. Instead, they were going to an orphanage somewhere in the east to host a party for the children there. One of Nela's charity contacts had arranged it, and they had to drive a cart there with supplies.

Shame bubbled up inside her as she remembered how moody she had been that morning. She'd never seemed to fit in at school, and all she'd wanted was to go to the festival like the rest of the girls. For too many afternoons, she'd been forced to pass the others outside the teashops, laughing as she trudged past with Nela. She'd wanted so badly to know what they were talking about. All she had to go on were her novels, where the characters only talked of one thing — boys. How wonderful their lives seemed! She had never even spoken to a boy outside of Alip Tellemuir.

As they rode out towards the orphanage, she had sat in the back of their cart by the onions, staring at the city and wishing that something would make them turn around. Luckily for her, though, she'd been wrong — it was still one of the best days she'd ever had.

After a few hours in the cart, they had finally left the main road, starting down a narrow path onto the sand. As they came over the last dune, she finally saw the beach. It had never occurred to her that the eastern districts were still on the bay. The water was sparkling in the sun, and dozens of children ran in and out of the surf, laughing in the spray.

The adults who ran the orphanage had set up three enormous bonfires, and on the leeward side of the beach, there was a long row of picnic tables with settings for some fifty people. As soon as they approached, the other children ran up, pulling crates from the cart. Some of them wore clothes that were either too small or covered in patches, but all of them were clean and smiling. They called out their thanks, running everything to the bonfires for cooking.

Sumi had stood watching as the adults speared the food on long rods. There was fish and corn and everything in between, all of it stuck in the sand by the fires for roasting. The other children went back to their games, but before long, they were calling for her to join them. They had seemed to accept her immediately, not questioning who she was beyond that she had arrived with the food. She ran after them, somehow feeling at home with them. After all, even with her grandparents, she was an orphan, too, in her own way.

They had passed the rest of that magical day on the beach, feasting and playing until they performed the rites of the sea as the sun set. Afterwards, her cheeks red from the wind and her smiling, she had ridden with her grandparents to the orphanage to drop off the leftover food. They had approached in the last light of dusk, but she still remembered the contours of the buildings against the purple sky. The orphanage looked like a giant school, with rows and rows of dormer windows were the children had their bunks.

While her grandparents went in to finalize everything with the Headmistress, one of the girls from the beach had called to her, waving her over to a barn. The inside was glowing with the light of dozens of lanterns, and the older children were buzzing between huge rows of shelves, organizing the donations. The girl who had called for Sumi took her hand, running towards the back of the barn.

As they approached a pile of hay, she could already hear the meowing. She remembered gasping, kneeling down in the hay as she spotted Amis, a tiny grey kitten in a litter of brown, his yellow eyes shining. The girl had explained that they raised the cats for ratting, but she had heard the Headmistress complain about raising such a large litter.

"You'll take one, won't you?" she had asked, clutching Sumi's hand. "They have rats in the city, too."

Wide eyed, Sumi had nodded eagerly before she ran out of the barn to look for Nela. She had never thought in a thousand years her grandparents would say yes, but without even looking at Grandpa for confirmation, Nela had said yes.

"I like cat," she said, "not enough cat in Berill."

"What the boss says, goes," Grandpa said, shrugging. "Besides, I'm sure a few ratters kept me alive in the navy, least I can do is return the favor." She'd sprinted back to the barn, wrapping Amis in a blanket and carrying in her lap the whole way home.

As she lay on the floor, almost fifteen years later, she felt like she was back on that wagon ride. She stared into Amis' yellow eyes, stroking his coat as he purred. She began to feel a lightness in her chest, a flutter like a thousand butterflies lifting her off the ground. It felt like she was made of bubbles, and as she began to laugh, there was a flash of light and a loud pop.

She opened her eyes, blinking. The world was wider and brighter than it had been just a moment before, like looking through a fun house mirror. She looked down at her hands and found…paws? Paws! She started to laugh, but it came out as a meow. She had turned into Amis! It was *real*!

She locked eyes with the real Amis. His ears were back as he crouched low, looking like he could pounce at any moment. He let out a growl, sniffing at her. But then, suddenly, he relaxed. Had he recognized the real her somehow? He pushed towards her, nuzzling her face as he began to purr again, tickling her whiskers — she had *whiskers*!

Apparently satisfied, Amis took off, running through the house. After one lap around the cottage, he stopped, meowing at her to follow before sprinting off again. She took a shaky step with one paw, a bit thrown by having two extra legs. As she forced herself to walk, though, it seemed her body did the work for her. The back paws followed the front, like the swinging of her arms when she moved her human hips.

She started to run, letting out a triumphant meow as she chased after Amis. When she caught him, he turned, tackling her in a roll of fur. Then, he ran off again, and they started taking turns chasing each other to the sitting room. After a dozen rounds of that, Amis finally stopped in the kitchen, leaping onto the counter by the sink. He reached for the window, tapping the glass with his paws.

She followed him to the sink and stopped, staring up at the ledge above. It seemed awfully high as a cat, but somehow, a strange confidence welled up in her, knowing for certain she could make the jump. She leapt, kicking hard with her back legs, soaring onto the counter like it was nothing. She hopped over to the window ledge, giving Amis what she hoped was a knowing look. There were benefits to having a cat-human on your side, after all. She took her paw, popping open the lock on the window and pushing it open.

They leapt out into the garden, but when she landed on the dewy grass, she froze, eyes wide. Despite the darkness, she could see *everything* — every leaf in the garden, tiny bugs as they crept across the plants. And as she breathed in, it fell like she could *smell* the city, as if she could see the chimney smoke as it mixed with the sea breeze. She meowed loudly, calling for Amis. She heard a rustling in the garden before he reappeared, sticking his head out from between the squash plants and meowing back.

She leapt after him, and the games began again. She felt like a doll in a full-sized house, chasing Amis past kale and rhubarb that seemed gigantic at the size of a cat. The night was cold, but with a body covered in fur, it felt invigorating. As they ran, a family of mice bolted across their path, and Amis turned, launching into the undergrowth after them.

Do as the locals do, she thought, running after him. She found that with her heightened senses, she could track the mice just as well as Amis. Her ears picked up the slightest rustle of the leaves, and her eyes caught the merest glimmer of movement. It felt incredible to hunt, every part of her brain prickling with the chase.

Suddenly, they were on top of the mice. Amis leapt and caught one, biting down hard on its spine with a crack. Sumi saw another up ahead and launched herself at it, trusting her newfound senses to keep her aim true. She got it, clamping her jaws around its neck. But as the blood poured into her mouth, she gagged, the thrill of the hunt vanishing.

"That's foul!" she yelled to Amis, though it came out as a low yowl. Apparently having a cat body wouldn't give her cat cravings... She stumbled towards a clump of mint, taking a huge mouthful to banish the awful taste. As she shook her head and turned around, she saw the mouse lying on the ground, writhing. In her haste to get rid of the blood, she hadn't snapped its neck like Amis had.

Oh no, oh no, oh no, she thought, running over to the poor creature. What should she do? She didn't want to take its neck in her mouth again, but still desperately wanted to end its suffering. A powerful guilt washed over her, and the lightness in her heart began to wither, the swarm of butterflies vanishing. Suddenly, there was another flash, and she found herself lying in a heap among the squash plants, human again.

She groaned, rolling over and pushing herself onto her hands and knees. She was crushing the squash, her body much too large to fit between the rows as she had as a cat. She leaned back, wiping the dirt off her hands before squeezing her temples.

"The mouse!" she gasped. She looked down, and there it was, still in the throes of death. She scrambled to her feet and jumped over the garden fence, running to get the large shovel that leaned against the side of the house. She put the mouse out of its misery with one clean blow as tears welled up in her eyes.

"I'm sorry, Mr. Mouse," she whispered before digging a little hole where she buried the poor creature. Amis appeared, his own mouse between his jaws. He dropped it at her feet and meowed.

"Thanks, Amis," she said, nodding sadly — he was doing the work of his species, after all. "Job well done. I'm sorry I'm not cut out for it myself."

She blinked, realizing for the first time just how dark it was with her human eyes. She breathed in deeply, and all the mysterious scents of the feline world were gone. At least she still got a deep breath of the sea, calming her nerves.

She walked to the back door and turned the knob, but it wouldn't budge. She slapped her forehead. They had come out the window! She looked through the glass pane in the door and saw her bag sitting on the kitchen table, her keys inside.

Well, you already fell in the squash, she thought, *what's one more indignity?* She walked up to the window, now at chest height, and tried to climb in.

"So much harder as a person!" she groaned, putting her hands on the ledge and hauling herself up. As she landed her knees on the windowsill, she looked back and forth, trying to decide how to turn her legs to reach the counter below. She swiveled her right leg over the windowsill but lost her grip, falling inward and landing in a heap on the kitchen floor. Amis was right behind her, landing on her chest and knocking the air out of her.

"Some powerful Shapewalker you are," she said to herself, chuckling as she squeezed the cat, "not going to be killing many kings if you can't even climb through a window."

She laid there for a long time before finally standing, massaging the back of her neck. That was probably enough for one night. She washed her hands and put the kettle on before digging out some bread to go with her cheese. Once the tea was poured, she sat at the kitchen table, chewing with her eyes closed. Wrung out as she was, a smile still came to her face. She had done it! The magic was real, and it was hers.

Still, there was one question she couldn't seem to answer — why give these powers to someone like her? There were so many people more deserving, people who were brave and strong. People like Nela, or even Mama, taken so young, who was so kind that her daughter remembered her nearly two decades later. What had Sumi ever done? She was too scared, too weak and alone to ever do a tenth of what they had. Had the gods been drinking when they chose her?

She took the block of royal cheese from the table and tore off another slice, placing it on top of her bread. As she bit into it, an idea suddenly struck her. Two strangers, first Darren and then the Royal Librarian, had changed the course of her day. Even though they hadn't done anything remarkable, their kindness had turned a day that should have been horrible into something magical. What if that's what her powers were for, to give her the courage to be kind?

The clock chimed in the hall, making her realize how much time she'd spent as a cat. She gulped down her tea, jumping up to head to bed. Even as she hurried up the stairs, though, something felt different. She wasn't just rushing off to sleep so she could work in the morning. Tomorrow would be something new. She would find someone to help, and everything else would follow after.

7

She stopped listening, suddenly knowing exactly what he was pointing to. There, in the middle of the room, was a gigantic flower, the color of moonlight. It was shaped like a lily, its petals tipped towards the night air as if waiting to capture dreams that drifted on the wind.

-Excerpt from The Borimol Plains

—:—

Aelibis stared out the dusty window of the warehouse, trying to keep his hands moving on the task the foreman had given him. The place was split into narrow aisles, each one divided by a long table. He had to empty crates of women's stockings and wrap them in tiny silk bags for stores. It was a good task for someone with plans to make, even if he couldn't seem to focus lately…

At least it wouldn't be long now. Running a scam was like baking bread — you had to trust your nose, and he could already tell this would be a fine bloody loaf! Anyone else might write off a company that did women's wares — the stockings certainly weren't worth anything — but after a week, he had finally figured out where they were hiding the jewelry.

The loot was only half of the puzzle, of course, but his other preparations were nearly finished, too. He'd even made a memory with the boss already! He still wasn't quite sure how that bit worked, but if he could find a way to tell a joke to the owner — anything to get himself laughing and happy — he'd be able to use that memory to imitate the man later. He always picked jokes that his old man had told him as a kid — those seemed to work the best for some reason. And once you imitated the owner of a warehouse, the rest of the job was easy.

At this point, he could probably plan a heist in his sleep. The problem was what came after… He'd barely scraped out of that police raid, and had lost half his crew in the process. Most of the loot, too — the half he hadn't been able to sell yet, anyway. Of the men who escaped the raid, only a few remained; the rest had decided to walk. Even worse, he was running out of savings, forced to spend far more than he'd liked filling out their ranks.

That was the nature of his business he supposed — easy come, easy go. But that strange bloke, Erso… The man had warned him twice now, and he'd been right, too — somehow the police *were* tracking him. It had something to do with his powers, though he wasn't any closer to understanding how it all worked. Part of him thought he should've taken Erso up on his training, but he hadn't made it this far by letting anybody get the best of him, and he wouldn't start now.

Besides, Erso had never turned back up after the raid. Aelibis had been careful, of course, making sure not to use his powers at all. That probably meant Erso couldn't track him any better than the police, and he would keep it that way until it was time to finish this job. That did make him wonder, though…shouldn't they just do this heist the old fashioned way?

No! he thought, a shiver running up his spine. He had to be better than that. His heists were clean, without a single death so far. Once he started cracking skulls, he'd be no better than his father. He had to have been made a Shapewalker for a reason; he had to be different.

He may be a bit rattled now, but he would find a way through. He had done three heists before the police found him. He'd gotten lucky before, and maybe he'd get lucky again. The police weren't magic, not like him, and it couldn't be that easy to find him. Either way, he couldn't turn back now. This was his destiny. He'd been given powers unlike any he'd ever seen, and he'd be damned if he was gonna sit on his hands, rotting away in some stupid slum.

He looked over his shoulder but didn't see the foreman anywhere in sight. He snuck his hand into his jacket pocket and pulled out the photo he had hidden there. He rubbed his thumb over its surface, the image already worn from overuse. He was afraid to ruin it, but he needed to touch it all the same. It was his good luck charm, and Umilai knew he needed luck now.

It was a picture of a woman, her hair done up in long, looping braids, a wide smile on her face. His beautiful Irieal. She had moved to Amoriai just before his powers appeared, looking for better work and a way out of their rough life. He was going to follow her, and once he made something of himself, he'd finally marry her. He was almost there, just a little more money and he'd be ready.

"Wait for me," he whispered to the photo, "just a little while longer now." He would find her, no matter what it cost him.

8

You fools who fear the darkness, do you think there no light in the depths?! The twinkling soul of the true gods, they will light your path better than some feeble sun! Come with me into the heart of things, where truth awaits your weary mind.

-Excerpt from the Poems of Boran Stonekeeper

—:—

Sumi woke with a smile on her face. For the first time since Nela died, she could remember dreaming, her mind finally able to cling to those tiny fragments. She remembered flying, wielding a sword, running as a deer — a hundred lifetimes in the span of a night. She popped out of bed without a single groan, suddenly seeing the possibilities a new day could bring.

She went out into the hall and splashed water on her face. Leaning close to the mirror, she pulled her cheeks tight and turned her head every which way. There didn't seem to be any stray cat hairs, though one could never be too sure.

"First an old woman and then a cat," she said to herself, chuckling. "What's next, knitting yarn?"

Before changing, she walked over to Nela's room, the perfume still heavy from the day before. She took a deep breath, sighing it out. Lifting the necklace from beneath her nightgown, she let the pendant dangle in front of her, the emerald sparkling in the morning light. The letter had said it was her great grandmother's — had she been a Shapewalker too? Of all the times to find this magic... She had so many questions, but the one person she wanted to ask was gone.

She turned back to her room, slipping the necklace under her gown. She'd need to remember to keep it hidden. As she dressed, she kept thinking about Nela. Had there ever been any signs that the woman was different? She hadn't been an "ordinary" person, but that didn't mean she had magical powers, either. But where would she even begin to look for clues?

Being Anushai had certainly made Nela unlike anyone else's grandmother. She'd tended to look down on most Berillai social customs, though who from the Continent didn't? As she brushed her hair, she wondered — could there have been more to that bias? When she was ten, she'd asked Nela why they didn't have a secret phrase.

"You want phrase with your Nela?" her grandmother had asked. "Only fool Berillai need phrase. I know you're my granddaughter, no need for phrase to telling that."

Sumi put down the hair brush and drummed her fingers against her chin. After what she'd read about King Rummon, it was painfully obvious why the Berillai like their passphrases — not that many were using them now with trolleys running everywhere. Still, could a Shapewalker's abilities make those precautions unnecessary? Like the book had said, they — she — could supposedly tap into some kind of power that connected all creatures…

What about the opposite; could a human ever tell what she was? A shiver ran up her spine, remembering the palace guards. They still followed the old ways, so carefully keeping swords out of the wrong hands. Would they ever recognize her symbol? What about the police? She clutched her necklace, her pulse quickening. She *had* to be careful.

She shook her head, finally moving to the wardrobe to put on her dress. She carefully placed it over her shoulders before doing up the buttons. Then, she slowly laced her boots, making sure the knots were done perfectly. She was like a knight donning her armor, getting ready for battle. Maybe she wasn't a fearsome knight, working in a shop all day…but it was something! She wouldn't ever want to leave Mr. Furttenhur anyway, but these powers *would* change her life, even if it was only in the stolen minutes at the end of the day.

As she went down the stairs, she saw a letter sitting on the floor just under the mail slot. Had she missed it coming home in the dark? She ran down the last few steps, snatching it up. It was from Seriai! It felt like ages since the last letter had come, though everything had been a blur lately… Still, it wasn't like she could blame Seriai; the mail service out to her farm was awful, and she'd hardly have time to write now with another baby around.

She ripped open the envelope, eagerly skimming the lines as she walked into the kitchen. Every detail brought up another question for her to write in reply. Hopefully she'd meet those babies someday… They almost never came to the city anymore, but she hadn't even met their first child yet!

She dipped into the sitting room and grabbed a piece of paper to start her reply when she froze. What was she supposed to say about her own life? Seriai was already worried about her with Nela gone, and she'd sound dotty if she started talking about Shapewalkers! She needed time to think... She put the letter in her bag; it would have to wait until things slowed down at the shop.

Sumi walked to the stove, excited to make a proper breakfast for once. She built up the kitchen fire before setting the tea to boil. Then, she went to the front porch and retrieved the milk. Once the fire was hot, she put the cast iron skillet over the burner, cracking a few eggs and frying them up while she chewed on the last of the royal cheese. As she finally sat down at the kitchen table, she turned back to the most important question looming in her mind — how would she use these powers?

She thought of her dreams the night before, the silver knight's sword gleaming in her hand. What did the heroes of her childhood stories do? They saved the day, obviously, but how did they figure out who to help? It seemed like they mostly just rode around on their horses and let trouble find them. The world was full of monsters and villagers in danger, and all the knight had to do was stay on their path and be in the right place when the time came.

Sumi nodded to herself as she chewed. *Let the world come to me, then,* she thought. Working in a flower shop wasn't exactly the same as riding through the kingdom on a horse, but the idea was the same. She could go on working in the shop and see what trouble came her way. If she could help just one person a day, it wouldn't be even a fraction of an afternoon's work for Nela, but it would be a start.

An hour later, Sumi ran into the shop out of breath. She may have done that every morning since Nela died, but this time felt different. She had never realized it could feel good to run late... Apparently all you needed was a good enough reason. It was like running from an angry mob versus running in a race. Both would make your heart pound, but the feeling was acutely different.

She'd been looking for someone to help, though she hadn't found anyone in particular. Still, the looking was its own joy. It felt like she saw even more of the city than normal with her focus dialed in on everyone around her. Even loving the beauty of this place as she did, the active searching brought a new keenness to her vision.

She greeted Mr. Furttenhur in the traditional way — even if she *was* the type of monster he'd been hoping to avoid — and slipped into the back room to don her apron. She stepped out in a flash and strode to the front of the counter, clicking her heels together like a soldier snapping to attention. She smiled at Mr. Furttenhur as he looked up, realizing she was awaiting her orders for the day.

"Ah, yes," he said, thumbing through a stack of papers he had placed on the counter. "We're scheduled to get a new shipment of fall pieces in today. Could you be a dear and remove the old summer ones to make room?"

Sumi's smile fell. There was nothing worse than discarding the old flowers. Especially at the change in the seasons, the previous month's stock fell out of favor, and the poor plants started dying on the shelves, never gracing a kitchen table or the arm of a date. Sumi nodded, glumly dragging her heels up to the first table, taking stock of what was wilting the fastest.

A while later, she was waddling back down the shop steps, arms laden with dozens of flowers to be discarded. She felt like some ancient Berillai queen, off to prepare the king's funeral pyre. At least a funeral would fit the mood of so much going to waste... At the bottom of the stairs, she turned left into the alleyway between their shop and the next. There was a large iron box there where they stored wood for the furnace. When Mr. Feirshin came, he would bring more wood along with the fresh flowers, taking the old ones with him.

She lifted the lid and dumped the flowers in, the petals hitting the bottom with a sad thud. She lingered for a moment, the lid still in her hand. She ducked her head into the box, emerging with the heads from two roses. She smoothed her hair, shooting a glance towards the mouth of the alley. Hopefully no-one had seen her face-first in the wood pile... She slipped the buds into her apron pocket. It wasn't much, but maybe she could keep this little bit from going to waste somehow.

It seemed she'd come down just in time. As she came out of the alley, Mr. Feirshin was pulling up in his cart. He sat tall on the box, his bald head covered with a wide, floppy hat. He must have been as old as Grandpa — had he still been alive — but somehow, he was still as strong as an ox. How did he do it, leaving the farms at dawn and riding to the city everyday?

"Sumi!" he called, smiling as he pulled the pipe from his mouth. He pulled the cart along the curb in a smooth sweep, coming to a stop right next to her. "Just who I wanted to see, the picture of beauty!" He winked, jumping down from the driver's box.

"Morning, Mr. Feirshin," Sumi said, rolling her eyes as she stepped up, petting the horse's mane. Mr. Feirshin was always sweet to her, saying she looked just like his wife. Was that a compliment, though? He never did specify — did she look like his wife now or in her youth? It could easily be either with a face like hers...

The horse, Elpitore, was a beautiful white gelding, and had finally taken to her after years of deliveries. Mr. Feirshin fumbled around in his coat pocket and found a sugar lump, handing it to her. Unfortunately, it was probably just the sugar that had made the horse like her... Still, she held out her palm, giggling as Elpitore smacked his lips over the sugar. Mr. Feirshin moved to the back of the cart where the deliveries were covered in a long, beige tarpaulin.

"I'm glad I caught you first," he said. "It's a shame wasting new flowers on Old Man Furttenhur." Never mind that Mr. Furttenhur was twenty years his junior, Mr. Feirshin winked again, chuckling as he ripped back the cloth.

"Oh!" Sumi squeaked, running to the back of the cart. It looked like a sunset, fall flowers splashed across the wood in waves of color. There was purple fountain grass, marigolds, and red chrysanthemums. "They're beautiful," she whispered, leaning over the flowers. She took in a deep breath, feeling like she was inhaling fall itself.

"Knew you'd like 'em," he said, moving to the back of the cart where the wood was piled up. Her smile fell, remembering what was waiting in the wood box.

"I'm afraid we have a lot of unused flowers today," she said. "You know how the late season can be."

Mr. Feirshin smiled. "Not to worry, dear," he said. "I pass an ironworks on my way out of town and they throw 'em right in the forge, no trouble at all." Sumi frowned. She'd already felt bad for the flowers; picturing them being burned to a crisp wasn't exactly helping. Mr. Feirshin groaned, picking up a large cord of wood in each hand as she scampered behind.

"There's no way you could use them?" she asked. "Give them to that beautiful wife of yours maybe?"

He chuckled, squatting down and dropping the wood beside the box before leaning in to collect the old flowers. "Afraid not," he said. "The wife would kill me — allergies like you've never seen. I'd rather give them to a beauty like you, but you already work here."

She rolled her eyes again as Mr. Feirshin laughed. Before putting the wood in the box, he pulled two logs from the cord, handing them to Sumi.

"Be a dear and run these to the boiler," he said. "Furttenhur's written to me twice this month telling me to hurry with the wood before the frosts come."

The boiler was off the alley on the ground floor, behind the bakery. She turned to stoke the furnace, and Mr. Feirshin went to haul the rest of the wood, shouting jokes to her the whole time.

The rest of the afternoon breezed by, a flurry of carrying in flowers and endless rearranging. Mr. Furttenhur stayed later than normal, as he usually did for large deliveries. They also ended up having a good number of customers. As they began to see splashes of color in the windows, dozens had climbed the steps to the shop, leaving with armfuls of blossoms they'd only just arranged.

Finally, things slowed down, and by the time Mr. Furttenhur left, she had about an hour left of work to herself. She did some last minute tidying before ducking into the back room, eagerly pulling out her letter from Seriai. Hopefully in the time she had left, she could think of something semi-sane to write in reply… She had glossed over the letter in the kitchen earlier, but she read it again more carefully, savoring it:

My dearest Sumi,

I was so happy to receive your last letter. I'm sorry it's taken me this long to reply. I think of you every day, and I re-read your last letter probably a dozen times. But with the new baby, it just took me forever to find the time to write you back!

Thank Umilai's Heart little Essie was born healthy. We named her after your Nela! Ekkel wanted to name her after the Queen, but I put my foot down. She was like my own gran, after all. I'm so sorry I missed her funeral. If I had been even a little less pregnant, I promise I would have pushed my way onto a train, no matter what Ekkel said.

Tears slipped down her face, and she reached up to wipe them away. What a relief it was to have a new life out in the world carrying on Nela's name! Her grandmother deserved a legacy, and at the rate she was going, it wasn't seeming likely she'd have her own family… Going through the funeral without Seriai had been heartbreaking, but this made up for it a hundredfold. To think that right when Nela left the world, a new little Essie was born into it… She dabbed at her eyes with her handkerchief and kept reading:

The farm is going well! We've been lucky with the rains this year, and it looks like the grain is going to come in better than last season. Ekkel is happy, of course. His father kept telling him not to take over the family farm, so he's relieved to finally be making something of it. I actually feel like Cullesil in The Borimol Plains — remember when she marries the count?

Sumi laughed out loud. She and Seriai had always bonded over their Anushai romance novels. By some strange quirk of fate, Seriai had read the same series that Nela had always loved. There was one final paragraph, the letter ending much more quickly than normal:

I'm so sorry, but I'll have to leave off here for now. I already hear Essie crying in the next room, and Ekkel is out with Pursal in the barn. I'm thinking of you always, and I can't wait until your next letter. Please tell me how you're doing, I'm worried for you all alone in the cottage. I'm wishing you only wonderful things.

Your dearest and best of friends always,
Seriai

She lifted the letter to her nose and breathed in, trying to catch some trace of Seriai's life. Maybe she caught just a whiff of hay and baby powder? Even if it was just in her head, she was glad to have Seriai feel even an inch closer. It broke her heart just a little to watch the letters growing shorter, though even a single sentence would've been enough. Seriai did make up for her brevity with constancy, never leaving a doubt about how much she cared. With no family left, that kind of friend felt like an anchor in a stormy sea.

Sumi pulled out a piece of paper from Mr. Furttenhur's desk and opened the ink well. She smoothed the paper and wrote a greeting:

My dearest Seriai,

That part at least was easy…

I'm so glad to hear that Essie was born healthy and happy. What a beautiful name! You know my grandmother; she would have acted like it didn't affect her, but it would have pleased her to no end. Please say hello to Ekkel for me. If you feel like Cullesil from the stories, is he your handsome Porsulair? If Essie is already two months old, then Pursal has to be walking by now! I want to hear everything about how he's growing. I'm sure he'll be just as brilliant as his mother once he starts talking.

Sumi stared out the window, scratching her head. How to tell her about what was happening in her life? There was finally something wonderful taking place, but she couldn't possibly tell her the whole truth, and anything vague would only make her worry…

Without realizing, she had stuck the end of the feather in her mouth and was chewing on it. She stuck out her tongue and shook her head. Might as well give the writing a go before she ate the whole pen.

Life certainly has been strange since Nela died, though things are finally starting to look a bit brighter. She left me a beautiful necklace that was a family heirloom. Hopefully I can show it to you next time you're in the city... I miss you dearly as always. Maybe I can take an extra day off during Umidiar next year and come visit?

My love always,
Sumi

That would have to be good enough for now. Maybe by the time they visited each other she'd have the whole magic business down... If she could tell anyone in her life, it would be Seriai, she just had to find the right words. She folded up the letter and stuck it in an envelope, addressing it carefully to make sure it didn't get lost in the maze of eastern farms.

"The flowers!" she said, jumping up before she sealed the letter. She reached into her apron pocket, slipping the rosebuds into the envelope. She always wanted to catch a whiff of Seriai's life, so why not do the same for her? It wasn't as good as pressing them, of course, but at least the flowers wouldn't go to waste!

As she put the letter in her bag, the clock finally struck six. The last hour had gone quicker than she'd expected! She quickly tidied up her things and got ready to leave. As she walked towards the door, she paused, taking a deep breath. Someone was out there, waiting her help. She was going to find them, and together, they'd start her adventure.

9

It seemed she was in for far more than she'd bargained for, though, as Mother liked to say, "the game wasn't good until you bet all your pieces." As they stepped out into the garden, the assembled party all looked up, with more than a few eyes widening at the presence of the duke.

-Excerpt from The Borimol Plains

Sumi merged into the evening rush like a drop of water in a surging river. She looked carefully at every person she passed, but how would she tell who needed help? Each of them wore a mask of invulnerability, the determined look of city folk trying to get home at top speed. Maybe it would be easier if she rode the trolley out to one of the neighborhoods... Of course, the palace square would be thronging with people in the evenings, but anyone who needed help would probably stay out of the fray.

She pulled off to the side and stood behind a mailbox, pulling out her coin purse. She jangled it by her ear, but it didn't make a sound. She sighed. No more trolley rides for her, apparently. If the reduced pension wasn't bad enough, the RTS lifting the prices last summer for the line expansion basically ensured she'd never afford the trolley again. She didn't mind the walk to the terrace, obviously, but she'd need speed to reach those further neighborhoods... Once people ducked inside for their dinner, there might not be anyone left on the street to bump into!

She drummed her fingers on her chin. What about the docks? They were within walking distance, and there *had* been an awful lot of travelers lately. She continued down Laeryia Boulevard towards the port. Since she was on the beach side, she could make out the statue of Umilai, the god standing proudly on his clam shell, coral sword in hand. She smiled; it was almost time for Alomidiar. The passing of the summer festival was finally losing its sting, and it was almost time for the city to celebrate again, transforming the beachfront around the statue with bonfires.

As she approached the port, she noticed a man with his hat in hand, begging for coins. Most of the people passing averted their gaze, with one or two openly glaring at him. He had a greasy beard but a kind face, and his clothes, while threadbare, seemed well cared for. One leg of his pants was pinned up where one of his legs would have been, and he leaned against a set of crutches. He must have had an amputation — a navy man maybe?

He was calling out to each passerby, asking for a trolley token to ride to the end of the line.

"Help a man get home!" he called. "Out of work, just wanna get back to m'boy! Riding to the end of the line!"

Sumi frowned; things certainly had grown harder the last few years. As farms were snatched up for the train line, more people seemed to be pouring into the city every day. If the warehouses or mills couldn't take them, where would they end up? It seemed the abundance of commerce still hadn't eliminated the greed and suffering that went with it.

Her heart ached as she approached the man, knowing already that she had no coins to give.

"You miss," he asked, "spare a coin please? Or a token?"

She smiled and shook her head. Why didn't she say something?! It was just like her to clam up at the most important moment. Nela would always stop and talk to the beggars that they passed, at least learning something about them or sharing some of the food they were delivering. How had Nela been so brave? She may have been a foot and a half shorter than Sumi, but you'd never know it by the way she carried herself.

As she walked away, she slowed her pace, finally stopping by a news stand. She hovered there, looking back at the beggar, wishing she could do something. She should at least find the courage to go back and talk to him! But she felt so ashamed for walking by in the first place — what would be her excuse now for walking back?

She fidgeted behind the newsstand, her nails digging into her palms. All she needed was a single token… She froze, her hand going to her mouth. Could she *transform* into a trolley token? Having done Nela and the cat, clearly any living creature was on the table, but an inanimate object? There was also the happy memory bit to sort out… If she was going to pull this off, she'd somehow need to conjure a memory with a coin in it.

77

"Oh!" she said out loud, causing a few people to stare. She blushed but smiled in spite of herself. Of course she had a memory of a trolley token! Memories of her first trolley ride began to flood her mind. To think that there were so many things she'd nearly forgotten, only keeping a few precious gems from a mountain of moments. But now she'd need every single one, any random moment potentially hiding the key to her Shapewalking.

She had been maybe ten when the trolleys went in? The prices were still low then, with the crown trying to get everyone used to the strange machines. It had been winter, and she could still remember how icy cold the air had felt. She had been wearing that wool coat Grandpa had gotten her. It was way too small for her by then, but it was still the warmest thing she owned. Nela had taken her down from the terrace with no destination in mind, only to ride the trolley for the fun of it.

The feeling of the memory entered her body, visceral and tactile. If you weren't paying attention, you'd think memories were only in the mind, but the *body* remembered just as clearly. She felt her tiny hand in Nela's, their mittens combining into a giant wool ball. She felt Nela opening her palm, putting a token in her hand. They were bronze then, the metal shining in the hazy winter sun.

She let out a long breath, her fingertips tingling. She turned and ran down the street, ducking into an alley before the memory overtook her. She held on to the old brick wall for support, rounding a corner where she could hide. She felt that coin in her tiny hand, focusing on its shape, its texture, the old king's face on its surface. Her eyes filled with a brilliant last of light, and she was gone.

_____

Sumi was a coin. She was a coin! She felt the stones beneath her and the air above, her metal surface radiating out the coolness of fall. It didn't feel bad to be cold, though, it simply *was*. She had no eyes as a coin, but by touching with her surroundings, it seemed she could sense them, as if seeing the world through a haze.

She had a growing awareness of herself too. She felt the ridges running along her sides, and she could feel the old king's face on her front. She couldn't explain it if she tried, but she simply knew those things were there. It was like knowing that you had legs without looking at them. She could focus on the details, but they would be there whether or not she paid them any mind.

Growing used to her form, her mind returned to the man on the sidewalk. He was only a block away on human legs, but it seemed like miles away now that she was so small. How was she supposed to get back there? She wasn't even sure she could get off the ground, let alone cover that distance. When she was a cat, she could do whatever a cat could do, right? But cats had muscles! What was a coin but a round object? Still, if she could do anything a coin could do...

She pushed with her mind, as if she were getting up from the floor with her arms, and the coin righted itself, lifting onto its edge. She froze for a moment, stunned, feeling the world around her again from her new position. Had she really doubted her magic so easily? A coin *could* be balanced on its side, of course, and if a coin could do it, so could she.

Now for the hard part, she thought. She focused her mind forward, and the coin rolled. She wobbled a bit at first, but after a few feet, she got the hang of it. As she reached the end of the alley, she slowed, pulling backwards with her mind. She'd have to time her exit carefully. People may ignore a runaway coin if they didn't look too closely, but she couldn't risk getting picked up by the wrong person.

She rolled to the edge of the alley, pushing outward with her mind. The traffic was thinning, though there were still more people than she'd like. Before her, the sidewalk ended abruptly like a yawning cliff. The curb! Maybe she could roll along it and stay out of sight. She just had to avoid the gutters. She shuddered; she could change back if she fell in, but she'd still have to escape a city's worth of filth... She stilled her mind, as if she had taken a deep breath. She couldn't turn back now.

She waited for a gap in the crowd before shooting towards the curb. She rolled over the edge and banked to her left, heading back towards the man. As she approached the first drain, she felt herself tense — if a piece of metal could even get tense — but rolled past it smoothly. She plowed ahead, unable to sense much in the way of landmarks. Finally, after what felt like an eternity, the man came back into view.

She started to slow her momentum, preparing to turn towards him, but there wasn't a gap in the curb. She was so close! She stopped, probing with her awareness when she heard the jangling of coins in his hat. That was it! If he couldn't see her, maybe he would hear her. The next drain was only a few feet away, and it had an iron grate...

She wobbled towards it, carefully tipping herself onto the grate, her bronze side making a crisp clink. She felt her weight teetering on the edge, her vision disappearing into the abyss of the drain. If she had eyes, she would have shut them tight. When nothing happened, she lifted and dropped herself again. She kept it going, knocking against the iron over and over until, finally, a hand appeared, reaching for her. She reached out with her mind and saw...the man with crutches!

She sensed his face getting closer as he picked her up, his hand warm against the coin. Hopefully he wouldn't be put off by the old king's face… Nela had always been finding old ones in her coat somehow, though, so she knew for a fact they were still accepted. It would have been nice to transform into a proper new token with Queen Welaya on it, but the memory was what it was. The man glanced around, probably looking for the owner of the coin, though, of course, he found no one.

"Looks like my luck's finally changed!" he said, smiling as he slipped her into his pocket. He fumbled with his crutches for a moment before swiftly moving down the street towards the closest trolley stop. She slid back and forth in his pocket, swaying to the rhythm of his gait. The wool of his coat scratched against her surface, sending static rippling across her that made her want to giggle.

They stood at the stop, and she reached out with her mind, trying to take in everything passing through her hazy vision. While they waited, the man began to whistle a tune. So he was a navy man after all! It was an old sailor's song called 'Mad Jaim', one she'd know anywhere from how often Grandpa sang it. As he whistled, some of the words came back to her.

'Mad Jaim was a sailor, Mad Jaim was a cat, the cook and the captain, the boy and the hat.' That actually sounded like a song about a Shapewalker! In the story, he was some kind of shapeshifting merman who boarded a navy boat and ended up doing all the jobs on the crew. He scrubbed the decks, lifted the sails, even took a nap as the captain's cat. At the end, he jumped back into the sea and swam away as his tail regrew.

Had Grandpa known about Nela's family? And if Nela did have the magic, would she have told him? Dozens of memories floated up of him singing it while Nela cooked, gently ribbing her as he sang the verses and laughed. That would have been so like him! Knowing some giant secret and choosing to spend his entire life teasing his wife about it. She chuckled, settling into the pocket as she buzzed along to the man's tune.

Erso was on Fort Street by one of those big ugly banks where the Berillai loved to worship money — or whatever 'god of the sea' bullocks they were about. Leave it to those pirates to land in a new place already full of gods and pretend there was something better to worship. What about Pe'ritrine or the Nine Saints? How could you live on land, enjoying perfectly good crops, and thank some giant sea monster for them? It was baffling.

He had finally taken a break from searching, sitting on one of those marble ledges by the bank, though he'd have to move soon judging by the way those guards kept looking daggers at him. Maybe he should just go inside? Aelibis might like hiding in there, lots of money about. He looked down at his shoes, grimacing as he found one of the laces untied. Well, it wasn't like he could blame the poor thing. It was a wonder his shoes even had soles anymore with how much bloody running around he was doing!

It was a pity he just couldn't shape it back into place, though. Leave it to the Berillai to take the fun out of everything — not that there were that many kingdoms left where a mu'amashdar could shape and expect everyone to mind their own bloody business. Still, it was the principle of the thing. He was still grumbling, leaning over to tie his shoe when he felt a giant ripple shoot through his mind, like thunder on a sunny day.

He nearly jumped, his eyes shooting towards the beach. Could that finally be Aelibis? In the middle of town in broad daylight? He forgot the shoelace, running toward the docks. He spared a glance towards the guards. They were still giving him dirty looks, probably trying to decide if he'd actually stolen something. Leave it to the bloody Berillai! They couldn't conceive that a regular bloke could be a Shapewalker, but they still believed in stone speakers and all that nonsense. As if he could call the metal out of the bank by whispering to it!

As he crossed over Laeryia Boulevard, he could still sense the Shapewalker, following their energy along the beach until he found a disheveled man waiting for the trolley. It was too soon after the ripple to tell for sure, but he was the only one around.

"The one leg is a nice bit," he said to himself, ambling over to the man, nodding. He was whistling some old sailing song. He hadn't heard it before, but the melody was simple enough, so he hummed along. The man flashed him a toothy grin, going on with their duet. Well, that proved it wasn't Aelibis, at least — he hadn't tried to spit on him or anything! Though it wasn't everyday you saw a felt a ripple like that... Had Aelibis wanted him to find this man? Maybe follow him back to a hideout?

As the trolley finally rang its bell down the street, a few other passengers strolled up to board. They seemed awfully casual about it... Could one of them be Aelibis? He didn't look too closely. If he was meant to stick with the first bloke, he'd do it. He'd certainly done stranger in his line of work...

Erso boarded after him, dropping one of his fake tokens into the trolley box. He'd shaped it alongside him just that morning, so it'd have

81

a few days before it turned back into a cheap coin. It wouldn't do to waste real money everywhere he went, especially not with the bloody Berillai who wouldn't know the difference! He drifted casually to the back of the trolley, taking a seat across from the man with the crutches.

Sumi clinked down into the token box, landing on the other coins. *Good luck!* she thought to the man as he moved towards the seats. She felt out with her mind, taking in her small confines as the trolley lurched forward. *Hello friends*, she thought to her fellow tokens, though none of them were Sumis. She sat there a moment longer, basking in her triumph when a thought struck her — he'd said he was riding to the end of the line...

Oh dear, she thought. Her job was done, but she could be stuck in this box for a very long time. How had she been planning on getting out anyway? She couldn't exactly wait until the clerks were counting up the tokens at the end of the night! Or even worse, trying to explain how she'd gotten into a locked treasury vault... If they didn't hang her for thievery they'd get definitely her for the Shapewalking!

You've really done it this time, she thought. She tried to summon the trolley map in her mind. She'd ridden to the end of the line once on an errand for Nela. There was a station there where the drivers switched out. If she waited until then, she could escape before they head back east...right? She took the coin equivalent of a deep breath. She shouldn't spoil her success with worry. Like Grandpa always said, "the storm'll hit your sails, best not to watch it on the horizon."

Erso eyed the other man, trying to gauge if he was a Shapewalker. He liked the flair for the dramatic, but why pose as a one-legged man? And where were they riding to? The energy was certainly still with them, but it was hard to pinpoint when they were moving. He couldn't sense a keyhole on the man, though it was always impossible to tell under a ripple that big. He looked around at the other passengers, though they all still seemed perfectly normal. Well, like Beysal always said, if he wanted the honey, he'd have to shake the tree.

"Lovely evening, eh?" Erso asked.

"Oh yes," the man said, flashing him that piano-key smile again, "couldn't be lovelier!"

Erso nodded knowingly — he'd be having a good evening too playing a one-legged man.

"Where you heading?" he asked.

"End of the line," the man said, "been lookin' for work by the docks." His smile disappeared for a moment. "Not much work for a gimp, I guess." Erso nodded sympathetically, but it was only a moment before the man was all smiles again. "Well, that's tomorrow's trouble, now I get to see my family."

Erso smiled back. This man was a natural actor, fully committed to the role.

"I'm actually getting off there as well," Erso said. "Thought it was time for a *change* in my environment." He stressed the word, but the man didn't react at all. "Since you live that way, any chance you could recommend a decent pub?"

"Oh, sure," the man said, nodding quickly. "You'll want to stop at the Queen's Passage. Very hospitable, always treat me just like anybody — good ale, too." He looked Erso up and down, finally noticing his tailored suit. "You a salesman or something?"

Incredible! This man was so good that he was making up Erso's backstory. "Exactly so," he said, smiling. He reached into his pocket and handed him a card. "Used to be a tinkerer to tell the truth, but with all these factories now, I sell aluminum kits."

The man nodded soberly, squinting at the Amoriai name on the card. "Well, thank you kindly, Mr...Milak'erat," he said, "but I can't rightly afford any aluminum kits myself." He moved to hand the card back, but Erso put up a hand, stopping him.

"Think nothing of it," he said, "it's still my pleasure to make your acquaintance. Maybe you'll have need of me at some...future date."

In truth, there wasn't much risk in handing out those cards. He actually made them the same way as his coins. In just a day or two, they'd transform back into little slips of paper. The person he'd given it to would likely just think it lint in their pocket, forgetting all about the strange man they had met. He turned back to the front enjoying the ride. Perhaps when they got to this pub, he'd finally get a grip on what Aelibis was about.

When they finally arrived, Erso got off first, waiting for the man was he stepped down on his crutches.

"Nice riding with you," Erso had said, extending his hand. "You said the Queen's Passage, right?"

"That's the one," he replied. "It's not far from my place, why don't I drop you off there?"

"That'd be a pleasure," Erso said, clapping the man on the back. Even better if he invited himself — it wasn't every day the fish jumped in the net for you. The two men walked out of the trolley station and into a nearby neighborhood. As they walked, the streets narrowed, the industrial smells of the station finally giving way to cooking fires.

After what had felt like forever, the driver had finally clanged the bell on the trolley, yelling back to the remaining customers.

"End of the line! Last stop!"

Sumi watched the customers shuffle off, waiting for the man as he hobbled by on his crutches again.

You were worth it, she thought to him, *good luck! I hope you see your family soon!*

It buoyed her again to see him arriving home at last. That's what it had all been for, after all. Now she just had to get out in one piece herself... The driver finally got up, groaning as he donned his cap and lit a pipe, grumbling to himself as he switched off the electric lights.

She waited to a count of ten to make sure the driver was gone. Then she lifted herself on her edge, balancing on the other coins. She could see the slit of light at the top of the box. She tried to roll herself up to it, but the tin walls were too slick, and she kept sliding back down. Apparently, doing whatever a coin could do didn't exempt her from gravity...

She vibrated in frustration, slamming herself into the side of the box over and over, the tin clinking as she struck it with her coin. She froze, an idea suddenly hitting her. It was a foolish one, but she had to get out of this box as quickly as possible, and that meant it was time to entertain any and all possibilities. The wall of the box didn't sound horribly thick, and even though she had fit into it as a coin, she certainly wouldn't as a human...

"I want to be me," she said, focusing all of her energy in her center, "I want to be me, I want to be me!" She shouted the last time in her mind, and a brilliant flash lit up the inside of the box, filling her eyeless vision with bright white light. Under the force of her body changing from a coin to a human, the box exploded outward with a loud bang. She was weightless in the air for a split second before falling to the floor in a heap, coins ricocheting off the ceiling and raining back down on her.

She groaned, but then she started laughing. It had worked! If you were going to a fool, you'd at least better have the luck to go with it. She didn't have much time to waste, though. If the explosion in the box was as loud as she thought, someone was sure to come looking. 'Sorry sir I was stuck in the box,' wouldn't sound very believable when you were covered in trolley tokens.

She scrambled to her feet, slamming her shoulder against the trolley door and spilling out onto the cobblestones beneath. Her eyes darted back and forth, frantically searching for a way out. The trolley yard was open, though it was surrounded by buildings. She got back to her feet at a run, sprinting between the docked trolleys to the first alley she could see.

Erso made polite conversation as they walked, the man moving along at a good pace despite the crutches. He must get plenty of practice with that form to move like that! The cobblestone streets were so narrow now that the windows of the boxy little houses ran right along the street. He glanced in a few as they passed, though he kept one eye out for a keyhole on the other man.

As they turned the last corner and the pub came into view, he felt another ripple tear through his mind. He hadn't missed the keyhole...it had never been there. He stopped dead in his tracks, leaving his companion a few lengths ahead of him.

"What's the matter?" the man asked, hobbling around on his crutches.

"I, uh, forgot something on the trolley," Erso said. He pulled out a sovereign bill and shoved it in the man's pocket before he could protest. "Just have a drink on me. I'll be back."

The man began to stammer his refusal, but Erso was already gone. He wouldn't be back, of course, but he had given the man enough for twenty drinks, so hopefully he'd forget Erso before the night was done. He thought about turning into something faster than a man, but the streets were still crowded with people. Besides, finding a place to hide in this maze would only waste time. Instead, he ran for all he was worth, his shoes slapping against the cobblestones. For once, maybe he'd catch Aelibis *before* he did something foolish.

As soon as he hit the station, he could sense the ripple again. If the Shapewalker had left, it hadn't been long. He looked around every which way, suddenly spotting a woman darting from a trolley towards a nearby alley. He smiled, sauntering in that direction. If he lingered by the exit, hopefully he could catch them on their way back out.

He reached the alley and poked his head in but found it empty. It stretched far into the distance with narrow corridors branching off every ten feet or so. She couldn't have made it all the way to the end of the alley yet, so she must have ducked into one of those branches on the side.

Erso shrugged; he could wait. No sense scaring someone in a back alley — there was enough to be afraid of in this city as it was. He stepped back, leaning against a lamp post. He pulled his pipe out of his pocket, carefully stuffing it with polis leaves. He had really been looking forward to a stiff drink at the Queen's Passage, so a smoke would have to do. He looked off in the distance and sighed, watching the sun set as a blue trail of smoke floated up around him.

Finally, he heard the click of boots coming back down the alley and looked, finding the same woman coming back onto the street. She walked quickly, with the nervous step of someone who wasn't where they ought to be. She was so nervous, she nearly ran into him.

"Oh!" she squeaked, jumping back. "Sorry, sir!"

He looked up at her and smiled, though she still looked scared enough to freeze to the sidewalk.

"No trouble at all," he said, nodding. "You have a good evening, miss."

She nodded back, smiling awkwardly as she stepped around him, re-shouldering her bag before racing down the street.

He watched her go, smoking the rest of his pipe. Eventually, the ripple disappeared, fading back into the depths of mu'lalat. Should he have followed her? A woman ran into the alley, sure, but the same woman had walked back out. She might be stealing trolley tokens, but that didn't make her a Shapewalker. Besides, it wasn't Aelibis; he'd never blush like that. Try to stab him, sure, but the man would never blush.

He chuckled, knocking out his pipe. Perhaps there was more to this city than he'd thought. He itched to look for her again, but he had to get back to Aelibis. He'd be on the run after that raid, and time was running out. Why couldn't he quit that fool? Maybe it was his face, forcing him to remember things from Mesopyn he'd rather forget... He shook his head, walking back towards the trolley station. Either way, he really owed himself that bloody drink.

10

There is no freedom like an open mind. Our people, so blessed by the gods, can read the wind and hear the stones. What place could be kept from us? We crossed the seas to rain fire on this place, and in its wake, we make the world anew.

-Excerpt from the Poems of Boran Stonekeeper

—:—

It was two hours later when Sumi finally reached the terrace. She reached up to undo her cloak and winced. Every part of her was sore. It felt like she'd run a dozen miles — which she basically had, rolling all that way as a coin — not to mention the walk back from the station. She hadn't exactly thought that through either, though it only made her more glad she'd stopped to help. Imagine having to make the same journey on crutches…

Besides, she should just feel lucky she'd escaped. She'd thought for certain she'd been caught when she ran into that man outside the alley! He hadn't been a conductor, not with that fancy suit, but he hadn't been there when she ran into the alley, had he? He'd been polite enough, though, just letting her walk away. She shook her head, this was no time to get sloppy.

She slipped into the cottage, yanking off her boots. It was pitch black on the street and even darker inside, but she didn't waste any time getting the lamp. Instead, she simply dropped her bag on the stairs and wandered up to her room, feeling her way along the wall. She face-planted on the bed, not even bothering to take off her dress. Still, she fell asleep with a smile. She'd done it, she'd helped someone, and with luck, there would only be more to come.

———

Erso stood at a bar, drumming his fingers on the counter. He'd searched the city for three more hours before giving up and ducking into the closet pub he could find. He'd downed his first drink in one gulp and was waiting on the second. Like they said in Amoriai, the first drink was like taxes — best to pay up and get on with the rest of the bottle.

As the bartender brought him another whiskey, he took a small sip, finally letting some of his tension slip away. Being in Berill felt like a weight on his chest, clinging to his lungs as he breathed. Everything in him wanted to run, to get away from the snare before the rope pulled tight. He grimaced, shooting back the rest of the second glance. The bartender raised an eyebrow at that, but he simply shrugged, raising his finger for another. So taxes were a little high this year, not his fault.

The third drink finally seemed up to the task, and he actually sipped that one, staring into the fireplace. His mind kept circling back to the girl from the trolley station. Could there really be another Shapewalker in the city? It wasn't like the Berillai to let weeds grow in their precious little garden, even if they hacked up the flowers doing it. More importantly, though, if there were two, should he really bother trying to save them both?

There was enough heat in this city to cook a bloody ham, and he never could juggle like Beysal. If he tried to save them both, he might wind up getting all three of them killed. Was he getting sloppy, feeling sentimental for another Shapewalker he didn't even know yet? He should really be thanking his lucky stars the police hadn't shown up at the trolley station. They preferred cracking skulls in the poor neighborhoods, of course, but now that they had the raids going, they weren't likely to let any sign of Shapewalking go unnoticed.

That was, unless his other plans didn't work… He took another sip of his drink and smiled. At least if he couldn't find the fox, he was working on muzzling the hound. He couldn't very well search for Aelibis every hour of the day, and causing mayhem at the police station was a good substitute. His uniform was nearly perfect now, and he'd even started getting nods from the bloody front desk blokes! It was astounding.

He'd started small, of course, misplacing important files and making things generally difficult. Eventually, he'd learned the name of the *ja'radena* who investigated Shapewalkers — a Detective Parimu. He had some ridiculous title like Director of Reality or something. If the Berillai were going to hang you for the crime of being born, at least they were gonna be fancy about it. Despite the title though, the guy wasn't exactly popular around the break room, so he'd started trying to hobble the man directly.

The week before, walking through the crowds at the market, he'd finally had a bolt of inspiration. What did the Berillai love more than their sacred god of commerce? This Parimu bloke, though, was a zealot, and he wouldn't let anything stop him from bagging another Shapewalker. More importantly, the man didn't have any staff of his own, borrowing officers from the department for his raids. If he could show him disrupting commerce, the Berillai would be none too keen to lend him those men.

He'd gone back to Wembly during the evening rush on Boraldi. It seemed like the entire bloody city had descended on the market to buy food for Queen's Day supper. Ignoring the fact that the Berillai couldn't even name their days of the week properly, it had made a perfect crowd for sowing some chaos. First, he went out behind the market building and transformed into a rat. He forced himself through the transformation, using a memory without suppressing his ripple at all. It was hard to do it the old-fashioned way once you were properly trained, but he could still just make it work.

Immediately after, he'd changed back into his normal form in the same way. That would look like a hundred fireworks going off to a trained eye, even a wool eater like Parimu. Then, he started making the rounds, looking for a mark. He had wanted someone who was almost done with their shopping, and just as the police whistles sounded, he'd spotted a well-to-do looking woman and her husband heading out the gates.

He could still picture her — blonde hair like a Three Sisters woman, and a fancy maroon coat that would be easy to spot on the street. He'd ducked behind a counter, silently taking the woman's form. As the police came into the market, he sprinted past, like a woman on the run. Police whistles sounding behind him, he tore into the night, sliding around a corner as he flashed back into a rat.

He'd watched as they chased down the poor woman and started barking at her. An argument ensued that ended with the woman slapping an officer across the face. He really knew how to pick 'em! If she was wealthy enough to strike a policeman, then she'd certainly be able to raise a whole heap of trouble for Parimu back at the station.

As he went through the memory in his mind, he actually laughed out loud, causing a few of the other pub patrons to look at him sideways. He nodded to them, lifting his glass before shooting back what remained of his drink. He took out a fake coin — a big one — and rapped it on the bar. It was probably time to buy a round for the house. Berill was plenty dangerous, but he'd eat his hat if he couldn't have some fun before he left.

11

Cullesil was such an odd creature. She loved the hunt of society ball's more than anyone she'd ever met, and yet, she seemed to only have eyes for the Earl. He would surely marry her, old as he was, if she gave the barest of hints, though she seemed content to play the fool. Did she hope to gain some grander promise from him?

-Excerpt from The Borimol Plains

—:—

Sumi woke up the next day, splayed across her bed like a star fish, her dress twisted around her in knots. Somehow, she disentangled herself, rolling to the edge of the bed. She looked down at her rumpled dress, shaking her head; apparently there would be a lot of ironing in her glorious Shapewalking future. She stood, wincing as her feet remembered the six mile walk the night before. She rolled her shoulders and tilted her head, earning a loud crack from her neck.

She'd felt sore last night, but she hadn't expected this! It was like her body remembered being a coin and didn't want to go back to having limbs yet. She'd need to think of some forms that weren't so rigid to balance things out. A snake? A sponge? What about a pile of strawberry jam? She chuckled, stumbling towards the water basin.

This magic wasn't a trick, though; she really *had* become a coin. She hadn't felt this way after being Amis, but she had been a coin for far longer. She probably shouldn't expect to spend that much time in a form without paying the price. She started brushing her hair, biting her lip more than once as she tried not to cry from all the knots.

She glanced at the calendar on the wall, breathing a sigh of relief. It was finally Queen's Day! She'd been so focused on using her powers last night she hadn't even realized it was her day off. She probably shouldn't have gotten out of bed, then… She chuckled; it was probably for the best. If she had stayed tied down by her dress another minute, she would have suffocated in it.

She planted both hands on the counter and stared at herself in the little mirror. She'd fallen asleep with her makeup on, so she looked like a crazed raccoon. But still, she smiled. She had really helped someone with her magic, and now she had all day to do it again. Although, judging by the new knot appearing in her shoulder, she'd need to find a better system before she killed herself from exertion...

For the moment, none of that was as important as taking a bath. She went down to the kitchen and lit the stove, actually bothering to heat the water for once. She soaked in the tub for close to an hour, until her hands were properly pruned. She thought about nothing in particular, floating in daydreams as the heat took away her knots.

Once dressed, she went downstairs and rummaged through Grandpa's desk until she found his ruler. Taking out her notebook, she drew a line down the center. She made two columns: 'Things I've Become' and 'Things to Become.' The coin idea had completely taken her by surprise, but if she could practice new ideas at home, she'd be much more prepared.

She turned the page, drawing a grid with the days of the week. It wasn't terribly romantic, but she'd need some structure to these adventures. It may be the navy blood in her, but she definitely thrived under a routine. Besides, if she was going to do a good job at the flower shop, she couldn't very well spend hours each night locked in a token box.

She walked into the kitchen to start breakfast, staring out the window as her eggs cooked. It felt like she was marooned on an island, dark storm clouds covering the sky and the city empty below. It was harder not to miss Nela on Queen's Day, the one day a week that was only for each other. If she'd been alive, the oven would already be humming, the smell of something baking filling the house.

She sighed, leaning against the sink. Would Shapewalking really change anything? It wouldn't bring Nela back. And it wasn't like it would make her any friends, hiding who she was. Still, the book had said this was the magic that connects all things. She had to keep hoping. If helping people made her even a tiny bit more like Nela, it had to lead to something, open some door to let the joy back into her life.

When the eggs were done, she sat back down at the table with her notebook. It was tempting to start with all the shapes she wanted to make, but the logistics ought to come first. She didn't want her adventures becoming rigid, of course, but she wouldn't last a week without some kind of structure. Like Grandpa always said, "a boat doesn't move because of the wind, it moves because someone woke up and raised the sails." Great gods above, but they had sayings for everything…

Queen's Day, at least, was easy. She could do exactly as she had that morning, bathing and cleaning before heading out in the afternoon. Most of the factories were closed, so hopefully there'd be more people out and about. On Umildi, she could look for someone to help on the way to work, hopefully feeling rested from her day off. On the way home, she could do the shopping and cook for the rest of the week.

She chuckled, adding a note to play with Amis on those evenings. There was no telling what that cat would do if he started feeling neglected… She went on like that, assigning different tasks to different days of the week. When she'd filled in the whole page, she held it up, smiling at her handiwork. Marking off the time for Shapewalking felt sacred, protecting it from the rest of her life and the endless chores at the cottage. It felt like a dance, coordinated and beautiful, each day weaving into the next. Now, all she had to do was think of fun things to become.

***

A few hours later, she was finally ready to head out into the city, her notebook filled with new ideas. They'd come to her as she cleaned the house, stopping back in the kitchen to jot them down between chores. Some of them had come to her fully formed with a memory attached, practically gift-wrapped just for her. She'd put stars next to those, hoping to find matching memories for the others later.

The first thing she'd written down was 'broom'. Not the most exciting idea she'd ever had, but she *had* been sweeping at the time… There probably wouldn't be many people in the city desperate to tidy up, though she could always use it as camouflage. A horse running down Laeryia Boulevard wouldn't be very inconspicuous, but a ratty old broom…

As she'd worked through her chores, her daydreams had taken over, the additions becoming more and more abstract. Halfway down the list, she'd been picturing herself sailing across the bay when she'd written 'Boat'. Was that even possible? Everything she'd tried so far had been no bigger than herself. Maybe a small dingy would do… She needed to know more about her powers, how far she could stretch herself.

Near the bottom of the page, she'd written 'Rainbow'. She had been thinking about the storm coming in when the image had popped into her mind. If a boat had a size problem, a rainbow would have one doubly, but what a way to cheer up the whole city if she could!

As she climbed the stairs to get changed, she noticed a steady drum beat of rain on the roof. There were lots of things to like about fall in Berill, but the rain wasn't one of them. As the weather cooled, storm clouds would roll in at least twice a week from the bay, drenching the city. Worst of all, the fall were so short. Once the rains hit in earnest, winter was never far behind.

She added an extra layer to keep from catching a chill before pulling out her wax cloth cape. It was Grandpa's from the navy and strong enough to rebuff almost any amount of water. Hopefully she could still find someone to help in the rain... With everyone off for Queen's Day, most people would probably just stay home, though the lousy weather should reveal who needed the most help.

She went down to the front door and peeked out the window, finding a waterfall pouring from the roof. She heard a meow behind her and turned, catching Amis staring at her.

"Sure you don't want to come?" she asked. She leaned down to scratch his head, but he shot back towards the kitchen. "Fine," she sniffed, standing back up, "suit yourself. Watch the house while I'm gone at least!" She took a deep breath, squaring her shoulders. When it came to rain, any delay could risk you staying in the whole day. She opened the door, ducking out into the storm.

She had to squint as she made her way down Fort Street, the wind driving the rain into her face. She had her cloak's hood pulled low and was leaning forward, hoping that gravity would prove more powerful than the wind. The water formed a river that rushed along the sidewalks, cascading down the gutters. Despite raising her hood every ten feet or so, she didn't see a soul.

It wasn't until the banking district that she finally saw signs of life, a handful of cart drivers out making deliveries. They all wore grim expressions, but went about their business as if it weren't raining, save for wearing their own rain cloaks. She watched them for a moment, but shook her head, moving on. Those were professionals. If anything, she'd be the one needing rescue from them when she got washed away.

At the bottom of the hill, she passed the palace. The fine gravel was being pelted by the rain, forming divots that were collecting water. A poor groundskeeper moved between the puddles with a rake, smoothing out the stones before starting again at the beginning. The guards were all out as well, standing at attention as if tiny waterfalls weren't coming off the front of their caps. They wore long cloaks, one hand firmly on the pommel of their swords.

She stopped at the corner and raised her hood again, scanning in all directions. There were a few more people on Laeryia Boulevard, though it was still mostly workers. What could she even change into to help someone in all this rain? She chuckled, slapping her forehead. Of course. She'd unconsciously written 'umbrella' about two-thirds of the way down her list. If anything would be useful on a day like this, it was that.

Luckily, the idea had come with a star as well, the memory already clear in her mind. It was the day Grandpa had taken her into town in the rain to run errands for Nela. She hadn't inherited his cloak yet, obviously, and she'd been forced to wear her wool coat. It had been cozy enough, but without a hood, it did basically nothing to keep the rain off. She still remembered how hard she'd been sniffling, her face dripping with rain despite her hat.

Grandpa had laughed so hard when they reached the bottom of the hill. "You look like a drowned rat, girl!" he'd said. "Come here!" He'd carried her the next few blocks until their first stop, her face buried in his shoulder.

Their first stop had been the sundries store for Nela's baking. She still loved that place, so full of odds and ends! She'd wandered the aisles while Grandpa put in their order, shuffling around in her soggy boots. She'd been too short for the counters then, but she'd still wandered the aisled until she found the umbrella display. Most of them were stodgy black pieces, but one was a brilliant red, propped open on the table like a setting sun. She'd stood there, staring at it until Grandpa tapped her on the shoulder.

"Almost done, dear," he'd said, leaning down and speaking in a soft voice. "Why don't you wait by the door?"

Finally snapping out of her trance, she'd wandered over to the windows, watching the rain. Eventually, Grandpa had come back, tapping something on her shoulder. She'd turned, finding the red umbrella in his hand.

"Shouldn't have a drowned rat for a granddaughter," he'd said, smiling as he handed it to her. She'd ran out into the rain, flinging open the umbrella, a beautiful pitter-patter sounding on the cloth. She'd spent the rest of the day jumping in puddles, twirling her umbrella as she followed him through the city.

———

Despite the rain, her heart felt warm as she stood there, deep in her memory. That decided it then — she'd find someone as wet and miserable as she had been, and she'd be their red umbrella for the day. But she couldn't just do one of those stoic workmen. They likely wouldn't be caught dead with a red umbrella, and besides, they probably liked getting to look tough. She needed to find herself a drowned rat.

She pulled her hood back up and headed down Laeryia Boulevard. It took another ten minutes of walking in the rain, but finally, she found someone. She hadn't seen her coming with her hood, tiny feet suddenly appearing before her on the sidewalk. She leaned back, finding an old woman crossing her path. She looked miserable, no brave look plastered on her face. She was carrying a wicker basket, shuffling as quickly as she could as she tried to escape the rain.

Sumi ran for the nearest alley, her boots sending up sprays of water. As she reached it, she looked both ways, but there wasn't a soul, only rain as far as she could see. It was only a few heartbeats before a light flashed in the alley. One moment, she was standing in the rain with her hands clenched, and the next, there was a beautiful red umbrella on the ground, open and propped up on its side.

The rain drummed against the canvas of the umbrella, rolling down onto the cobblestones below. She no longer felt cold and miserable. Just like when she was a coin, the cold water running down her side was simply a fact that entered her awareness. In fact, it almost felt good. There was a rightness to the way the water ran off her, like she was achieving her highest purpose by simply being.

She needed to get on the move. The old woman was short, but she had been moving at a good clip in the opposite direction. How did an umbrella move, though? The coin had rolled easily enough, but she couldn't exactly roll like this. Just then, a squall slammed into the alley, the wind ripping between the narrow walls. The wind filled her, lifting her off the ground before it passed. That was it! She'd have to use her body like a sail and fly after the old woman.

She rolled along her edge, wheeling at an angle as her octagon shape clicked against the stone. She went back and forth, turning until she was nosed out of the alley. Without the alley walls, the gusts that swept along the street began to pull at her. She judged the direction of the wind, turning directly into it. The canvas rippled, and she leaned back, shooting into the air.

She sailed along the street, soaring some ten feet before skittering back down onto the pavement. She rolled again, turning to the side to catch another rush of wind. As she flew ahead the second time, she could sense the woman passing below. She tried to stop, but another squall hit, shooting her twenty feet further than she'd intended. *No, no, go back!* she thought. Luckily, another gust came along in the other direction, and she took, tilting lower and hitting the ground just in front of her target.

The woman slowed, cocking an eyebrow at the umbrella. She looked up the street for its owner, but, of course, saw no-one. They got hit with another squall of rain and the woman shrugged, stooping to pick up the umbrella.

"Don't ask the fish where it found the silver," she said, lifting Sumi above her head. The rain dropped down onto her canvas, pouring from her edges to the street below. It felt like running in the rain with your face to the sky. The woman smiled below her, slowing her pace now that she didn't have to be exposed. The wind grabbed at her, but she subtly shifted herself with it so the woman wouldn't have to struggle.

They went on like that for ten blocks or so, crossing through the west gate of the old city wall. Where could they be going in all this rain? Finally, they turned onto a side street, running into the Royal Hospital. It was a beautiful building, done in sandstone and surrounded by a walled-in park. The building rose above the trees that ringed its walkways, the paths flanked by benches for the convalescents.

They went up to the wrought iron gate at the front of the hospital gardens where two guards were waiting. One stood by the gate while another sat in a small hut. She'd never been to the hospital herself, though supposedly anyone could get help there if they were sick enough. Why was this woman here? Most of the old timers — Nela excluded — were terrified of the hospitals, only trusting the neighborhood apothecaries.

They approached the guard in the hut, the man smiling as he recognized her.

"Mrs. Berkin," he said, touching his hat, "lovely day for a stroll, eh?"

Mrs. Berkin laughed.

"I was getting soaked! But I found an umbrella on my way here. Isn't it beautiful?"

The man leaned forward in his seat to look over the counter at Sumi.

"Well I'll be," he said, "what a color. Some people have all the luck, they do." He leaned back into his chair and pulled out a clipboard. "Well, umbrella or not, we'll try to get you inside quickly here. Let's see... We've had some room changes. Had a ship go down last night near Averly, whole mess of men came in."

The guard scanned the pages for a time, flipping back and forth until he found what he was looking for.

"There we are, looks like Tethel was moved to 314. Nice view, though, he should be happy there." The woman smiled again, nodding in gratitude. "Alright then," the guard said, "just the last little formality, sorry, ma'am. If you don't mind, what's your passphrase?"

"Only open hearts receive the true reward," she said without hesitation.

The man looked down at the sheet of paper, nodding.

"That's the one. Thank you kindly, m'am. If you don't mind my asking, where'd you get that one?"

The woman laughed.

"Tethel's always loved his fairy tales, so I picked a quote from *Elkor's Allumin*. Do you know the old stories?"

The guard laughed, scratching his chin.

"Bit above my head, ma'am," he said. "I s'pose that's why I'm out here in the rain, and Tethel's inside getting proper cared for." He laughed again, rapping on the wooden frame of his hut. "Corporal, please see Mrs. Berkin through."

The other man snapped to attention, saluting before opening the gate. The iron moved smoothly on its hinges, digging into the gravel of the drive. Mrs. Berkin reached into her bag, smiling again as she slid a wax-wrapped loaf of bread to the guard.

"Thank you, Mrs. Berkin!" the guard called after her. "Remember, Room 314!"

They stepped through the gate and started down the gravel path. The building that loomed above them was easily as tall as the Royal Library, only with four times the windows, each divided ward with its own source of daylight. It looked almost like a manor home, with tall copper gables rising off the roof and subtle wave-like shapes carved into the wood of the dark eaves.

They stepped through the large doors at the entrance and into a quiet marble hall. There were torches on the walls and a large candlelit chandelier above, giving the stone surfaces a soft glow. Supposedly, there were electric lights in the operating rooms, but they wouldn't be in the entrance with how many people found them off-putting.

Mrs. Berkin tucked Sumi under her arm, walking up to the sweeping front desk. She winced as her canvas dripped on the spotless floor, though no-one seemed to mind. They secured directions to Tethel's room before taking the main stairwell into the belly of the hospital. The place had been built in a large rectangle, centering on a courtyard filled with more benches. Great gods but the Berillai loved their sunlight! She was lucky Nela didn't go in for all that, or she'd have wound up lying in the garden every time she had a cold.

Mrs. Berkin stopped to catch her breath at the first window, looking out at the rain. After a few more minutes of climbing, they finally landed on the third floor. They moved down the well-waxed halls, winding around the sides of the rectangle until they came to Ward 314.

Mrs. Berkin stepped inside, hanging her coat on a rack and leaving Sumi propped up against the wall. There were eight beds in the ward, each with an imposing iron frame and crisp white linens. Strangely, only one bed was filled despite what the guard had said. Sumi followed Mrs. Berkin with her mind, the old woman stopping at the end of the row and sitting next to... a child. *Oh dear,* Sumi thought, her heart wrenching.

Tethel was a small boy, maybe eleven, and he looked up with a weak smile at who must be his grandmother. Mrs. Berkin reached into her bag and pulled out another set of wax-wrapped treats along with a stuffed bear.

"Grandma has good things for you today," she said in a quiet voice like the coo of a mother bird. "I found some chocolate at the docks and made your favorite. Can you believe it, at this time of year?! And look who else came — Doctor Bearkin, with his arm all healed up!" She went on like that in a constant stream of sweet words, like dusting Tethel with a soft layer of snow.

As Mrs. Berkin cut a slice of bread for Tethel, Sumi heard a voice approaching down the hall. She switched her awareness behind her, finding two men turning the corner. Only one spoke, while the other scratched notes with a quill.

"This is Ward 314," the man said. "This'll be the new children's ward with that shipwreck taking over the second floor. Just one for now." The man paused, flipping through a chart on the door, sighing. He lowered his voice before going on. "Terrible case this one, tumorous lesions of the bone, unlike anything I've seen. The Queen put us on it personally, but we haven't found anything that works yet. Miracle the boy's still alive."

The man peeked in and saw Mrs. Berkin, waving before he stepped back out.

"The grandmother's in just now, let's let them enjoy their visit. I'll show you the boy after our rounds." With that, the men walked off.

Poor Tethel, and poor Mrs. Berkin! An image popped into her mind of Nela walking through the rain to see her in a hospital. She desperately wanted to cry, but had no eyes. At least the trails of water coming off her canvas felt like tears. She had set out to help, but there was really so little she could do for them. She could sell them flowers or be their umbrella, but she felt so useless against a horrible disease...

She looked at Mrs. Berkin. She probably felt just as helpless, left to baking sweets and mending bears. Still, she had fought through the rain to make her grandson smile. And by the sound of the doctors, they were shocked he'd lasted so long. When there was nothing medicine could do, there was still the strength of a grandmother. She steeled her resolve. Useless or not, she would get Mrs. Berkin home safe and dry, at least letting her save her strength for Tethel.

Sumi let her mind wander, trying to give the Berkins some privacy — even if they didn't know she was there. She started feeling sleepy, the radiators blasting out coal-fired air. As badly as she wanted to slip under the blanket of warmth, she fought to stay awake. In truth, she had no idea what would happen to her transformation if she fell asleep... It certainly wouldn't do to have your umbrella snoring in the corner.

After an hour or so, she did hear snoring in the room, but it was coming from Tethel.

"Sleep well, sweet child," Mrs. Berkin whispered. "Grandma will be back soon."

She struggled out of her chair and leaned over, kissing his forehead before gathering her things. Wrapped back up in her coat, Mrs. Berkin appeared next to Sumi, scooping up the umbrella and heading out into the hall. As they reached the stairwell, rain was still pelting the windows in sheets.

"Well," Mrs. Berkin said to Sumi, "at least I have you, eh?"

Mrs. Berkin made her goodbyes to all the guards and attendants on her way out, receiving smiles and nods in return. *She has this whole hospital wrapped around her finger*, Sumi thought, smiling to herself. *She'd bowl the entire Navy over if it was for Tethel.* It reminded her of Nela in a way. Maybe that was its own magic power, granted to women the day they became grandmothers...

They moved back through the city, crossing block after block without seeing another soul. They passed the palace and the flower shop, finally reaching the corner where they'd started. They walked another five or six blocks after that before turning into a street lined with narrow townhomes. *You poor thing!* Sumi thought. *You walked all that way before you found me?*

As they turned onto the residential block, Mrs. Berkin pulled out her keys. So they'd be home soon... She needed to escape before they got inside. She'd give the poor old woman a heart attack if she transformed in her house! Gusts whipped at Mrs. Berkin's coat as she pressed onward, the narrowing street making a perfect wind tunnel. Sumi had to lean forward with all her might to keep from being snatched up. Actually...that might just work.

As Mrs. Berkin turned up the steps of a tiny townhome, Sumi leaned the other way, catching the next gale and whipping into the air.

"Oh no!" Mrs. Berkin shouted. She turned to give chase, but stopped as she realized Sumi was already halfway down the hill. It felt wrong to disappoint her after just finding such a nice umbrella, but it was a cleaner escape than any of the alternatives.

"Goodbye, Mrs. Berkin!" Sumi yelled in her mind as she skittered away on the wind. "I hope Tethel gets well!"

She titled back, soaring higher until she cleared the rooftops. The umbrella shook in the uneven wind, rocking back and forth as the rain kept washing down. She felt like a boat lost in a storm. But she was just low enough to make out the ground, and she shakily guided herself towards the flower shop. As she crossed the alley, she snapped herself shut, dropping like a stone as the sail lost the wind. She landed on the pavement, changing back into herself with a giant pop.

She groaned, lying on the ground in the rain. She was back in her original form, the wax cloth still covering her, though rain pelted her face. Still, she felt good, like a boxer after a worthy fight. She rolled over, staggering as the blood flowed back into her legs. She moved towards the back door of the building, pulling out her key. She went into the storage room, sitting on a stack of empty burlap sacks from the bakery. She added a log to the boiler, warming her hands by the fire. The rain continued to howl outside as she sat there, dripping as she smiled.

12

Why does the northern wind sing so sadly? Was it not her voice that freed us from our bondage? Was it not her whispers that taught us to ford the winter seas?

-Excerpt from the Poems of Boran Stonekeeper

—:—

Sumi sat in the flower shop's basement until it grew dark. Like most rainy days, the sun had simply disappeared. There was no brilliant sunset to cut through the clouds — the grey had simply become less grey, fading into the black of night while the rain kept on. She'd grown drowsy by the heat of the furnace, very nearly falling asleep as she drifted through thoughts of Nela.

Realizing it was dark, she shook herself awake and stood. She was much drier than when she'd sat down, though droplets of water still rolled off her cape. She'd felt such a thrill from helping Mrs. Berkin, but now all she had left was fatigue, that familiar sadness flooding her.

It was that same well of icy water in her heart, the one that had lodged itself there the moment Nela died. Or had it always been there? All her pain was so familiar, like shadows that trailed behind her. Being orphaned, the ache of loneliness, it was easy to forget them, especially when losing Nela felt so…impossible. She avoided looking at those shadows, staying busy, staying positive. But there they were, waiting for her.

She had been so happy earlier… What had knocked her off course? Had it been seeing Mrs. Berkin? There was a part of her that knew she would trade places with Tethel in a second if it meant seeing Nela again. Maybe she was just exhausted, but it all felt so pointless now. Even with all her Shapewalking, she was still cold and alone, with nothing left for her to go back to but an empty cottage.

Why was it that some days her guard slipped, leaving nothing to protect her? Where was all her beauty? It seemed like the moment she stopped clinging to her joy, the well of ice would break apart, sapping all her strength as it flowed through her veins. Still, even this sadness was a blessing. The far more terrifying thought was that one day, she simply wouldn't be grieving Nela anymore. Even mother's face had started fading, leaving only echoes in her mind.

Finally, she pushed herself up and walked out into the rain. The storm hadn't seemed to weaken at all, resuming its relentless drumming against her cloak. Her bed was so far away, if she could have only lain by the boiler forever. She wanted to get out of her wet clothes and curl up under the covers, pretending the world didn't exist. Though what she really wanted was to walk through the door and find Nela there, force-feeding her soup until the cold left her bones.

Most of all, she just wanted to tell Nela *everything*. All the things she'd been carrying on her shoulders since the funeral. The highs and lows of learning this magic, how hard things were without her — she wanted to lay it all down at her feet. Nela had been a rock, and she wanted to feel that solid ground again. Why did these powers have to come when she was already gone? She could picture them, sipping tea by the fire at night, going over the transformations she used each day. Instead, all she had was rain.

―――

She finally made it home, having lost all the warmth from sitting in the shop. She stumbled in through the front door, kicking off her wet boots as she wandered into the kitchen. She brewed a mug of tea in the dark, gulping it down before heading upstairs. She didn't bother drying off, dropping her dress on the floor as she crawled into bed. If only there were someone there to chide her for making a mess.

She may be under a roof now, but she could swear the rain was still falling on her as waves of sadness crashed against her mind. With her all her wretched positivity, she liked to pretend this sadness was a foreign feeling. But in truth, there had been hundreds of times when she'd felt like a ghost inside her own body. Times when she had drifted along for what seemed like an eternity until she could see the light again.

She pulled the covers over her head and closed her eyes. She may have been thinking of Nela nonstop the last few hours, but in that moment, she tried to really distill her, to draw on her strength and guide her through the fog. What would Nela say if she found her hiding in bed? She'd probably give her speech about 'seizing your power.' Somehow that had always worked. Even when it didn't make the sadness leave, it would at least push her forward until she was feeling better.

She smiled sadly under the covers, remembering the first time Nela had found her hiding in her room. She drifted off into the mist of those memories, willing herself away from the present and into the past.

———

Twelve Years Ago

Sumi looked in the mirror and sighed, pulling at the black lace on her dress. Grandpa had died a month earlier, and they were still stuck in mourning clothes for another five. Their life had already exploded into a thousand pieces; why did they have to wear these horrible clothes, too? She already looked awkward from growing a span over the summer, and this only made her stick out more. Nela said it was normal for Anushai girls to grow early, but that didn't help much when she was surrounded by Berillai classmates.

It wasn't like she had many friends to lose anyway. Mother had lived on the east side of the city, past the old wall, and by the time Nela switched her to the terrace school, the other girls were already friends. Mostly they ignored her, though she'd heard them call her 'the orphan' once or twice behind her back. She didn't expect much, of course, but after six years in class, these mourning clothes were upending the careful balance she'd found.

At least she had Seriai… That thought, at least, made her smile. Seriai had started in the school just that year. She had giant round spectacles and was about half of Sumi's height, but it seemed they were destined to be friends. The first day in class, she'd caught Sumi doodling in her notebook. She'd been drawing one of the necklaces in *The Borimol Plains*.

"Is that Vorseyai's moonstone necklace?" Seriai had asked, suddenly right next to her.

"You read those stories too?!" she'd asked, her jaw dropping.

"Yes, I love them," Seriai said, picking up the drawing and holding it closer to her face. "You drew it exactly how I imagined it!"

They'd talked about the books all the way home — the best twists, their favorite characters, which of the suitors seemed the most handsome — and ever since, they'd been friends. Nela sometimes let her sleep at Seriai's house, and they'd even gone to the library together to read.

Realizing there was no point to pulling at the black lace anymore, she finally stepped away from the mirror, pulling on her boots. Just then, there was a knock at the front door. She grabbed her schoolbag, racing down the stairs to open it. It was Seriai, her face beaming up at Sumi with a toothy grin. She was fidgeting, her hands behind her back.

"Bye Nela!" Sumi called out, shutting the door behind her. "What do you have?" she asked Seriai, stepping onto the porch.

"You'll never believe it," Seriai said. She pulled a book from behind her back and stuck it under her nose. Sumi gasped.

"*The Borimol Plains*," Sumi said in a reverent whisper, taking the book from Seriai's hands. "Where did you get this? You didn't…steal it from the library did you?"

"No!" she said, pushing Sumi's shoulder. Sumi handed back the book and they started walking towards school. "My ma went by a bookseller to do some sewing. He had a pile of books that no-one wanted, and this one was on the top. He just gave it to her!"

"Are people crazy?" Sumi asked. "They're only the greatest books ever written. But now we can read it whenever we want!"

Seriai nodded eagerly. "We don't even have wait for the library anymore! I'm glad no-one wants them — more for us. Besides, we already know from school that the people here are most definitely crazy."

They both laughed, gushing about the book as they walked the rest of the way to school. They were having so much fun that for a moment, she forgot they were walking into a snake pit. Unfortunately, their classmates hadn't. The moment they entered the classroom, Vorsal looked up, her obnoxiously perfect hair bouncing as she spoke in a mock whisper.

"Look out everyone," she said. "It's Ciersein and her imp." The rest of the girls started laughing as her face flushed. Nela said the goddess of death wasn't real, but it was *definitely* not a compliment.

Seriai's face screwed up in anger, but they both slunk to their desks at the front of the class. Fighting back would only make it worse. They had both learned the hard way to ignore Vorsal until the teacher arrived. For some reason, though, it seemed she wanted more blood than usual that morning.

"I think black is your color, Sumi," Vorsal said to the back of her head. "Did you kill your grandpa just so you could wear it again, or was it looking at your face that did him in?"

Laughter rang out behind them again, though it seemed more halfhearted than before. Still, whether they liked the jokes or not, none of the other girls would challenge Vorsal. It was better to be with the hunter than the deer.

105

"I wouldn't blame you if you stopped talking to me," Sumi whispered to Seriai out of the side of her mouth. "You'd have more friends if you stayed away."

Seriai scoffed, but reached out and gripped Sumi's hand on her desk. "If those monsters are friends, I'd rather not have any."

Sumi met her friends eyes, forcing a grin onto her face.

"Thank you," she said.

Finally, the teacher walked in and the laughter died.

_____

At the end of the day, Sumi left in a hurry, rushing for the door before anyone could see her cry. She'd lied to Seriai about an errand for Nela before slipping out the back. She took the long way home, walking through Rekip before making her way up the other side of Ebun.

When she finally made it to the cottage, she stood in the garden for a long time, desperately trying to wipe away her tears. With Grandpa gone, she didn't want to be more of a burden than she already was. Nela had been putting on a brave face as always, but she could hear her crying at night. Finally choking back her tears, she stepped through the door. The smell of dinner was wafting from the kitchen.

"Sumi!" Nela called. "Dinner almost ready!"

Sumi swallowed hard. Her voice sounded strained, but somehow, she still managed to answer.

"I'm not feeling well, Nela," she called. "I'm going to climb in bed."

She charged up the stairs, diving under the sheets just in time to muffle a wave of sobs. Her breath came in ragged bursts, her eyes squeezed shut as tears poured out like tiny rivers, soaking her pillowcase. After a few minutes, she heard footsteps on the stairs. She tried to stop crying, but the doorknob was already turning, and Nela appeared at the foot of the bed.

"Sumi child, what happened?" Nela asked, sitting on the bed as she rubbed one of her feet beneath the covers.

"Nothing, Nela," she said, sniffling. "Just girls at school, nothing important."

Her grandmother sighed, clicking her tongue.

"*Shash golm zhey neyom,*" she muttered in Anushai. She didn't know those words, but they sounded...dangerous. "These girls," Nela continued, "death they treat like is — contagious, no?"

Sumi flipped the covers off her face, narrowing her eyes.

"How did you know that?" she asked.

Nela was shaking her head and looking out the window. Her face was red with anger, her jaw tight. But when she turned and saw Sumi, she smiled.

"People not so different, child," she said. "Even fool Berillai." She swung her arm through the air as if smacking something. "They…lash at what they are afraid."

Sumi sat up, leaning against her headboard. She reached for a pillow and held it tight.

"But why me?" she asked. "Can't they tell that it hurts me?"

"They push away you," Nela said, "they push away death. They are weak, but they attack you because they not understand this."

"But I don't want them to think I'm death!" she cried. "How do I get them to stop?"

Her grandmother laughed, patting her arm.

"No child, their game do not play. One day, when they are still in tiny cage, you be free."

Nela stood, walking towards the window. She leaned with one hand against the glass, the sunlight shining off her white hair. "You stronger than them, Sumi. You lost much, but you are still kind. Life has many losings, sweet girl. Is about losing well. Be kind and you are free. If that they don't see, they are like leaving gold on dirt."

Sumi sighed. She didn't want to be strong, she just wanted to be left alone. Still, she felt a tiny flame of pride sparking to life in her heart. She could honestly never tell if Nela thought she was a good granddaughter or not, but here she was, saying she was strong. And her opinion mattered a lot more than any of those girls'. But Nela couldn't follow her to school…how was she supposed to survive the next two years?

"But how am I gonna make it, Nela?" she asked, wiping her eyes. "School feels like forever, and the girls just do whatever Vorsal says. How do I make things better?"

Nela turned back from the window and smiled. "You don't child," she said. "Let them have their power, and you have yours." She touched the side of her nose in that strange Anushai way she was always doing. "Yours lasts longer."

It was true that she and Seriai both took the path of least resistance. So in that sense, they were already following Nela's advice, weren't they? Still, letting the other girls say and do whatever they wanted didn't exactly feel like power.

"How is that power?" she asked, shaking her head.

Nela sat back down, taking Sumi's hand. Older people were usually cold, but not Nela. Her hand was like a furnace.

"Little minds love little kingdoms," she said. "Even Anushai, many think power is power *over* — power to control. But power is not to do child, power is to *be*. You be same sweet Sumi, and you be really free. There is strength to be with others, but not if you cannot be you. You cannot be in bouquet without own color, little flower."

"But don't you feel it Nela?" she asked. "This…emptiness without Grandpa? I wish I could be this strong girl you're talking about, but everything's just so…hard."

Nela patted her hand, looking out the window. Her eyes focused as if she could see something more than the mountains past the terrace. She stayed that way for a long time before she finally spoke.

"My father was a sad man," Nela said.

Sumi perked up. Nela never talked about her past.

"Many days, he cannot face life, my father. But he was good, good man. Better than any in Anushai. Though sometimes," she said, wiping away a tear that had escaped her eye, "I think he too good; so good he broke himself. Even this man, though, he do more good than anyone I ever meet. He was strongest and weakest man I ever knew."

Nela turned to her and they locked eyes. It was hard not to look away, her gaze like a magnifying glass on her heart.

"It is okay to be sad, sweet girl," she said. "To feel, so much better than to not feel. What they see weak, is really strong. I can no promise you when sadness end. But after I lose my father, I find Grandpa. You never know when sunlight come."

Nela finally stood, leaning over and kissing Sumi on the head. "You keep fighting my sweet girl. Keep fighting for your Nela, she not be here forever." She crossed the room, stopping for a moment by the door. "You come eat now, yes? Vorsal can no take your stew, else I thump her."

Sumi finally laughed, nodding as Nela shut the door. She took in a deep breath, squaring her jaw. Nela was right; she was stronger than Vorsal. Just by being herself, she had met Seriai and made the best friend she'd ever had. She would fight by being herself, by not giving up. It was horrible to think of a day when Nela would no longer be around — that was the last thing she ever wanted to think about — but she had to keep her promise and go on fighting no matter what.

Finally, Sumi smiled a real smile, leaving her memories behind. She had never had her grandmother's boldness, but she had somehow found the strength to survive, and Nela had been proven right. She and Seriai *had* found a way through school, making lives for themselves. She had started working in the flower shop right after graduation, and Seriai had married Ekkel before moving to the farm. More importantly, though, they had their friendship. Like Nela would have said, friends were like golden snails, and she'd take one Seriai over a million Vorsals any day.

Now she had to find the strength to carry on again. She felt so alone, but she wasn't truly. There was powerful blood in her veins, a blood that had been filled with love every day of her life. Even her great grandfather, who she would never know, was proof that you could be strong and fragile; that you could still do good with your life, even at your weakest. Now she had to spread that love, to keep on fighting like she'd promised.

She yawned, the bed finally providing something more than a place to hide. The chill on her skin seemed to fade, and the rain drumming on the roof was just rain again. She drifted off to sleep, determined to do battle again in the morning.

13

All of this was meaningless. Her father had at least tried to grow something to help people. Even if the plants took a hundred years to cultivate, at least he had tried. That had to be better than this gilded life in town, constantly trading away your years for what…more power? A marriage with a few thousand a year? There had to be more to life than that.

-Excerpt from The Borimol Plains

—:—

Early the next morning, Sumi stepped out on the porch, a hunk of bread in her mouth and her bag on her shoulder. An idea had come to her in the night that if she woke early enough, she could take a different route to work, hopefully giving her a better chance at finding someone to help. She had put Amis out the back door before leaving, but he had already rounded the house and stood in the garden, meowing at her.

"I know," she said waving at him as she passed, "Sumi is so strange. Go hunt something!"

Instead, he followed her out of the garden and onto the street. She decided to turn left, away from Fort Street and deeper into the terrace. Ebun ran for a mile or so before tapering back into the hills that ran along the city wall. There was a cart path there that she wanted to take, winding down towards the Royal Park.

The smells of autumn floated up around her. The leaves had started to turn, and the mossy wetness of the ones that had already fallen drifted on the wind. The sun had just begun to crack over the eastern mountains, filling the sky with the blue light of morning. As cook fires were lit, grey columns of smoke floated above the cottages until they were struck by the sunrise, evaporating into dissipating sheets of gold.

Eventually, she reached the end of the terrace, the cottages growing fewer until the wall arced down towards the bay. If Grandpa was right about those Mesop arrows, it would make sense to not want to live too close… Amis peeled off, disappearing into a nearby garden without saying goodbye. She stuck her tongue out at him before continuing on.

She turned left at the end of the road, finding the cart path snaking through the unkempt grass. There was an imposing iron fence there with Royal Navy forge marks. She hadn't thought about it as a kid, but it must have been an old supply line for the fort. The gate had no latch, so she pushed it aside, stepping onto the path.

She began down the hill, the green oval of the park looking like a perfectly cut rug from the top of the terrace. The packed earth of the path crunched under her boots, and she let gravity pull her along the switchbacks, feeling like she was on ice skates as she rushed downward. When she reached the bottom, she caught her breath, leaning on another iron fence as she looked out at the fancy townhomes.

The whole neighborhood felt like a doll house, the roofs covered in carved shingles painted in hundreds of colors. Apparently, that's what Berillai cottages had looked like on the Isles of dawn, the style only recently coming back into vogue. Their ancestors must have been desperate for the color with how brutal the winters on the Isles were supposed to be, though they looked just as pretty in Berill. At least there seemed to be no shortage of pigments, the royal stonekeepers always finding something new in the mines.

She passed through the neighborhood, not seeing a soul on her way to the park. Just as she started to worry, though, she spotted an old man, sitting on one of the benches across from the statue. He was leaning forward, his elbows on his knees. He was holding something metal, the bronze color shining in the morning light. She made her way around the gravel path, aiming to walk past him in case he needed something.

As she approached his bench, the man finally leaned back, propping the metal object on his knee. It was a spy glass! Grandpa had let her play with one once that he brought home from the barracks. She'd loved looking through it from the terrace, zooming in on the people below. Why did this man have one at the park?

"Good morning, miss," he said, smiling as she passed.

"Good morning," she said, returning his smile. As she walked away, though, she heard him let out a long, sad sigh. She froze on the path, her hands clenching. She couldn't always wait for an invitation. She turned on her heel, marching up to the man.

"Um, excuse me," she asked, "but is that a naval glass you have there?"

"It is," he said, beaming. "Have you seen one before?"

"I have," she said, sitting on the bench as he patted the place next to him. "My grandfather was in the navy."

"Ah, lovely," he said. "I was a crow's nest man myself. They let me keep this when I retired, Velloni bless the Queen. I use it for birding now — that's how I used to pass the time on watch."

"Oh, wow," she said, nodding. "Were you looking at any just now?"

"Trying," the man said, sighing again. "Not much luck, I'm afraid."

"What kind of bird were you looking for?" she asked.

"A fire hawk," he said, turning to her with a glint in his eye. "They're supposed to be nesting this time of year, but that blasted rail line they're building seems to have scared 'em off."

"I love fire hawks!" she said with an embarrassingly high-pitched squeak. The man, however, didn't seem to mind at all.

"Oh, that's wonderful!" he said. "I can never convince my grandchildren to come with me. A fellow ornithologist, are you?"

"Afraid not," she said, chuckling. "But I still remember the menagerie five years ago. I stood in the bird house for hours. I'll never forget those feathers."

The man removed his hat and turned it around, showing her one of the silver and red feathers attached to the hat's leather band. Her jaw dropped; how had she missed *that*?

"May I?" she asked. He nodded, and she very gently ran her finger along the edge of the feather. The plumage was smooth and slick, the flame-like pattern nearly jumping off the side.

An idea suddenly exploded like a firecracker in her mind. This would be an easy one! She already had a memory locked in and everything. She could never forget the afternoon she and Nela had spent at the menagerie. How had she not thought of any of those animals for her notebook? She smiled, standing up from the bench.

"I've have to run," she said, "but thank you for showing me your feather. I really hope you see a hawk!"

"Me too," the man said, smiling. "You have yourself a lovely day, miss."

She took off down the gravel path, her boots crunching on the stones as she walked as quickly as she could out of the park. She spotted an alley, rushing over to it as she pictured that day in her mind, the joy of the memory pulsing through her.

The Royal Menagerie was only held once every ten years. While the crown put it on for free, you had to get tickets weeks in advance at the trolley office. She'd marched there right after work on the first day of registration, singing up for her and Nela. She barely remembered her first menagerie, but she had been determined not to miss her second, dragging Nela down the hill well before their appointment.

It had felt like Umidiar, thousands of people wandering between the tents, buzzing with excitement. Everywhere you looked there was something to do or see — food stalls, strange plants, performers wandering about — but it was the bird house that had really captured her. Instead of a tent like the other animals, the birds had a great glass structure where they were allowed to flit around, landing on large branches set up along the walls.

As she entered the alley, she saw a trash can and skipped over to it, crouching down out of view. She was already beginning to feel the lightness coming on, and she shut her eyes, focusing on the fire hawk. She'd gone back to see it after Nela went home, sneaking behind the velvet curtain that separated it from the other birds.

She and the hawk had stared at each other, its keen eyes seeming to search her soul. It was a naval hawk, used to carry messages between ships. The bird keeper had said they were fiercely intelligent, refusing to serve falconers they hadn't chosen themselves. She had stood there as it stretched its wings, imagining it soaring over the ocean, feeling jealous of that soaring freedom.

Suddenly, as she hid behind the trash can, the lightness grew to a crescendo. It felt as if hundreds of balloons had been released in her chest, pulling her towards the sky. A bright flash filled the alley and she opened her eyes, blinking. She went to stretch her arms, but instead, began to flap long, beautiful wings.

She cocked her head, finding that her neck could turn far more freely, far enough to spot the red plumage spilling down her back. She looked at her feet and found powerful talons with gleaming claws. She flexed them together, feeling a swell of innate power. She'd learned her lesson from hunting mice, but she could sense how good it would feel to clamp down with those claws.

Eagerly, she ran out from behind the trash can, her talons clicking on the stone. She leapt into the air, flapping her wings — and came crashing down on her face. Apparently it wasn't as easy as being a cat… She tried to get back to her feet, but it was harder to pick herself up without hands. She flailed around for a moment with her beak on the ground before finally managing to get herself upright.

She spread her wings again, carefully flapping them. Walking had been easy because she already knew how… What was similar to flying, swimming? That was the freest she'd ever felt in her human body. Cutting through the ocean like a fish, she always felt weightless and invincible. What if flying was like swimming, but in the air?

She looked up at the crack of blue that stretched above the alleyway. She was going to swim through that sky. She flapped harder, like she was parting water with her wings. Instead of dropping on her face, she began to lift off the ground. She pumped harder, hearing the determined flap of the feathers against the air. She kept her gaze locked on the sky, and it slowly grew closer and closer. Finally, she burst through the top of the alleyway, crying out in victory, the sound erupting out as the high-pitched shriek of a hawk.

She tested a glide, letting her wings carry her forward on the air. She wasn't a fish — she was a boat! Now that she was moving, the feathers seemed to lift her with little effort. She tried pointing her beak downward, and her wings pulled into a dive, her body gaining speed. Laughing, she began to beat her wings again, climbing higher as she crossed the street and landed on one of the library's turrets.

She turned towards the park, catching the glint of the old man's spy glass. *Great,* she thought, *he's still there!* As a human, she'd barely been able to make out his hat, but as a hawk, she could see every detail of the man's face, like a drawing under a magnifying glass.

She let out a sharp cry, pushing herself from the library roof and beating her wings as hard as she could. She tore across the sky, swooping overhead as the man looked up at her. His jaw dropped and he leapt to his feet as he watched her sail by. She soared past the park and over the houses before turning back, landing on the statue.

The man laughed below, staring at her through his spy glass. She chuckled to herself, perching on King Rummon's arm. This must be what those sea gulls felt like! She turned around opening her wings so he could see the plumage. Then, she turned back, cocking her head back and forth like she'd seen hawks do. The man's eye was still glued to the looking glass, his mouth hanging open as his breath puffed out in the cold morning air.

Maybe she could do this for him once a month or something. Once you got the hang of flying, being a hawk wasn't all that hard really. She looked out over the bay, eyeing it eagerly. Everything in her wanted to soar again. The sky and the sea seemed to be calling to her. Could she? She probably had just enough time before work, and the man had gotten a good look at her...

She let out a cry of farewell, taking off into the air. She beat her wings in the direction of the water, soaring over the man and the last stretch of the park. As she lifted up over the street, a few people turned, staring as she sailed overhead. One little boy ran after her, pointing as he jumped up and down. This last flight might be for herself, but at least she could give the city a show.

Finally confident in her wings, she pushed higher, reaching the beach as the city disappeared behind her. The sea rocked back and forth, as if it were a single stretch of cloth, rising and falling with the undulations of something underneath. White caps dotted the horizon, flashing above the mass of blue as they rolled over. There were a few low hanging clouds over the bay, and she burst through them, emerging with her beak covered in dew.

She flew a mile out over the water before she turned, soaring west along the coast to take in the city she loved. The vantage point was surreal, like looking at the maps of Berill that hung in the library. The roads looked like perfect stone-colored lines instead of the bustling scrums she knew them to be. The mountains swept out behind the city like another wall, stretching to protect Berill with their embrace.

As she flew, she heard a rustling below and looked down, finding another hawk climbing towards her. She started, glancing at her talons and hoping she wouldn't have to use them. Instead of fighting though, the other hawk simply let out a shriek and began to glide alongside her. She looked closer, spotting a letter tied to its leg. *A naval hawk!* She shrieked back a greeting, soaring in formation with her new friend.

After ten minutes or so, she looked down, realizing they had gone far west along the coast, crossing well beyond the city wall. She hadn't mean to go that far! She called out a hasty farewell to the other hawk, banking hard and heading back to the city. She dove, gaining speed as she slipped along the beach. She swung low past the palace, arcing past the turrets towards the library.

As she soared past the Peerage, she caught sight of the clock on one of the banks. Her eyes almost popped out of her head as she realized how late it was. She had to be at work in ten minutes! She dove towards the ground, crashing in the alley with a giant flap of her wings. She looked both ways and saw no one, rushing on her talons behind the trash can from before.

"I want to be myself," she whispered in her head. "I want to be *myself*." But no pop came. She opened her right eye and glanced at her arm, still finding feathers there. *No no no,* she thought, *I don't have time for this!* What was the problem? Her mind raced through the other times she'd transformed back into herself. The first time had been a shock, of course, and the second had been biting the mouse. But with the coin, she had simply popped back, hadn't she? But she had been happy then...now she was desperate to get to work.

"Always undo a knot the way you tied it," Grandpa liked to say. *Okay*, she thought, taking a deep breath, *how did I tie this knot?* She had used a happy memory, just like always. So maybe she needed another memory to return? She thought of the menagerie, staring at the hawk. This time, however, she pictured being herself. She felt the cold air on her skin, tasted the sweetness of the caramel apples. Suddenly, there was a flash, and she was crouching behind the trash can, human again.

She breathed a sigh of relief, wiping sweat from her forehead. It had never occurred to her that she could change into herself. She thought of herself as a default, not a state of being that inspired joy. But it was her eyes that had experienced all those memories, her mind that remembered them. She would have to learn to harness that, the feeling when just walking down the streets of Berill felt like soaring.

She picked herself off the ground and started to hurry towards the end of the alley. As she reached the street, she almost cried out as she ran into the old man from the park.

"Oh, miss," he said, panting. "Did you see the hawk?!" He leaned against the nearest brick wall, breathing heavily.

Sumi looked up at the sky, trying to hide her shocked expression. *Fool!* she cursed herself. She should have picked a different alley!

"I did!" she said, trying to sound excited. "I work nearby, so I ran over, but it flew right back out." She huffed, pretending to pout.

He put his hand on her shoulder and smiled.

"It was glorious, miss. Now that they're back in the area, I'm sure you'll see another."

"I think we both will," she said, smiling. She made her excuses and ran off to work, soaring across the cobblestones like only a bird knew how.

Erso woke up with a jolt, a powerful ringing in his mind, like a cannon had gone off. He groaned, rubbing his eyes and sitting up in the bed he'd rented. He winced as he stretched, feeling stiff from the lumpy mattress. It was probably about as much as he could expect moving from one seedy pub to another every night, but still…

He shook his head and shut his eyes, focusing back on the ripple that had woken him up. It wasn't every day you had Shapewalkers transforming just after dawn. Could this be Aelibis' big play, to shape in the morning when the police least expected it? Or was it that other Shapewalker? He ignored the throbbing in his temples, reaching out with his mind.

At first, he felt nothing but a void, the empty halls of Mu'lalat stretching into eternity. But then...there! He felt the ripple moving. It felt distant, somewhere near the center of the city, though it was coming towards him. And it was...above him? He sat there for a time, tracking the ripple in his mind until it faded away.

He opened his eyes, rubbing his temples. It actually wasn't a half-bad plan. The police probably hadn't been drinking all night like he had, but they certainly kept late hours. If the ripple was already gone, there probably wasn't much chance of them rallying the troops. Although, a ripple in the sky usually meant birds, and that didn't seem to fit any robbery he'd ever heard of...

He threw his pillow across the room, flopping back on the bed. Despite spending weeks in this miserable city, he was still fumbling blindly. No-one in the pubs seemed to know of any big jobs coming up, and every bloody ripple he chased led him nowhere. Like his old man liked to say —'the best thing a man can know is what he doesn't know' — and he knew absolutely nothing; at least he was clear on that.

He looked longingly at his pillow across the room, lumpy as it was. He'd take a rock for a pillow if it meant five more minutes of sleep. But he shook his head, standing and stumbling over to where he'd laid out his clothes and pipe. He may as well start his so-called 'investigations' for the day. At least Aelibis seemed to be getting better at playing the game. Either that, or he was trying to kill Erso with a lack of sleep. Luckily for him, being raised by a moody actress had him used to odd hours.

A few minutes later, Erso stepped out of his room with his suit on. He'd shaped it so it would look freshly pressed. It didn't do much for the bags under his eyes, but at least he looked presentable. He stumbled down the stairs, entering the common room of the pub. The landlady was there already, wiping down the bar and not looking much more refreshed than he did. He sauntered up to the bar and leaned against it, receiving a withering stare.

"Any chance of getting some eggs this morning?" he asked.

She started laughing hysterically, stopping what she was doing to wipe away tears with her dirty rag.

"Sounds like a no," he said, sighing. He turned towards the door and out into the too-bright sunlight of the street.

"Who knows, Aelibis," he said to himself, "maybe your little games will kill me after all."

———

117

Aelibis stood in the shadow of an alley, watching the police station. Who'd of thought he'd end up like his bloody old man, looking for omens in the fire grate. Still, this ritual, at least, felt important. If you were risking death, you should always spit in Ciersein's eye.

There was honestly nothing left to set up on this job. He'd just come from seeing the basement where they'd stash the loot, and all the men were in place. All he needed was the courage to go past the tipping point. That's why he'd come here, wasn't it? To prove he could look in the serpent's mouth? Maybe they could track him, but he had the magic. It would work; it *had* to work.

Just then, he heard a shriek, and looked up, seeing a hawk soaring over head. He laughed, shaking his head. Now *that* was an omen. His father had believed in all that wind-reading rubbish, not him, but even he couldn't deny something like that. He supposed that decided it. Dithering was for men who had no purpose. He was the man who would choose.

"I'm not afraid of you," he whispered to the station, as if those bloody sheep herders could hear him. They could sit in their little tower all they wanted, it changed nothing. The real power, the strength of the gods was in *his* veins.

"It's time," he said to the man beside him. "Go grab the others; we move tomorrow."

14

Even gold could not sing like the stone of the gods. It is enough to make me weep, their rhythms shaking with the power of the earth! There is no time in the song that sings forever, no loss as it sets your spirit free.

—Excerpt from the Poems of Boran Stonekeeper

—:—

That night, Sumi came straight home from work, eager to practice her forms. She hadn't planned on practicing until Ebundi, but she had filled in so many lines in her notebook that she couldn't wait any longer. She threw her bag on the hall table and sped around the house, closing the shutters. No one really came by the terraces at night, but she couldn't risk a neighbor seeing flashes of light bursting from the windows.

After making her rounds, she grabbed her notebook and went to the sitting room. It was shrouded in dusk, the last remnants of evening light in the back of the cottage. Even the shutters wouldn't mask the flashes if it was pitch black... She went to the kitchen, returning with the oil lamp. Then, she set her notebook on the desk, opening it to the page she'd made for practicing. There were three columns: *Past Forms, New Forms,* and *Returns.*

First, she wanted to test a few of the things she'd already been to see if she could get back into them easily. With everything prepared, she stood in the middle of the room and closed her eyes, taking a few deep breaths.

"Okay," she said to herself, "let's start with Amis."

She brought up the memory, smiling as the lightness bubbled up in her heart. It felt like it was rushing upward more quickly this time, less like a rising tide and more like a volcano. She didn't even get to the end before there was a flash of light and she found herself on the floor.

She let out a triumphant meow. That had felt so easy! So that was one hypothesis settled — it *was* faster to turn into something she'd already tried. It was like her body had already known the way and led her along, like a horse leading its rider home, eager to get back to the feeding trough.

She looked down at her paws and kneaded the thick wool carpet. Without meaning to, she started purring, the luxurious feeling sending shivers up her spine. She didn't like killing mice, but scratching was really something! She shot a guilty look towards the hallway before taking a claw and dragging it across the rug. It was hers now, though a part of her still felt like Nela would come around the corner and catch her.

She went on like that for a while until the clock chimed the hour in the hall, snapping her back to attention. How long had she been standing there scratching the carpet? *No wonder cats never get anything done.*

Now it was time to work on getting back to her own body. Hopefully that would get easier too; she didn't want a repeat of that morning… She had added her own name to the notebook to find memories for transforming into herself. For now, though, she could stick with the one from that morning, the memory still fresh in her mind.

She closed her eyes, returning to the menagerie, thinking again of herself instead of the hawk. She noticed the scent of spiced nuts, and could audibly hear the laughter filling the park. Just like with Amis, the flash came sooner than she expected, the sateen of her dress shimmering in the lamplight where there had been fur just moments before.

She pumped her fists in excitement, putting a star next to *Amis* under the column for past forms. She also put a tick mark under *Returns*, marking her success at changing back smoothly. Then, she flipped to the back of her notebook where her list of forms was. With one previous test out of the way, she was eager to try something new. That wouldn't only mean trying out new shapes, but new memories as well.

She scanned the list, her eyes locking on *broom* again. She laughed. Not yet, too boring. Finally, she found one halfway down the list that she liked: *Flower*. It had a star next to it, too, the memory already prepared. She wasn't positive it would work since it had so bittersweet, but she wanted to try it anyway.

The month before he died, Grandpa had bought her flowers on her birthday. He'd picked out long, yellow-stemmed roses, with thirteen flowers to match her age. The memory wasn't only wrapped up in Grandpa's death, but was strangely entangled with her life now, the roses coming from Mr. Furttenhur's where he'd been a regular.

Right after he and Nela got married, he'd started stopping in the shop on his way home from the barracks. When she graduated, Nela had used that connection to get her the job. So the memory of the roses also intertwined with her long, lonely days behind the counter. Days that had only grown lonelier since Nela passed… She shook her head, clearing her mind. Bittersweet or not, she could already tell the memory was strong.

She'd been upstairs, darning a sock on the bed. She remembered the familiar sound of Grandpa's boots in the hall, his deep voice calling up the stairs. He had hidden around the corner with the flowers, and as she came rushing down, he had popped out, the burst of blossoms in his hand. She'd squealed, grabbing the bouquet as she threw her arms around him. She could still smell the flowers mixing with his cologne. And just when she thought it couldn't get any better, Nela's voice had called from the kitchen to say the cake was done.

She started to feel the lightness in her heart. This time, it was slow and deliberate, her first time navigating the memory. She pushed ahead, leading her body behind her this time, through the haze of the past. She pictured them all sitting around the kitchen table, one of the last times all three of them had been together. She tasted the richness of the cake, saw the flowers in their vase. Finally, the lightness reached a peak, and the air popped, flashing Sumi into a bouquet of flowers sitting in a vase.

She dipped into her field of awareness, feeling her long stems reaching down into the vase, the water cool against her thorns. There was water in the vase?! How oddly…specific. It felt strange, completely different from being a coin. She was inanimate, true, but she was also *alive*. There were sensations all along her stems, the water stretching into her blossoms, like drinking in reverse. She could even wiggle her leaves a bit — nothing drastic, of course, but there was a tension to the stalks that she could use.

It was absolutely delightful, though the form did raise questions… What would happen if she got stuck somewhere, like on someone's kitchen table? Would she wilt? What if they threw her in the rubbish bin — would she still be a whole Sumi if she tried to change back into herself with her roses scattered all over? Was she the flowers or the vase? Hopefully she'd figure it out before a dangerous situation presented itself…

I'll worry about that later! she thought. With another success so soon, she was ready for the next challenge. She couldn't really move the vase, but she made as if to raise herself straight and tall. Then, she brought her consciousness within, the equivalent of closing her eyes. She conjured up the image of herself at the menagerie again, transforming back into her own form even faster than the first time. She stood on the carpet again, gratefully moving her fingers and toes.

She lifted a hand to fix her hair and winced, a deep ache setting into her muscles. It was like her night as a token, when she felt like she'd run a hundred miles. But this time she hadn't gone anywhere... She hummed to herself, tapping her chin. It was hard to think of it like labor, magical as it was, but it clearly took a toll to string so many shapes together.

"Thank you," she said to her body, rubbing her shoulder. "I guess I've put you through a lot lately." It was probably time to switch to something familiar before she got too tired. There were still chores to do, after all. Amis needed to be fed, and she ought to cook a real meal for herself before she collapsed.

She pulled out her notebook, moving the flowers to the completed column before scanning the list again. One look, though, and the choice was clear: she had to do the hawk again. She wasn't about to go flying around the neighborhood, but there was something about animals that felt *realer* somehow. She thought of the menagerie again, and after a moment, she was standing on the carpet as a hawk.

She shifted her talons, gently squeezing the carpet. It didn't feel as good as it had as a cat, but it still felt nice to flex her claws. She flapped her wings, stretching them out. Then, she let out a shriek. Hopefully it wouldn't carry to the neighbors, but it was too satisfying to skip altogether... As she stood there, the real Amis came around the corner to investigate. He poked his head past the sitting room door, freezing as his eyes went wide. After a moment, he snapped out of it and hissed, running back into the kitchen. She laughed to herself — poor Amis!

After a minute, though, he was back. With the sharpness of her hawk ears, she easily heard him padding back along the hallway. He poked his head around the door again, squeaking out a tentative meow. It seemed he'd recognized her innate Sumi-ness again. Finally, he gained enough courage to creep up to her, nuzzling her leg. Then, he walked over to Grandpa's chair and jumped up, curling into a ball on the seat.

She flashed back into her own body, reaching up and stretching as high as her hands could go. Despite the soreness, she smiled. It felt good to run, to work, to strive — using your body to its full potential. She yawned, covering her mouth as the air escaped in a long burst.

"I guess I really am getting tired," she said, turning to Amis. She made a few more markings in her notebook and then shut it. That was enough for one day. She leaned over, scratching Amis behind the ears.

"Alright," she said, "this hawk's gonna to get you some dinner." Not to be left, her own stomach growled right on cue. Magic or not, she had to remember she was human. She headed to the kitchen, ready for some food and then some well-deserved sleep.

15

*She thought herself so clever, so far above the whirling of the pool. In
the end, she was a fool, no different than the rest.*

-Excerpt from The Borimol Plains

—:—

A day later, Erso strolled towards the police station, whistling as he
twirled his nightstick. He'd transformed his cane to make it, always
eager to have some prop to play with. It was so much easier to create
dramatic emphasis with something in your hand. Besides, the sun had
gone down an hour earlier, and the nights in the city could be awfully
dangerous.

The day had slipped by all too quickly, another grain of sand slipping
from his hourglass. How many had it been since the raid on Aelibis'
hideout? They were starting to blur together. He had been alternating
between the police station and the taverns, desperate for any clue,
whether it came from policemen or thugs. So far, there hadn't been a
peep. He just had to hope that was a good sign...

The day before, though, he'd finally felt another ripple, a strong one
in the upper part of the city. It was completely across town from his
tavern, but at least he'd been awake for it. He had rushed across the city
to find it, but just as he reached the highest terrace, the ripple died out,
just as it had before.

He had wandered around in the dark for a while, but none of the little
cottages had looked much like hideouts. It had to be a second
Shapewalker, though it was hard to tell how much they knew about their
powers. Clearly not enough to suppress their ripples, but it was uncanny
how they always seemed to stop just in time. At least they knew well
enough not to constantly call attention to themselves... *Just stay smart
a little longer,* he thought, picturing the beautiful woman from the trolley

station.

At least it didn't seem like Parimu was having much luck either. He seemed to be growing desperate, working late nights as he dragged his squads throughout the city. No matter where the searches took place, though, Parimu was always there. When it came to Shapewalkers in Berill, he was clearly at the center of it all. The man must have been a fellerhurn to get his position — without one there'd be no way to track Aelibis in the first place…

He ground his teeth at the thought. How evil would a Shapewalker have to be to hunt their own kind? Calling someone like that a fellerhurn was almost a compliment — and an insult to those little rodents. He'd actually never seen one, but apparently they liked to hunt mulakerri, the giant shape-shifting birds that could touch Mu'lalat. The fellerhurn couldn't shape itself, but it could feel their ripples, crying out to attract lions when they sensed a flock in the wild. Once the lions had their fill, the bastards would swoop in to scavenge the corpses.

Parimu clearly had some talent, though there was no telling how good he actually was. Not all fellerhurns knew what they were, of course, and their abilities came in a wide range. If he had to guess, Parimu's skills weren't particularly refined, or he would have found Aelibis well before that first raid. It seemed the police here relied on some combination of tracking and detective work. If you already knew all the shady taverns and thieving dens, you could zero in on a ripple, using manpower to make up for your lack of precision.

Erso spit on the street as he approached the station, trying to clear the foul taste of Parimu from his mouth. He stopped by the door, taking a deep breath. He'd blow his cover if he walked around steaming about fellerhurns. So far, at least, he'd blended in, like the ugly couches in the break room. He stayed likable and forgettable, letting him wander wherever he chose.

He tipped his hat to the front desk clerk, sliding him a packet of pipe leaves. They'd chatted about smoking once to stay awake on the night shift, and ever since, he dropped the man a packet on his way in. Hopefully it kept his comings and goings feeling welcome and familiar. Then, he turned left, heading eagerly towards the canteen. Say what you want about their lack of compassion or obsession with commerce, but the Berillai Royal Police had excellent pastries.

He sauntered in, smiling when he saw a tray of pear wheels. He took one before filling a mug with coffee. It was rubbish, of course, but at least the police didn't drink tea like the rest of the bloody Berillai. Then, he sat down, waiting for gossip. The canteen was a gold mine, already giving him a few delightful bits over the past week. The prank he'd pulled on Parimu's task force was still the talk of the station. It turned out that the woman in the maroon coat had been Elisal Pont'dulairn, the wife of the bloody Vice Peer himself.

She and her husband had raised a mountain of trouble for Parimu, well beyond his wildest hopes. He only had a rough understanding of Berillai politics, of course, but as it turned out, Pont'dulairn had been fighting recently to reorganize the Royal Police. From the sounds of it, the man was making a killing on the train lines, and he didn't want a single coin falling into the wrong hands. He wanted the police patrolling the factories and trolley yards, not chasing fairytales like Shapewalkers.

Apparently, not all his bills had succeeded in the past, but the horrible disrespect shown to his wife was the perfect ammunition for a fresh round of reforms. His most recent would give the Peerage control over police staffing, something usually done by the Queen. She didn't have to accept his bill, of course, but all those peers loved counting money, and that should put enough of them in Pont'dulairn's camp to make the Queen think twice.

The canteen was quiet that evening, so he finished his pastry and headed for the telegraph room. He'd been flirting with one of the operators for the past few weeks, and she'd been more than happy to keep him informed of police movements. The telegraphs were set up in a long bank with operators on both sides of a divided wood-paneled desk. He walked quietly into the room, casually leaning against the end of the row. His target, Solisae, sat just beyond the nearest divider.

She was finishing a transmission when he walked up, but he pulled a bottle of perfume out of his coat pocket and slid it across to her. There were only two other operators that time of night, and they were both on the other side of the bank. He was sure the others had noticed the attention he paid to Solisae, but no-one seemed to mind. Apparently, interdepartmental marriages weren't unheard of in the RPS. Finally, she pulled off her earpiece and looked up at him with a smile.

"Fancy seeing your here, Corporal," she said.

"The only fancy thing here is you, my dear," he said in a low, cooing voice. She blushed and looked away, slipping the perfume into her purse. "I'm about to start my shift," he said, "and I didn't want to miss seeing you before you clock out. Anything interesting out there tonight?"

Her smile faded as she picked up a heavy sheaf of papers that had been lodged beside her large machine.

"Absolute madness," she said with a huff.

"More Parimu?" he asked, trying to show the exasperation the other officers did without revealing too much of his hatred for the man.

"How'd you guess?" she asked with a grin. "Chief wants the men on Parimu's detail back walking their usual beats. But technically," she added, raising a finger, "they're still under him for two more weeks. So he's got them all checking in at telegraph stations every thirty minutes. Just makes a nightmare of paperwork for us."

"Glad I'm not on that detail," Erso said with a whistle. "He got 'em doing anything, or just checking in?"

"Nothing at all," Solisae said, rolling her eyes. "But if he sends in an order, we're gonna have to ring it in as an emergency, pull everybody to wherever Parimu says."

Just then, the lights on all the telegraphs started to blink and a tiny bell chimed on the top of each machine. Erso looked up at the clock and found it was exactly on the half hour.

"Sorry," she said, putting her earpiece back on. "I'd much rather talk to you, but we got the next twenty reports coming in for Parimu."

"Not to worry," Erso said, waving a hand. "I know where to find you, my sweet." He blew her a kiss, walking off as she turned back to her machine, another blush coming to her cheeks.

He headed back down the hallway. He couldn't stay at the station all night without doing anything, but maybe he could hang around a little longer to see if Parimu's units got deployed. Eventually, though, his pretend shift would have to start. At least there'd be emergency whistles if Parimu found something. He'd heard one a few weeks back when a ship had some trouble outside the port. They were awful, shrill as could be, but at least you couldn't miss it.

He poked his head into the canteen again. There was still some time between shifts, so there wasn't anyone there. Couldn't hurt to have one more pastry, could it? He slid up to the counter, pouring himself another coffee. He lifted the lid on the pastries, realizing there was only one pear wheel left. He looked both ways before sliding it onto a plate and slinking off to a nearby chair. In the eyes of the Berillai, he was already a monster; may as well add pastry hog to the list.

He picked up a newspaper and started browsing through it. There was an article about a recent pirate ring that had been broken up by the navy. For over a month, they'd been striking ships in a small schooner and slipping away just under the cannon fire. But just recently, the navy had laid a trap for them and sunk their ship. The men who didn't die at sea were to be hung in few days. Hard to know how much of it was true — the newspapers were all owned by peers — but it was never a good idea to throw a stick at a shark.

Despite the coffee, he started feeling drowsy in the warm canteen. He blinked, folding the newspaper and standing. It was time to go before his fake police officer was found sleeping on the job. He moved to put his mug in the sink when he felt a jolt of energy shoot through his mind. The mug fell, shattering as it hit the floor. There had been a powerful ripple somewhere to the north, near the water by the feel of it.

His eyes widened. That had to be Aelibis, and if he could sense it, so could Parimu. He stared down at the broken mug, his mind racing. Suddenly, the emergency whistle started to blare from the direction of the telegraph office. He snapped out of his fog, running down the hall towards Solisae.

"Solisae!" he shouted as he slid into the room. "What is it?!"

She jumped in her seat, turning in surprise.

"It's Parimu," she said, "something near the docks, warehouse district. All his men are supposed to report immediately."

Erso bolted out of the room without saying goodbye. What was Aelibis thinking being so blatant at night with the city crawling with police? So many weeks without another raid must have gotten the man complacent, but no heist was worth his neck.

"Bloody fool!" Erso shouted as he ran out the door of the station. He needed to get there before Parimu, but he wouldn't have a head star this time. He sprinted across the street, ignoring the stares of passersby. Let them watch! He needed something fast, something unnoticeable in the night. He disappeared into an alley, turning into an owl with a flash. He soared above the rooftops, flapping his wings as hard as he could. He stayed low, not wanting to lose even a second in his descent.

As he came over the last rooftop and crossed Laeryia Boulevard, he saw police carts pulling up to the warehouses.

"NO!" he shouted in his mind. He veered for the closest alley, careening towards the ground like a meteor. He tucked his wings, dropping hard the last ten feet. He slammed into the ground, transforming back into his police uniform. Springing to his feet, he sprinted towards the warehouses. More police carts were pulling up, the men in Parimu's unit already swarming the area.

He slid around the corner, not losing any speed as he raced into the dark courtyard between the dingy buildings. Men were running in all directions, and he could see torchlight through the hazy windows. He ran in the same direction as the others, like a pack of hounds all searching for the same scent. As he reached the end of the courtyard, police were coming back out of the warehouse on the end.

Two policemen emerged from the shadow of the doorway, carrying a manacled Aelibis between them. It was undeniably him, black beard and all, a silver ring clamped around his neck. Erso stopped, frozen to the ground as he watched, his eyes wide in horror. Aelibis looked up, smiling as he caught his eye. Erso just stood there, watching as they carried Aelibis away and put him in a police carriage. He stayed as wave after wave of police poured into the warehouses around him, scurrying back out with Aelibis' accomplices in tow.

Finally, Erso snapped out of his trance, pulling off his hat as he walked away. It was over, Aelibis was finished. He looked down at his police uniform, his brain tingling for a moment with the possibility of breaking him out.

No, he thought, *this has to stop.*

He had already broken enough of his rules staying on this case so long. Aelibis had refused his help, and he hadn't been able to save him. He never followed anyone into custody, and he never tried to break someone out once they were behind bars. He had to work at the fringes, abiding by his code and keeping himself alive. That was the only way he could continue this futile work. Trying to stop the deaths was like catching rain in a sieve, but he would carry on, just as he always had. Aelibis was dead, it was time to move on.

Erso walked back to the alley he had landed in, his fists clenched. It took every ounce of strength he had just to keep moving. He had to get away from that scene, had to disappear. Most of all, he had to forget. As he walked by the dumpster, he stopped, punching it as hard as he could. He leaned against the brick wall, slumping to the ground.

He put his head in his hands, his breath coming in ragged bursts. He wished he could cry, but all he felt was numbness as a horrible realization began to crush him — this was all his fault. The prank he'd pulled on Parimu had wound up with the man's forces scattered around the city. Last time, he had been able to catch them grouping up at the station, beating them to Aelibis' hideout. But this time, his stupidity had put the police exactly where they needed to be. He had tried to move all the pieces on the board, but all he'd done was hand them the bloody game.

He sat there with his head in his hands for a long time, until the cold of the cobblestones began to numb his legs. He finally stood, grabbing the dumpster and hauling himself to his feet. He wiped his face, finally noticing the coppery blood that had spread across his hand. He shook his head, transforming back into his usual self.

"This wasn't the first, and it won't be the last," he said to himself as he staggered out of the alley. He hadn't created this world, after all, and they would keep killing his kind with or without him. He emerged from the alley and looked left towards the warehouses. There was no-one on the street now, all of the police having ridden out. It was deathly quiet, as if nothing had ever occurred. He turned, wandering off in the other direction, unable to bear passing by that empty courtyard.

He saw the light of a pub in the distance and trudged towards it. He needed a drink, and then he needed to start the process of forgetting. Unfortunately, it was one he knew all too well. He had seen enough blood spilt, failed enough times. But this feeling would pass eventually, it always did.

"You did what you could," he said to himself. He finally reached the door of the pub, that mantra in his mind. *You did what you could.* But he didn't believe it, and he hadn't for a long time.

16

You think our power from the gods alone? I tell you truly, it is our nobility that brought this strength to us. You think the gods would choose just any ore to make a hammer? It takes strength to be placed upon the anvil, and power to be made new by the roar of the sea.
-Excerpt from the Poems of Boran Stonekeeper

—:—

The rest of the week went by in a blur. Sumi had spent every spare moment she had walking the streets or writing new shapes in her notebook. Her first practice session had unleashed a flood of ideas, inspiring her to go through as many old memories as she could. There hadn't been another opportunity to transform, but it was still invigorating to have so many arrows in the quiver.

The new schedule seemed to be paying off, too, giving her more energy. Although, after burning the candle at both ends, it was still a relief when Queen's Day finally arrived. Unlike the week before, she took her time getting out of bed. Then, she carefully made a list of chores before heading down to breakfast.

As she sat down to eggs, toast and sausage, Amis stood there watching her suspiciously. He cocked his head, meowing at her. She cut off a tiny piece of egg and pushed it towards him. He eyed her for a moment before wolfing it down with a flick of his jaws.

"I must seem like a stranger, eh?" she asked, laughing as she stroked his ears. "You know, it's only been a week or so since we played in the garden. I could become a hawk again and carry you out there." He apparently didn't like that suggestion, jumping off the table and leaving out the kitchen window.

She shrugged, taking a sip of her tea with a satisfied sigh. She had sweetened it with a thick pour of cream and brewed it extra strong to wake her up. Feeling much more alert, she opened up her notebook to the most recent page. She'd started a tiny map of the city, highlighting the routes she had walked and adding markings for alleyways with good cover.

She looked down at the map, trying to plan the best route for the day. Since it was her day off, she could cover a lot more ground. She hadn't tried the docks in a few days, but they seemed to be busiest on Queen's Day when the passenger ships docked. After her chores, she could start by heading east and then loop back along the beach to end up at the port around sunset. She traced her finger along the route, imagining herself on each street, picturing the landmarks and people she might pass.

When breakfast was done, she jumped up to get started on her chores. For the first time in months, it felt like she had the energy to do a deep clean of the cottage. She hadn't really bothered since Nela's funeral, and it was starting to show. She planned to scrub the base boards in the hall and brush out the tub with lye. It looked like there was a good breeze outside, so she could open the doors on both ends of the house and dry everything while the day was at its warmest.

After a few trips to the water pump and a round of boiling water, Sumi found herself on her knees in the hall, a bucket of steaming water by her side and a brush in her hand. She scattered some cleansing salts before dunking the brush and rubbing the coarse boar's hair back and forth along the old boards. Nela had hated this job the most, delegating it to Sumi as soon as she was old enough. For her, though, it had always been soothing for some reason. The rhythmic motion seemed to whisk her worries away, leaving just enough room in her mind for a daydream or two.

After working her way down the right side of the hall, she stood, stretching her back as she rolled her neck from side to side. She looked at herself in the mirror, finding a glow to her cheeks. She smiled before kneeling back down to scrub the second half. Now that she was Shapewalking, every bit of manual labor was a chance to prepare for adventure. That thought had kept her jumping at difficult tasks all week, even offering to carry the water buckets up the stairs for Mr. Furttenhur.

Amis came by to check on her a few times, hoping for a chance to play. Of course, after one step on the drying floors, he would run back to the gardens. A layer of water on the ground wasn't exactly his idea of playtime. On his last visit, she dipped her hand in the bucket and flicked a bit of water at him. He huffed, shaking his face before running off again.

"You could use a bath, you know!" she yelled after him, laughing. He didn't come back after that, and she finished the hallway, moving upstairs to do the bath.

A few hours later, with everything shining and clean, she came back down the stairs, her hands pruned and her face flushed. She had been on a roll after the bathroom, and hadn't stopped cleaning until she'd done the landing and all the windowsills. As she passed the clock, though, she squeaked, realizing it was already late afternoon. A little darkness was good for Shapewalking, but she didn't want to miss the sunset altogether!

She flew back upstairs, putting a quick braid in her messy hair, randomly plastering some makeup on her face. She inhaled a biscuit so she'd have something in her stomach, choking it down with some leftover tea before she shot out into the street. As she reached the hill, she noticed a chill to the air. She had worked up such a sweat cleaning, she hadn't felt it, even with the windows open. So winter would be coming, then… But fall had only just begun!

She strolled east through the Lournoy District and down to the water. She passed small pockets of people, families out for a stroll and the like, though no one looked to be in dire straits. She passed Mrs. Berkin's neighborhood before crossing Laeryia Boulevard and heading west towards the docks. As she passed the beach, the sun was heading for the horizon, cutting through gaps in the clouds with a beautiful golden glow.

She walked on at a leisurely pace, finally reaching the bend in the road where she took the ramp down onto the docks. They were about ten feet lower than the street, surrounded by a tall crescent of stone. A pier ran parallel to the boulevard, some fifty feet wide and filled with vendors selling food and anything else a traveler could need. There were dozens of navy men milling about, waiting to report to their ships. Merchants were barking orders and tourists wandered around, looking dazed by the crowds.

With the pier as their base, the dark wood of the docks stretched into the water, like fingers on a hand. The two closest to the palace were reserved for the navy, and the wall on that side of the port had a full array of cannons. There were a dozen naval ships at port and the same number of empty berths for the ships at sea. The naval docks were crowned with giant gatehouses, where a knot of guards stood waving the sailors through after inspecting their orders. The other docks were for merchants and tourists, with wide customs buildings guarding the way into the city.

Sumi wandered through the crowd, enjoying the chaos of laughing and yelling, the smoke of grills and pipes lifting above. She gave a few tourists directions before weaving her way forward, looking for anyone else that might need something. At the end of the docks, the pier merged with a large stone platform that held the main naval fortress, its parapets hiding the long range canons that protected Berill from blockades. At least, that was how Grandpa had explained it... Luckily, there hadn't been a blockade in her lifetime.

She planned to walk to the end before passing through the crowd again, but as she approached the stone platform, there was an odd change in the crowd. A nervous energy seemed to seep from between the rows of people, a strange magnetism pulling them towards the fort. The crowd had grown more dense, and she had to struggle to move forward. Curious, she wormed closer, though it was hard to see anything with all the people packed so tight.

She finally found a break between the shoulders of two shorter women. She peered ahead, gasping as she finally got a clear look. The crowd had formed for a public hanging. A lump formed in her throat; there was nothing she hated more in the city. It was barbaric, and she didn't want any part of it. She turned to walk back out of the crowd, but something stopped her. She couldn't put her finger on it, but something was buzzing in her mind, drawing her to look at the men that stood on the large wooden platform at the front of the crowd.

She gritted her teeth, her stomach twisting as she edged back into the crowd. The men all had black cloth over their heads, and sigils on their chests indicating their crimes. There were some ten in all, and she squinted, trying to make them out. She recognized the first two as the symbol for piracy: a snake eating its own tail in black ink, a ship in the middle. The second one she didn't know on sight, a knife in red ink, but it seemed like some kind of violent crime. As her eyes scanned down the row, her heart skipped a beat. On the next man's chest, in purple ink, was the shape of her necklace, the sign of the Shapewalkers.

Her temples pounded, and she struggled to breath. She bumped into the man behind her, realizing that she had been unconsciously backing away, trying to escape from the platform. She whipped around, raising a hand in apology before rushing off into the crowd, desperate to escape. She was afraid she would faint, the pounding at her temples growing harder as she stumbled away from the fort.

The crowd gasped as the switch was thrown. She clapped her hands over her ears, trying to block out the sickening sounds of the ropes snapping tight. She pushed forward more quickly, knocking into people without stopping to apologize. Finally, her boots clicked against wood, and she knew she was out of the crowd and back on the pier. Her head swam. She put out her hand, almost falling as she reached the stone wall that ringed the docks. She gulped in lungfuls of clean sea air, grateful for breaths that were untainted by the malice of the crowd.

She wasn't sure how long she stood there gasping for breath. Some woman came up to her, touching her shoulder and asking if she was alright. Sumi had her eyes clenched closed, but she nodded, managing to push out that she was seasick. Finally, her heart slowed, and her head stopped spinning enough for her to open her eyes.

She snapped her head down, her hand reaching for the necklace, making sure it was still hidden beneath her shirt. Her eyes darted around, but luckily no one was looking in her direction. The last thing she needed was the naval guards being called to check on the strange woman having an outburst. She staggered on, trying to act calm and keep her head high as she walked away from the docks, using all of her willpower not to run.

———

Erso gripped the top of his cane so hard that the sharp top of the handle started drawing blood. He gritted his teeth but didn't look down. He kept his eyes locked on the grisly tableau on the docks below. Aelibis' body hung from the end of a rope, sentenced to die alongside a few other criminals and what little remained of his crew. Erso watched until the man's legs stopped twitching and the executioner moved to cut him down. Aelibis' keyhole finally blinked out; his star no longer in the sky, his soul disappearing to the deepest halls of Mu'lalat.

Erso had failed him. Sure, Aelibis' own pride had played a part, but he hadn't been able to save him. All he could do now was watch as the man's life ended — he owed him that much, at least. There didn't seem to be anyone else mourning the man. Not that anyone would openly wail at a Berillai hanging surrounded by police... Still, it wouldn't have surprised him if Aelibis didn't have anyone; it wasn't like Erso did. If it had been his neck in that noose, there certainly wouldn't have been anyone in the crowd struggling to hold back a tear.

Wasn't this the life he had chosen, though? The freedom of anonymity and the shadow of isolation were just two sides of the same coin. It was safer living the way he did, and without a doubt easier. What little family he still had alive were safe in Amoriai, and he didn't have to put them at risk. There was a power in that anonymity, but it was days like this that reminded him it came at a cost.

Two hundred years ago, if a Shapewalker walked into a village, they'd be run out of town if they weren't already wearing the face of a local. Now, you could take any form and not a single person in the city would look at you twice. He'd looked like himself the entire time in Berill, and it hadn't made a shred of difference. It was powerful that you could be anyone, but it was only because you were no-one to begin with.

He supposed it was the life Aelibis had chosen as well. He made it a point to never judge what his kind used their powers for. After all, there were only so many options when society labeled you a monster. Still, whether they chose this life or not, all too often, it ended in the gallows. He tried to take some solace in their ability to choose for themselves, but at that moment, it only felt like numbness.

He finally broke his eyes away, looking at the crowd on the docks. He had been focused on Aelibis, but he could have sworn he'd felt the other Shapewalker, their tiny rhythm pulsing at the fringes of his mind. Had it been the woman from the trolley station? As the men were hung, the other Shapewalker had faded away, disappearing just as Aelibis' aura had died out.

It had taken every bit of his will power not to follow. But he had been determined to give the man's death a witness, to finish things the right way. There would be time to find the woman yet, though maybe not much. Aelibis' transformations had likely covered for this other Shapewalker. The detective wouldn't have been able to distinguish between them, especially with his searches focused on the rougher neighborhoods. But with Aelibis dead, it wouldn't be long before even a thick headed fellerhurn like Parimu was on her trail.

Erso turned and left the docks. He would find her before the police. With Aelibis gone, there was nothing to take his focus away. He would circle the city til his feet bled, avoid sleeping if he had to. The winter festival was coming up, and the whole city would be out on the beach. That would be the perfect time to find her. If he couldn't find her there, then he could admit defeat. He wanted to be done with this wretched place, but he'd be damned if he let the police have another of his kind without a fight. He walked out of the crowd and back into the night, eager to make things right for once.

_____

The sun had set during the hanging, and by the time Sumi emerged from the docks, the sky was dark. She rushed ahead, wandering into the city without thinking of where she was going. Her only desire was to get away from that horrible scene. After turning down a half dozen streets, she looked up, realizing she had made it to the Royal Park. She wandered inside and sat on a bench, leaning forward with her head in her hands.

As she slowly emerged from the fog in her head, she replayed the last hour in her mind. Something had drawn her to that hanging, something making her eyes see what was on that last sign. She looked all around before fumbling with her dress and pulling out her necklace. There was no mistaking what she had seen — it was the exact same symbol.

She had no idea it was so dangerous to be a Shapewalker. She had known instinctively that it should be a secret, of course — it wouldn't be very smart to brag about being the same kind of monster that killed King Rummon — but being hung? It wasn't as though Shapewalkers were a regular topic of conversation. Before this all began, they had only been fairytales. She certainly hadn't considered that there were others like her in Berill, let alone that it was a crime punishable by death…

She sat up straight, closing her eyes and taking a deep breath.

"Okay," she said to herself, "it's okay, nothing's changed. You were being careful, and you'll be even more careful still."

She opened her eyes and looked around the park, finding the neighborhood empty around her. At least it was dark. Dark streets used to seem ominous, but now they offered her a place to hide. She couldn't run off with her tail between her legs. There was finally something she could do for the world, of course it would come with some risk. Nothing had changed, she just had to carry on.

She stood up tentatively, her legs feeling shaky. She should call it a night for now; she wasn't in any shape to transform. She could get back on her schedule tomorrow. She was shaken, but she would be alright. She felt so close to the life she wanted, she couldn't give it up yet. Assuming she lived long enough to seize it… Her mind shot back to the image of the hooded man about to be hung, and a shudder shooting up her spine. She couldn't think about that now, she just had to keep moving forward.

She wandered off into the night, heading towards the cart path, the most direct route back to the cottage. She pushed through the darkness, eager to block out the images of the dock with the familiar comforts of home. Even with no-one there, the cottage was filled with memories of Nela and the hope she'd need to face tomorrow. She likely wouldn't sleep a wink, but was still longing for her bed all the same.

17

The empire hasn't stood because it was more virtuous, my dear. It remains because our forefathers had the strength to see it through. You think magic is something only given to the kind? It is blood, like any other, and it can be spilled or hardened, like metal in a forge.

-Excerpt from The Borimol Plains

—:—

The sun rose the next day, only to disappear into a sea of low-hanging clouds that had blanketed the city. Sumi stood by the window in the kitchen and sighed as she sipped her tea, looking out over the only home she had ever known. It seemed different somehow, now that she knew she was a criminal in her own kingdom. Each street was still full of promise, but now she saw the danger, too. She had gone from a valiant knight to someone lost in the jungle, each turn holding a beautiful flower or a tiger ready to pounce.

Her eyes were bleary, still holding onto the nightmares that had woken her over and over. Once, *she* had been the one in the noose, the black cloth blocking her mouth. She had struggled to breathe, trying to claw her hands free from the ropes that bound them. Just as the platform gave way, she had woken with a jolt, finding herself twisted in her sheets, the bedspread over her mouth.

As little as she had gotten, the sleep still seemed to have done her some good, putting a bit of distance between herself and that horrible scene. She still felt a weight on her heart for the other Shapewalker, like she should be mourning them, a life just like hers cast aside. And she couldn't help but wish that she'd been able to meet them. To think of getting to talk with one of her own kind, all the questions she wished she could ask…

The grief she felt also seemed to come with a sense of resolve, crystalizing her need to do as much good with her powers as she could. The fear still needled at her, but for the moment, her resolve was stronger — if only just. Hopefully some time in the flower shop would clear her head. She was supposed to help someone in the morning since it was Umildi, but she needed calm before she'd have any chance at Shapewalking. After work, she could try again.

She pulled her warmest coat out of the closet and bundled it tightly around her. As she closed the front door, she kept her hand on the wood for a moment. She was trying to hang on to her courage, but it still felt wrong to leave behind the safety of home. She finally stepped off the porch, looking back at the cottage until it was out of view.

With the sun gone, it was even colder than the day before. There was no denying winter now. At least the early sunsets would offer her a few extra hours of darkness to hide in... As she walked down the hill, she kept thinking about the other Shapewalker, trying to imagine what kind of person they had been. Admittedly, she didn't know anything about them. Had they tried to use their powers for good, or had some other crime gotten them killed?

Other than being a Shapewalker, it wasn't like she was doing anything wrong. Maybe it wouldn't matter if some silly girl wandered around the city helping a few people. There had to be legal books at the library or something that could help, right? Still, she had to be careful. Just because she'd had the privilege of never running up against the law didn't mean that justice was on her side.

Once she got to work, thoughts like those seemed to consume the rest of her day. The shop was slow, and there wasn't much to keep her mind off things. After Mr. Furttenhur left, she stood by the window, watching people slip past on the street below. They all rushed by, holding tightly to their coats, not a single one glancing up at the shop.

"You'd think they'd want more flowers on a cloudy day," she whispered to herself. Unfortunately, it seemed customers only came in on the best of days. Aside from the occasional funeral arrangement, all their business was for celebrations: weddings, first dates, parties. What was it that made people try to magnify the days that were already glorious? It was like wanting a sky with two suns.

The shop slowly darkened around her, and she lit the stand lamp for the first time since spring. She was fine with wearing a coat, but why did winter have to be so dark? It was one thing to miss the sunset, but it was another thing entirely when it disappeared before her shift was even over.

With a few minutes to go, she put on her coat and stood by the door, closing her eyes and taking in a deep breath. She was still afraid. She would probably never get the image of that hanging out of her mind. But she refused to quit, and that meant it was time to leap into the unknown. When the clock chimed, she locked up, stepping onto the tiny balcony.

As she watched the crowds, a smile finally came to her face. Despite the darkness, the street lamps glowed brightly, and snippets of laughter drifted up from the crowd. These were still her people, and she was here to help them. She could do this. She went down the steps and into the street, wandering towards Wembly Market. She wasn't ready to go back to the docks, but the happy crowds at Wembly would be perfect for getting her feet wet again.

As she made it up the hill, the smell of roasted nuts filled the air. She quickened her step, her mouth watering. Now that it was winter, the booths would be setting up outside for Alomidiar! She reached into her purse and shook her coin bag, hearing a few soft clinks. Maybe she could squeeze just enough money together for a pick-me-up…

Bubbles seemed to dance in her chest as she wandered the stalls, the familiar sights of the holiday finally banishing that image from the docks. There were small wooden figurines to burn in the fireplace, and large salt blocks for carving. They even had the centerpieces made of seaweed, each one having been intricately braided before drying.

Holding up one of the centerpieces, she finally frowned. This would be her first festival without Nela… Even though she hadn't believed in the Berillai gods, Nela had always made sure the cottage was full of seaweed and snacks. She couldn't afford much now, but maybe she could find some by the beach and decorate in Nela's honor? She pulled out her notebook, making a note to look. Unfortunately, there were only going to be more firsts like this. From now on, every holiday would pass without her.

Further down, there was a stall roasting squid, the fragrant smoke filling the air. She smiled again, one of Nela's sayings came to mind — 'Only foolish squids want the moon when they could have the sea.' Like all of them, she only halfway understood it, but it seemed to be about living in the moment. Her heart would likely never stop aching for Nela — and it would only hurt more on holidays — but Nela would have wanted her to celebrate anyway. All she could do now was laugh so hard that Nela heard from wherever she was watching.

Finally, at the end of the row, she found a vendor roasting elden nuts in a giant metal drum. She wound up having enough to buy a small satchel, eagerly tucking the first one in her cheek. They were slightly sweet and hot, tossed in ocean salt and oil. She held it in her mouth for a full minute, savoring the flavor as she breathed in deeply. Then she crunched down, chewing the nut completely before she tossed the next one in. If she could only afford a handful, she ought to make them count.

Finished browsing the outdoors stalls, she went into the market proper. She stopped by Mr. Tellemuir's stand, finding Alip there again. She didn't want to run this time, suddenly needing a familiar face. It was relatively quiet, so she stood by the edge of his table and waited as he finished making change for a woman buying snow melons.

"Lousy luck you've had," he said, turning towards her with a wink. "Catching me twice when I know you're looking for my father."

"Well," she said, laughing, "you know I'd rather have the wrong Tellemuir than none at all."

He grunted, scratching his chin philosophically.

"So, what'll it be today? As you can see," he said, sweeping his arm across the stand, "we're awash in snow melons. I'll give you a good deal if you take some off my hands."

"Nothing for me today, actually," she said. "Against my better judgement, I came over here to give you some of my elden nuts."

"Well, look at that," he said, putting his hands on his hips, "Sumi Elerair, of all people."

"Just be quick about it," she said. "I'd hate for people to think I'm getting cozy with an oaf like you."

He laughed, extending his hand where she deposited half of her remaining nuts.

"I'll ignore that since you come bearing gifts," he said, tossing a few in his mouth. He closed his eyes, lifting his chin toward the sky and humming with satisfaction. "Thank the gods," he said, "I didn't know I'd be this lucky today. You get these by the door?"

Sumi nodded, tossing another nut in her own mouth.

"Good taste," he said. "Errond's got the best in the city. But tell him you know me next time and get the discount."

"Just followed my nose," she said tapping it with one finger. Just then, another customer came up to Alip's stand. "Well, I'll be off," she said, smiling, "nice seeing you."

"Thanks Sumi!" he called, waving as he turned to help the customer.

Sumi rounded the end of the market and started walking up the other side. Halfway down, she passed by a young woman who was kneeling on the ground and picking up a bunch of fallen apples. There was a man standing over her, and as Sumi passed, he whispered in a rough voice.

"Look what you've done," he growled. "If you were a good girl, we wouldn't have had any problems."

Sumi pulled aside, pretending to look at some baskets as she snuck a glance back at the pair. They'd been standing so close she thought they were a couple, but she didn't like that tone… The woman's face was bright red as she scooped up the last of the fruit and stood.

"Come on now," the man said, grabbing her wrist, "let's get you back to mine."

The woman snapped her hand out of his wrist.

"I told you to leave me alone," she hissed. "We're through — stop following me."

She stormed off, holding tightly to her basket as she headed towards the exit. The man followed her, rushing to keep up. Sumi's blood boiled. *How dare he,* she thought, *that poor woman!* Her mind raced. What could she do? The man was huge, at least a foot taller than her. She whirled around, looking for Alip, but more customers had appeared, and she couldn't catch his eye. Her pulse was fast as she clenched her fists. If only Grandpa were alive; he would have had no trouble with a man like that.

That was it! He may not be alive, but he could still make an appearance. She took off, running out of the market, her mind spinning as she tried to land on what version of Grandpa she wanted to be. It wasn't hard to think of a memory — just like Nela, he was in hundreds — the problem was picking the right one.

She turned out of the market and saw the woman at the far end of Esile Street, rounding the corner with the man close on her heels. Sumi ran as fast as she could, sprinting along the outside of the market before sliding around the corner of a nearby alley. Grateful for the dark, she crouched behind some crates as the perfect memory came to mind. Grandpa had come to an event at school, about six months before he died. He had still been strong as an ox then, and was wearing his naval dress uniform. She had earned a pin for good marks, and he had looked so proud, his eyes sparkling as he looked up at her on stage.

The dark alley flashed, and Sumi sprinted onto the street, moving quickly with Grandpa's long legs. She wore the dark blue dress jacket and white pants of a navy officer, her black leather shoes slapping against the pavement. She turned right out of the alley in the direction the woman had fled. She heard shouting ahead and ran faster, speeding around the next corner.

The woman was in the middle of the street, the man shouting as he pulled at her basket. Sumi slowed her run before they noticed her, trying to put on the dignified air of a navy officer. She strode up to the man and found with satisfaction that she was easily a head taller than him now. And despite his age, Grandpa's muscles were quite a bit bigger too. She grabbed the man by the shoulder, gripping hard.

"I'd let the basket go if I were you, son," she said in the angriest voice she could. She almost scared herself as she heard that icy voice, one Grandpa had only had to use on her maybe twice in her life. It was calm and quiet, but deadly serious.

The man spun around.

"Mind your business, you old—" he started to say, but his voice fell silent when he saw the pins on the uniform.

"I hope you're not a Navy man, are you?" she asked, staring right into his eyes.

"Uh...yes, sir," he stammered. "I'm a...uh...second cadet on the Jade Mistress."

Sumi laughed. "Well, you won't be for long if I have any say! I could have you strung up from a mast pole for less. At least for the Queen's sake you weren't in your uniform."

"N-no, sir," the man said hastily, "it's nothing, just a personal matter."

"Don't give me that, boy," Sumi said with a growl. "There are no personal matters for a navy man; you represent the Queen and her laws just as much on land as at sea." The man's face went white, and she decided to press her advantage. "You get back to your ship now and start praying I don't rip up your commission before you get there. And if you *ever* bother this woman again, you'll have worse to fear than losing your post."

She released her vice grip on the man's shoulder, cocking her head towards the water. He took off, running for the docks like he was escaping a fire. The woman was on her knees, picking up her produce for the second time, the fruit flying across the ground the moment the man let go in their tug of war. Sumi picked up the last few apples before offering the woman a hand, lifting her easily with Grandpa's strong arms.

"Are you alright, miss?" she asked. The woman's cheeks were red again, but she nodded, streaks of mascara running down her face.

"It's over now, dear," Sumi said, patting her shoulder. "What's your name?"

"Barine" she answered in a small voice. "I'm...sorry you had to go out of your way, sir. I do beg your pardon."

"It's nothing," Sumi said, waving her hand. "I'm the one who should be apologizing for that sailor. If you don't mind me asking, what's the story with him?"

"Well," Barine said, "we were sweethearts once." She shook her head as if trying to banish the once sweet memories. "I found out he was writing letters to three different girls and broke things off while he was at sea. Now that he's back in port, he hasn't left me alone. He turned up at my work, followed me to the market…" She trailed off, sniffling as she wiped her eyes.

"Well, he won't be bothering you again if I have anything to do with it," Sumi said, reaching into her pocket. Thankfully, her grandfather's old notepad was still there. How had that made it into the transformation? She shook her head, scratching down her address. "This is my personal address. If you ever hear so much as a whisper from him, write to me here."

She reached into another pocket and handed the woman Grandpa's handkerchief.

"Now, why don't I walk you home? You've had quite a night."

Barine nodded, fixing her shawl and pointing to the east. Sumi followed next to her, asking the woman about her work and her family. It turned out that she was an orphan, too. Her last remaining relative, a brother, had passed away fairly recently. He had been in the navy as well, but now she was all alone, trying to make ends meet doing bookkeeping for a leather factory.

"I'm so sorry, dear," Sumi said, letting out a sigh. There was so much pain all around them. It hit especially close to home that Barine had no-one left. She had to be careful about revealing too much, but her heart yearned to offer the woman a little friendship.

"You know," Sumi said, "one of my neighbor's has a niece who sounds just like you. She works in a shop as well, Furttenhur's Flowers just down Laeryia Boulevard from the palace. It's hard being alone; you should look her up some time."

"That would be lovely," Barine said, smiling. "I could use a friend my age, all the neighbors here are getting on in years."

"Sounds like me," Sumi joked, laughing.

"Never!" she said, grabbing Sumi's arm. "Sir, you're like a knight, you are."

They both laughed, turning a final corner where Barine pointed out her door. Her place was a narrow two-flat, with fading grey brick and a tin roof. Hopefully Barine's brother had qualified for the naval pension; she knew all too well how hard it was to hang onto a house alone.

"I'll be alright now, sir," she said. "I appreciate you walking me back. And I can't thank you enough for earlier."

Sumi smiled, feeling her grandfather's dimples on her cheeks.

"All in a day's work," she said. "Just write if you need anything, alright?"

She turned away, spotting another alley. Barine didn't live far from the warehouse district, and the streets were dark and quiet — perfect for Shapewalking. She whistled as she walked, the tension finally easing from her shoulders. She had really helped this time, not only getting to embody someone like Grandpa, but doing something only a Shapewalker could have done. If mousey Sumi had tried to fight that man, she and Barine would have both ended up in the hospital!

She turned into the alley, the dark cloud hanging over her finally seeming to dissipate. The alley jogged to the left before branching off into corridors, each one servicing a different warehouse. She turned at the first corner, leaning against the wall as she prepared to take her usual form.

Transformed back into herself, she turned to go, a smile on her face. She was starting to feel at home in these hidden spaces. She had always sort of liked the mystery of alleys — the high walls, the dim light, corridors into the unknown. Once inside, though... Well, there had always been enough trash and rats to disrupt any fantasy. But the more time she spent in them Shapewalking, the more she felt a kinship with them. Now they were a place of safety and possibilities. Perhaps one day they'd crown her — Sumi, Queen of the Alleys.

She was still chuckling to herself as she turned the corner, finally hearing the shouts coming from the street. She shot backwards, slamming her body against the nearest wall. Her eyes went wide as she listened, trying to hear over the thumping of her heart. She heard the slamming of carriage doors and the heavy smack of boots. It was too late for this many people to be in this neighborhood, wasn't it? Still, she was in her own form... She was about to slip out when a voice yelled over the din.

"Search them all men! This is the right district, but the Shapewalker could be in any of these buildings! Don't stop until you find them!"

She gasped, air rushing into her lungs as she clapped a hand over her mouth. Her mind shot back to that horrible hanging, the symbol — her symbol — pinned to his chest. How could they know she was here? No-one had seen her, had they?

Footsteps started down the alley from the street. No more time to think, she bolted back the way she'd come. She sprinted hard, not looking back, her lungs burning as she ran. She heard a police whistle blow behind her, and she pushed harder, regretting the loud clack of her heels as they struck the stone.

The length of alley she was running down split again, forming an L-shape to the right. She rounded the corner, almost slipping in a puddle, but she kept her feet, dashing forward. Her eyes were scanning for an escape, jumping from wall to wall. This alley had seemed perfect, but she'd trapped herself in a maze! She panicked, the footsteps and shouts growing closer.

The next length of alley ended in a t-shaped fork. She went left, trying to orient herself off the mountains poking above the walls on the horizon. She couldn't outrun them, but she could get out close enough to a terrace, maybe she could slip onto the path by the school... She turned right again, but as soon as she did, she saw a dead end. She slipped, falling to her knees.

"No no no!" she cursed under her breath. There was no going back; she'd fall right into their trap. There was no going forward either...the wall in front of her was twenty feet high with no handholds for climbing. The only other thing in the alley was a large iron barrel. She scrambled off her knees, diving behind it.

Her chest heaved in and out as she tried to think. Somewhere in the alleys nearby, there was a great crash that sounded like trash cans being thrown to the ground. The yelling of the policemen carried from that direction. They were probably tearing the place apart, and it wouldn't be long before they found her...

She clamped her eyes shut, her nails digging into her palms. She'd have to change into something that could help her escape. But what and how? How was she going to think of a happy memory now? The fire hawk sprang into her mind. If only she could soar out!

"Nela, help me," she whispered. She fumbled for her necklace and clutched it in her hand, the gold of the pendant cool to the touch. She took a deep breath, suddenly finding a stillness amidst the panic. It was either over for her or it wasn't. Now wasn't the time for fear, it was the time for change. This would be her only chance.

The hawk suddenly reappeared in her mind, along with a strange realization. She didn't need to become the hawk, she *was* the hawk. She had felt the wind under her wings, seen the ocean below, waves rolling onto the beach. She had done those things, she was that hawk. Suddenly, her body felt like just another transformation she had learned. She took one last breath, and as she breathed it out, she saw a soft glow through her eyelids.

She didn't stop to look at herself. She turned and frantically flapped her wings, taking off into the night. She lifted up, gaining speed as the wall approached. At the end of the alley, she finally risked a glance back and saw a policeman just coming around the corner. He shouted at her, pointing in her direction as more men poured into the alley.

She shot forward like an arrow, leaving the police behind as she cleared the wall. She was finally out of the alley and speeding over the rooftops. She flapped hard, trying to gain height so she could orient herself. She could tell she was heading east by the water, but it was hard to make out anything specific.

Finally, she crossed over Fort Street and knew exactly where she was. She dove lower, trying to avoid giving the police a clear view. She stayed parallel with the hills, not wanting to turn towards the terraces too early. After another mile or so, she crashed down into an alley. The moment she hit the ground, she lost the transformation in a brilliant flash, the pop like a cannon in the dark night. She got up from the ground, trying to run, but the world rocked around her and she stumbled into the nearest wall.

She leaned there with her head down, her hand against the rough brick. She closed her eyes, breathing in and out in desperate gasps. Her muscles ached from her flight, and her temples were wet with sweat. The cool wind that gusted between the buildings barely made a dent in the heat pouring off her skin, like a glass of water on a blazing fire.

Her head finally stopped spinning and she opened her eyes. She stared out into the night, listening hard for approaching footsteps. That had been far too close. That policeman had been looking for her specifically. She wasn't sure how, but they had known that there was a Shapewalker in the area. Even a second more and she would have been finished…

She reached for her pendant and shoved it back under her blouse, the cold metal feeling clammy now against her boiling skin. The police knew more than just that symbol. The tiny voice in her head that had told her to stop transforming after the hanging had been right. She was so naive. It didn't matter to them if she was trying to help people. They could find her, and she knew already what the punishment was.

But how had they known where she would be? Had she been caught earlier and followed until now? There was just so much she didn't know, things the police knew all too well. It was time to stop transforming. She had been wishing so desperately for a different life, but she wouldn't have any of that from the end of a noose.

She headed out of the alley and onto the nearest road, trying to figure out what part of the city she had flown to. She walked as fast as her legs would go, navigating as she moved, not wanting to risk stopping for even a moment. The night slowly cooled her until she shook despite her thick coat. Worst of all, the cold air seemed to grip her heart as well, that icy well of sadness rearing its head.

She had brought this on herself. What had made her think herself clever enough to use a magic she knew nothing about? She had been given an incredible gift, and she'd already squandered it. A powerful shame burned in her heart. She had been using this power as a crutch, trying to be more like her grandparents. But the truth was, she wasn't like them at all, she was nothing.

This would be the end of her games. Whether the police knew her face or just how to spot her kind, she was done. She wouldn't draw attention to herself anymore, and if she was lucky, this wouldn't be her last month alive.

18

Sometimes, only the words of the ancients can truly speak. I seek their wisdom now—
   'Vilodash um'ilai rissage mulan'
   By the gods, the seas we take them, they are ours!
                     -Excerpt from the Poems of Boran Stonekeeper
                  —:—

Detective Parimu woke in a jail cell. His uniform coat was propped under his head as a pillow, his overcoat serving as a blanket. He pushed himself to a seat on the hard bench and rubbed his neck. It was tempting to groan with the aches, but luckily, he was too disciplined fo that. Besides, he had almost certainly slept on worse during his years in the Royal Navy.

He felt his face, grimacing at the stubble. Unlike the other fools in the department, he'd much rather be clean shaven. The fashions of beards never seemed to stop, but a clean face had been good enough for King Rummon, and it was good enough for him. At least he kept an extra razor in his office, but shaving took time, something he seemed to have precious little of these days.

He stood, crossing the small cell and pushing the iron door open. He had spent most of the night crisscrossing the city looking for the Shapewalker, and hadn't stopped until just before sunrise. At that point, he hadn't wanted to bother going home, figuring a few hours of sleep in the jail would get him an earlier start on finding his new quarry.

He didn't know whether to laugh or cry. He was ecstatic they'd discovered another Shapewalker so quickly, but the vile things seemed to be everywhere, spreading like rats. It was almost unheard of these days to find so many in one year. Could it be related to the thieving ring? Hopefully it was just his diligence rooting them out and not an actual increase in their number...

He worked his way down the basement hallway, a few of the early risers watching him from their cots. They were none of his concern. Most of them were petty criminals, and at least they were human. He didn't begrudge his fellows the occasional error in judgment, provided that the Queen's justice set them straight. When it came to what he hunted though, there could be no quarter given, no second chances.

The basement was squat, with brick walls and hard stone floors. It was cramped, though it certainly wasn't meant for holding parties. The jail was only temporary, anyway, the real prison on a barren rock off the western coast. When you left this place, you were either free, heading west, or riding to the gallows. Parimu came to the end of the hallway and knocked twice on the steel door. A slat opened, another officer locking eyes with him.

"Timber trees are thicker than tangerines," Parimu said, offering the weekly passphrase for the holding cells.

The man nodded and closed the slat again, a heavy bolt shifting before the door swung open.

"Morning, Sir," the officer said, offering a crisp salute.

"Morning, Officer Ailurn," Parimu said as he climbed the stairs, the door slamming shut behind him.

At the top of the stairs, he emerged into the clerical office, the sound of typewriters greeting him. He smiled at the rhythmic clicking. That was the sound of progress, of justice being served. He turned right, striding past the well-kept desks. Now this was an office! Everything was in its proper place, clean electric lighting humming from the green glass fixtures.

He went through another door to the jail's canteen. He preferred stopping at this one when he could, the one at headquarters full of men who disliked him. He made himself a strong tea to take the sleep from his eyes and wolfed down a pair of biscuits, standard fair for anyone in the Queen's service. He had been eating them since he was in the navy, and a morning didn't feel quite right without them. He quickly washed out his cup before walking out into the morning light.

He took in a deep breath, savoring the crisp winter air. He wasn't much for drinking, but navy men always swore by the sea air for their hangovers. The same seemed true for just about any ailment, though, including his lack of sleep. He walked quickly towards headquarters, eager to be in his office.

It was going to be another long day. Combing through the city hadn't worked the night before, so he needed to cast a wider net. Unfortunately, that meant he needed more men just as he was being stripped of his task force… It would be awfully difficult to do proper reconnaissance without enough bodies. Still, he'd see it done, even if he walked his own feet to nubs.

As he crossed over Fort Street, he smiled, passing a bunch of children on their way to school. They were jostling each other and laughing as they surged over the sidewalk. That was how the world should be — full of people who knew each other — not those lonely lines of drones pouring into factories. The children gave him hope. There was no telling if they'd stay close after they left school, but at least he could give them a city safe enough to live in.

Once he reached the station, he stopped by his box in the mailroom, chewing on his lip as he read through the endless drivel. Lines and lines of talk from his superiors, all while they ignored the Shapewalker problem. Still, he refused to sigh and moan like the others. There was a right way to do things, and he would do it. There was no point in wearing the silver badge if you besmirched it with a lack of backbone.

He pulled his pocket book from his coat and licked his pen, scratching out a few notes in his schedule. Then, he placed the letters inside and snapped the book shut, returning it to its proper place in his coat pocket. As he looked down, he caught a piece of lint on his collar and quickly removed it, dropping it in a nearby rubbish bin with a scowl.

He moved down the marble corridor towards his office. Well, his shared office anyway. In the old days, the Director of Reality had been a position of honor. Now, he shared a space with the Inspector of Alleys and Rubbish… Not that he needed a fancy place to work, but the kingdom deserved proper protection. Still, for the first time in a long while, he felt hope. It had been years since so many Shapewalkers were discovered. If he was successful again, maybe it would remind the upper brass just how dire the threat was.

Not that it wasn't still an uphill climb… He may have the support of the crown — at least the Queen still had honor — but he faced constant pushback in the RPS. Not even murder seemed to engage them as much as the "efficient allocation of police manpower." But if they stopped policing Shapewalking, how long until the fabric of society simply came apart? If you didn't know who anyone was, what was the point of being a person in the first place? That was the problem with those creatures, they just didn't—

"Ah, Parimu," an officer at the front desk said, breaking into his train of thought.

Parimu turned to find Cadet Nichols smiling smugly, his uniform a mess as he leaned back in his chair. The fact that this loathsome man was allowed to man the desk was a disgrace to the department. Parimu had seen him on multiple occasions flirting with women who came in to file police reports. And now Nichols just thought to interrupt him when he had important business to attend to?

"Yes, Cadet Nichols?" Parimu asked, standing tall before the slovenly man.

"Sergeant wants to see you," Nichols said. "Told me to send you up whenever you got back. Said you were to go right away."

Parimu nodded calmly, though his insides roiled. Why did no-one understand the gravity of his work?

"Is that all?" he asked.

The younger man smirked.

"That's it," he said. "Though, if you want some advice, you might actually like this job if you weren't such a zealot."

"Thank you, Nichols," he said, turning to go. As he reached the stairs, everything in his body longed to keep climbing towards his office, but he forced his feet to turn, heading towards the Sergeant's office.

The Sergeant's secretary, Mrs. Pommelroy, was at her desk. He'd always liked her, her notes almost as detailed as his own. At least someone in the upper ranks did good work… He stopped in front of her desk, his heels clicking together. She glanced at him, her beetle eyes magnified by her thick spectacles.

"Ah, Parimu," she said, "the Sergeant is expecting you. Just let me make sure he's free."

She scuttled back into the office, disappearing behind the glazed glass of the Sergeant's door. While she was gone, he looked around, nodding in satisfaction. At least the Sergeant kept a good office. Unlike some men of his rank, he only used regulation materials. Nothing was gilded or out of place, simply iron and polished brass, the only things an officer needed.

Pommelroy returned, sitting back at her desk.

"He can see you now," she said, nodding in the direction of the office door, which she had closed again on her way out.

He stepped up and turned the knob. There was no point in knocking when he had already been told to go through. That was the kind of timidity that came from a weak mind. A keen man knew his place and did what was required simply and efficiently. The Sergeant was at his desk, his uniform jacket on, smoking a cigar as he read some papers. He read on for a moment before looking up.

"Two red hens at midnight," Parimu said, using the official code from his personnel file. The Sergeant raised an eyebrow at his propriety. Not all stuck to the old ways, but at least the man still responded in kind.

"The fox lurks where the farmer is not," the Sergeant replied.

He put down his papers and crossed his arms, looking Parimu over. He kept puffing on his cigar without using his hands, like a freight train blowing smoke as it went down the coast.

"Now Parimu," the Sergeant said, "why did I come into my office today to find a fresh request for men? I thought I made myself clear after the market incident."

Parimu winced, but kept his stance straight. He knew what he saw, but ever since that trouble with the Peeress, it seemed the usual disdain for his department had tripled. It had to have been a trap laid by one of those wretched creatures... But couldn't the Sergeant see his thoroughness was an asset? He may be overly keen at times, but the risk was real. Just as certainly as there would be murders in the sleepiest village, there were Shapewalkers in Berill.

"I'm sorry, sir," Parimu said. "You know it's my duty to investigate every trace of Shapewalkers. And I swear to you that we were close on one last night. If you give me more time with the men I'll—"

The sergeant cut him off.

"If there really was one, then where is it now, Detective? You had forty men running around the warehouse district all night and nothing to show for it."

Parimu started to protest, but the Sergeant cut him off again.

"Listen, Parimu," the Sergeant said, putting down his cigar and rubbing his temples. "I've got an entire district to run. And while I appreciate the risks, you've gotta realize this isn't the olden days. I'm grateful for the one you just caught, really, I am. But you know if we find three a decade now we're lucky. I can't have you hurting commerce for the sake of a fancy."

Parimu clenched his fists. He knew he should hold his tongue, but why couldn't the man see the truth?! When he finally spoke, his response came out in a firmer tone than he expected.

"Don't you see how this can tear everything apart, sir? If a baker isn't a baker, and a cobbler isn't a cobbler, how can we keep any of it straight? We'd be back in the dark days when assassins lurked around every corner. The people are losing their vigilance sir, and I'd rather resign than let the kingdom crumble around me."

"Peace, Parimu," the Sergeant said, raising a hand to stop his outburst as he puffed out a ring of cigar smoke in exasperation. Parimu took a breath and calmed himself. He spoke again, softly and more slowly.

"I just want this kingdom to stay as it's always been, sir. In the world I grew up in, we had a community, people who worked together. Now, it's all factories and pubs. And just when we're pulling apart, no one in leadership seems to give a damn about Shapewalkers anymore. It's as if they've forgotten King Rummon altogether. I took a vow for a reason, and I mean to see it through."

"Now listen, just take a seat," the Sergeant said. He sat in one of the green leather chairs. He'd rather stand, of course, but he couldn't disobey a direct order.

The Sergeant took another deep puff of his cigar.

"I'm a good Queen's man, same as you," he said. "And don't tell me I'm just like the others. You know my grandfather was save from an assassination by the DoR when he was chief.That's why I let you work out of this building, and that's why I generally try not to meddle in your affairs. But—" he raised a finger in warning, "—I won't let you take that long leash and hang yourself or the department. If you've got a hunch, bring it to me, don't kick down half the doors in the city first. Do you understand?"

"Yes, sir," Parimu said, standing back up at attention. "Is there anything else, sir?"

"No," the Sergeant said, "just mind what I told you. I'm denying this troop request for now. When the storm you've cooked up in the Peerage blows over, we can talk." He turned back to his papers and waved his hand, dismissing Parimu. "Just come to me first, Parimu."

"Yes sir," he said, "thank you, sir."

Parimu strode from the room, closing the door behind him. He wouldn't technically disobey. He had taken this case to the Sergeant and had his request denied. Any future hunches would, of course, be taken to his superiors. But the Shapewalker he was chasing now was no hunch, it was a certainty. This was an active and urgent case. He would capture this Shapewalker, he just needed another way to get the resources...

He went back the way he had come, walking down the hallway as quickly as possible. He needed to lay a trap for this Shapewalker. Unfortunately, last night's near miss guaranteed they were aware of his pursuit. He had been so close! He had just turned the corner when it soared out of the alley as a hawk. He wished he had brought his bow, though he likely wouldn't have been able to get a shot off in time anyway.

This was the most difficult hunt there was — a creature that could become *anything*. They had flown so quickly! Even if the squad of police backing him had been worth their salt, he still may have missed his quarry. Still, if he couldn't outrun them, he'd just have to outsmart them.

He ran up the stairs, taking them two at a time. His office was buried deep on the third floor, and he hated the wasted time to get there. He turned three times through the maze of hallways, finally coming to his door. He tried the knob, but it was locked, his office mate likely off on inspections. He pulled out his key, letting himself in. It was a small space, just enough for two desks and an extra chair they shared for interviewing witnesses.

The office had no windows, so it was always dark, the department still not bothering with electric lights for the lower ranks. He lit the lamp by the door, the flame spreading a warm glow as it crackled to life. His desk was on the left, a sturdy oak piece with few possessions on it. There were a couple of photos, a standard-issue typewriter, and a dark-stained inkwell his father had given to him when he joined the force.

He paused for a moment by the coatrack, looking at the portrait of King Rummon behind his desk. His heart swelled with pride as he locked eyes with the king. To think he served a the family of a hero! Without him, there would be no Berill, no virtue on the Continent worth protecting.

"I will avenge you," Parimu whispered, "with every breath of my life, until your kingdom is secure."

He closed his eyes, taking a deep breath. No matter what, he would keep his oath. It may be a long shot, but he had a plan. He had thought the Sergeant may deny his request, and had spent much of the night thinking of a contingency. Technically, in an emergency, the Director of Reality had the ability to request supplies and troops directly from the crown. He came around the desk and sat in his chair, sliding a blank piece of paper into the typewriter.

Parimu's predecessor had always said the royal family still took such requests very seriously, the threat of Shapewalkers instilled in each monarch from an early age. He had to hope that was still true. Queen Welaya hadn't been on the throne terribly long, but she had the true blood. If he couldn't count on that, then this battle was already lost.

According to the papers, there was no love lost between the Queen and Pont'dulairn, especially on matters of security. Unfortunately, with that incident at the market, he had given the Vice Peer the perfect weapon to use against his Queen. But if he caught the other Shapewalker... Two in the same year would be all Welaya needed to regain control of the police department. He began to type, his fingers furiously trying to keep up with the flood of inspiration. Now that he had decided on a course, he wouldn't rest until he accomplished it.

If only he had more time… Alomidiar was coming, and he needed to use the festival to lay his trap. He didn't know what this one wanted, but crime always seemed to peak around the holidays, when the Berillai were lulled into complacency. If this one was a thief like so many others, they wouldn't be able to resist the valuables on display.

But if he failed to catch them during the holiday, the creature may well sneak out of the city and back to the safety of the Continent. If that happened, it would only risk more of their kind coming, convinced they could use their magic here with impunity. He shook his head, typing on, desperate to make his petition to the Queen before time ran out.

19

"Would he truly be of Fire House if he weren't?" Vorseyai asked. Perhaps she was better than generalizing by house affiliation, but she'd met few exceptions to the rule thus far.

-Excerpt from The Borimol Plains

—:—

Sumi stood at the back fence in her garden, looking out at the sea. It had been five days since the police chased her, and still nothing had happened. She had barely slept in that time, every creak of a shutter in the wind sounding like an imminent raid. As she fastened the deadbolt each night, she had caressed the wood, an immense guilt weighing on her heart. It would be her mistakes that ruined Grandpa's beautiful door when the police came to kick it in. But they never came.

Of course, if they hadn't come by now, they probably never would. She kept waiting for the other shoe to drop, but if they knew who she was, they wouldn't have waited. A detective wouldn't have to stake out the cottage long to realize she was an easy target, one silly girl living alone in the terraces. Even with her "powers", what could she do to defend herself? It wasn't like she could make the earth shake like the ancients, and a cat's claws wouldn't get her far against a battalion.

Even if they never came, she still felt shaken to her core. How could they have known where she would be? There were the bright flashes of light, of course, but she had sworn there was no-one on the street... There had to be another way to track a Shapewalker. She couldn't believe now how lucky she had been to not get caught before, but she had pressed her luck far enough. She would live quietly again, and hope she could avoid being hung by the docks, a crudely drawn symbol of her people pinned to her chest.

That morning, she had woken before dawn after drifting into a light, worthless sleep. She was so sick of tossing and turning, she had gotten out of bed as the roosters crowed, taking some tea into the garden. Winter had truly begun, grey clouds covering the ocean in a thick blanket. They were so low, they looked like they were touching the water, the bay a billowy sheet of dark blue ripples. The sun had tried to make a dent in the clouds as it rose, but after a brief moment of orange over Fort Hill, it had disappeared into the grey.

She sighed, barely tasting her tea as she sipped it. At least she could still feel the warmth on her lips. She absently looked back at the cottage through the crumbling foliage of the garden. She hadn't lit any lights on her way out, and it looked desolate, like a graveyard, just a collection of stones marking the memory of another time. Over the past few weeks, for the first time since Nela died, the house had felt alive again. Now, she felt further away than ever, her legacy slipping out of grasp.

The first day or two, she had tried to keep her spirits up. Nela's voice had been in her mind each day as she got out of bed, urging her to be stronger, to carry on. The first morning, even though she had been a ball of nerves, she still found herself watching the crowds on her way to work, looking for people to help. Slowly though, like a crack in a vase, her heart had leaked out until it was empty.

What did she think she could do for those people? She was just a lonely girl afraid to live a full life. The magic had changed nothing. Had she thought if she helped enough people, they'd throw a parade in her honor? If they knew who she really was, they would hang her for being a monster. But without her powers, she was truly alone again. She slipped in and out of the shop each day without a trace, back to the way she had been before — less than a ghost. And one day, she would pass away, never having touched the world or made it any brighter.

It was her day off from the flower shop again, but how to fill her time? She sluggishly thought through her list of chores, deciding that everything could wait for another day. There was no-one in the house to disappoint, after all. She would feed Amis and ignore the rest. She finished her tea and wandered back into the house. There wasn't much food left, the shopping forgotten in her panic, but she found a sausage in the larder, cutting it up and frying it for the cat.

But when it was ready, Amis was nowhere to be seen. Maybe he'd forgotten her too... She put the sausage on the windowsill before shoving a stale hunk of bread in her mouth, knowing she should eat, even without an appetite. She wandered into the sitting room, chewing listlessly as she flung herself down in one of the chairs.

She sat in the dim room for a time, her mind blank. Eventually, though, she looked in the hallway, catching the edge of Nela's picture in the mirror. She groaned, throwing an arm over her face. She didn't want to do anything, but she couldn't stay in the house either… Every room was too thick with painful memories, the past piling up like sand in an hourglass. She needed to escape. She got up, put on her coat, and wandered into the city with no destination in mind.

———

Sumi worked her way down the hill as an icy wind blew up the slope. It pulled at her coat, but she didn't mind, the bite on her skin feeling better than numbness. There weren't as many people on the street as in the summer, but with the weather finally dry, it seemed like more than she'd seen in a while. Still, seeing families out for a stroll only made her wish she had one of her own. She sighed, heading for the beach. The water always seemed lonely in the winter, and at least they could keep each other company.

She crossed the street by the palace, stepping onto the sand. There were a handful of walkways that crisscrossed it, but she stayed off them, forcing her way through the dunes. She stayed near the edge where tall grass lined the hill, the long fronds turned brown by the cold nights. Near the center of the beach, there was a flurry of activity as workmen prepared for Alomidiar. They were building a large wooden sculpture, though she couldn't tell what it was yet.

As she crested the dunes, she followed a gentle slope down to the water. She stood there for a long time, staring out into the endless blue. She saw the occasional ship go by, but mostly she just watched the point in the distance where the clouds and the water merged. Suddenly, she stooped down, untying her boots and kicking them off. She pulled off her stockings and tossed them onto the sand before running into the water until the waves hit her knees. She held her dress in her hands and danced back and forth as the water numbed her legs.

It was an old trick Grandpa had taught her, marching her down to the water as a teenager whenever she was moody. It was something he had done in the navy, and he would run alongside her until they were both laughing, her troubles forgotten. She didn't laugh now, but as she finally slowed her dance through the frigid surf, she felt much more alive than when she'd begun.

She left the water and dropped down on the sand with a thud, wiping the sand from her legs with her handkerchief. The best part of the ritual was pulling your stockings back on, making your feet feel ten times warmer. She carefully retied her boots, but stayed sitting on the ground, her knees pulled up to her chest. She looked out to the water for a while longer until she heard footsteps coming up behind her.

She turned to find one of the workmen approaching, a smile on his face. He had a grey beard and a weathered look, but kind eyes.

"I like your spunk," he said, chuckling. He had a steaming cup of tea in his hand, which he offered her. "I used that trick once or twice myself in my navy days."

"Thank you," she said taking a sip of the tea. It was a winter tea, floral and spicy, and it felt good to hold the tin cup with her hands. "The tea's lovely," she added. "My Grandpa taught me the trick with the water, he was in the navy, too."

The man smiled, nodding knowingly. He stood there next to her for a moment, staring out at the water.

"Well," he said, turning back, "I'll leave you to it. Nobody jumps in winter water if they don't have something on their mind. Just drop the mug off when you're done, eh?"

Sumi smiled, nodding to the man as he went back to the worksite. She stayed on the ground, trying to gulp down the tea before it lost all its steam to the cold air. She'd gotten lucky with the workmen, but she needed to move on soon. It was still odd to sit on the beach in winter, and if she stayed too long, she might attract the police. It felt strange to have to think that way, but that was her life now...

She rolled over and pushed herself up, dusting off the back of her dress. She marched over to the men at the worksite and tried not to blush too much as they all laughed, the original man coming down off his ladder to accept the mug. She gave them her thanks a half dozen more times before wandering back towards the street. She didn't deserve it, but it truly was a kindness he had done for her.

When she reached the end of the sand, she stopped, staring up at the city. All of Berill rose before her, climbing the hills and reaching for the sky. What was her place here? She felt a surge of love for the city, but it felt like staring at an old photograph, some artifact remembered but lost long ago. Maybe it was time for her to leave, but where could she possibly go?

She crossed back onto the sidewalk, wandering aimlessly through the streets. She didn't want to return to the terrace yet, where the silence of the empty house waited for her. She passed a bakery and splurged on two honey rolls. She probably couldn't afford them, but she needed the wind in her sails. She put one in her bag and began to chew on the other, forcing the sweetness into her body.

She turned from street to street, her eyes passing over shops and gardens without seeing them, willing herself forward. She walked uphill from the water, only vaguely aware that she was somewhere east of the palace. As she finished her roll, she emerged from a narrow street and found herself just a block from the Royal Library.

She thought back to that first day. What had it all been for? She had found her magic, but it hadn't been enough to overcome the weakness in herself. She hadn't learned to be strong or fearless like her ancestors, and now it would all end with her. It felt like such a tragedy to end a powerful bloodline on such a flimsy branch. She leaned on a nearby fence, staring at the stained glass windows as she felt her pendant beneath her blouse.

She wished she knew more about her family, their beliefs, their hopes, their way of life. What had kept them going when they were hopeless? What had given Nela the courage to leave her home? She needed to know how to be like them, to be worthy of the gift they left behind. She wanted to feel their faith, their goddess, Essomuai, the light in all things. There had to be a way to fill in all the things that Nela never told her.

She found herself pulled towards the library as if connected by a string. Before she realized it, she had her hand on the heavy door. The library was quiet, its ancient walls reflecting the quiet light of a dreary afternoon. Everything was perfectly still, but instead of a cave full of treasures, this time, it felt like a tomb. Still, there was peace there too — a place where she could hide and bury all her burning questions in the safety of a book.

Her heart lifted just a bit as she saw the Master Librarian sitting at the desks. He was exactly as he was before, leaning over his filing boxes with his wine-bottle glasses stuck on his nose. He was almost like a statue, placed there to teach future generations about what librarians did. As she approached, he looked up at her, blinking for a moment before a smile washed over his face.

"Ah, Miss Elerair! What a delightful surprise. I'd hoped you'd be back. You know, I went right home after your last visit and told my wife, 'There's still eager young minds in our kingdom!'"

She smiled at him, her cheeks lifting despite the sadness clinging to her eyes.

"It's nice to see you again too, sir," she said. She suddenly thought of the other roll in her bag. "You were so kind last time, I thought I'd return favor." She took out the parcel and placed it on his desk. "I brought you a honey roll from Duke's".

He took in a sharp breath of air.

"Wow, and a mind reader too!" he said. "I adore Duke's honey rolls.

My wife made me stop going — said she'd kill me herself if the sweets didn't first." He chuckled, apparently delighted at his wife's murderous show of affection. "But I think you and I could handle just one more secret, eh?"

"So," he said, stashing the roll beneath his desk, "is there anything I can help you find? Or did you really just come here to see an old man?"

"Well," she said with a grin, "this library does seem to have the handsomest men in the city. But... I suppose I also wanted to know more about religions on the Continent. Something on Anushai if you have it?"

"Hmm...religions," the librarian said, stroking his beard. He returned his glasses to his face and started to pull out racks of cards. "Aha!" he exclaimed after a few moments, pulling one out of its box. "I thought I might find his name here. It's your old friend, Sir Arteir Pallinayum. I remember the work you pulled last time, *Creatures of the Continent*. It was a favorite of mine when I was an archivist."

"My wife would tell you I can't remember anything — not that she's wrong, of course. I forgot to eat breakfast twice this week. But I haven't forgotten a book yet, thank Velloni." He turned the card to face her and pointed to a name about halfway down. "You see, Pallinayum did indeed live long enough to write his treatise on religion."

She leaned forward, squinting at the card in the soft blue light. There was Pallinayum's name alongside the title: *Beyond Alomus, Religious Rites of the World*.

"That looks like just the thing!" she said, taking the card. It was two floors higher than last time. The Master Librarian placed his hands on the desk, starting to get up.

"Oh no," she said, waving her hands frantically. "I couldn't want trouble you again after all you've done." She lowered her hands and sighed, leaning closer. "And if I'm honest, I feel like a bit of wandering would do me some good."

"You do seem a bit sad," he said. "Hope you don't mind my saying. But this is an excellent place to hide from your troubles." He chuckled, scratching his head. "I suppose I got so good at it they let me run the place."

He rang the bell on his desk and a porter came up with a lantern, bowing as he handed it to her.

"Enjoy your visit dear," the librarian said. "I hope there's plenty of happiness ahead." She nodded, curtseying as she thanked him before heading to the stairs.

When she finally reached the fifth floor, she stopped for a moment, leaning on the railing to catch her breath. The blue light from her lantern bobbed back and forth, the familiar smell of dust and leather filling her nose. It was a good thing she hadn't let the librarian make the climb, he might have never recovered.

She began wandering through the rows, hope suddenly blossoming in her chest. What if the secret she needed was really here? She scoured the shelves in the dark, looking for the bronze plates on the ends. It took her three times longer without the Master Librarian, though, and more than once she passed by the stairwell again, unknowingly traveling in circles.

"How many rows could there be?!" she asked herself, laughing at the absurdity of it. The shelves were supposed to be organized, but it felt more like a forest, the books like birds that had simply flown in and decided to roost. In some sections, the shelves grew closer together, new ones crammed in wherever they would fit, and the numbers seemed to jump about at random. One shelf was three hundred lower than the one before, and she couldn't fathom what had changed.

Finally, her lantern shone on a placard that miraculously matched all of the numbers. She rushed into the stack, running her fingers along the dusty spines. Halfway down, she found a book bound in thick wood and inlaid with silver. The metal shined blue in the hazy light as she took it in her hands. There was the title, and set into the cover was a strange symbol of three upside down triangles that intersected in the center.

She thought for a moment about finding a study room, but she didn't want to wait another moment. The floor was still silent, so she eased herself down and leaned against the nearest shelf. She crossed her legs, propping the book on her lap as she eagerly opened the cover.

She thumbed through the dense introduction — it seemed he could have written a whole book about the book! — until one section caught her eye:

Many a Berillai priestess has called me a blasphemer for writing this volume. They say that to discuss the Continental 'gods' would be to deny that Alomus created the Wellonaians, disparaging the hallowed name of Umilai. But know this — it was with the express permission of King Ulrechekt that I write this book, and every priestess in this kingdom serves at his pleasure.

We long ago left the seas behind us and established this kingdom, not through superstition, but with mercantile grit and the pursuit of knowledge. I would not disparage the beliefs of my people, for they are my own, but so neither would I cast out the beliefs of others as wholly without worth simply out of shortsighted pride.

She couldn't even remember the last time she had seen a Berillai priestess... Grandpa had followed the rites of the sea, of course, like every good sailor. But aside from celebrating the festivals, they hadn't exactly participated in the religion. In fact, she didn't know anyone who did. Still, she had vivid memories of Nela telling her to say her prayers each night. But to whom or what had they been praying?

She tried to remember, the ritual flowing like a river, crossing thousands of nights. She distilled them, the memory coalescing in her mind. Nela would always bring a lamp to her room, setting it on the window sill and turning it low. The faint orange glow would only light a small circle, its warmth like a distant star. She remembered the feeling of being tucked into the bed in the perfect way, the quilt heavy on her chest, her breath deepening as Nela leaned in to kiss her.

Nela would always whisper a few words in Anushai before taking her hand, leading her through a prayer she'd translated into Berillai. How had it gone? It only came in snippets, but it was something like: 'Flower, boulder, raven, brook; wood and boat and fisher's hook...' and then, 'love of kin and light of day, give what is and take what may'. There were parts missing in the middle, but she remembered the ending, Nela always making her giggle with a kiss on each eye. 'You to I, and I to you, love we'll give and duty do.'

She opened her eyes, smiling as the flood of memories warmed her heart. She hadn't thought of that in years! It felt foolish now, how eager she'd been to put herself to bed as a teen. If only she had let bed times go on a little longer... But what a lovely prayer! How long had Nela spent getting it to rhyme in Berillai? Had she said the same prayer with mother? With her eyes closed, she'd felt transported back to those nights, the blue lantern twinkling in the dark like Nela's lamp, giving her a peace she thought she had lost.

She took a deep breath and returned to the book, finding the table of contents. It seemed to be in west to east order of the kingdoms, as if it had followed Pallinayum's travel route. She found Anushai on page 207, turning as fast as she could without tearing the old parchment. There was a brilliant ink etching with the name of the kingdom surrounded by curling leaves, the symbol of the Shapewalkers in the center. She rubbed her thumb carefully over it before flipping the page:

The religious beliefs of the Anushai were the hardest to discern, and I spent many months there, visiting again and again to piece together what is still likely only a paltry understanding. This stems not only from the natural reticence of their culture, but their penchant to speak in metaphors. They have a great many sayings in their native tongue they believe provide the necessary context, but which may sound like absolute nonsense to an outsider.

She chuckled, thinking of Nela's many strange sayings. She *had* always acted as though their meaning should be obvious to Sumi or anyone else she spoke to. It was good to know all Anushai were like that. She pictured a flustered Pallinayum pressing Nela for answers. She'd likely start hitting him with the kitchen spoon before he made a dent in her religious beliefs…

Pallinayum went on: *Similar to many Continentals, the Anushai consider Wellonai to be the goddess mother, the creator of the world. They believe she had three daughters: Itorunai, Vilodai, and Essomuai. They speak most often of Essomuai, though, and this "daughter goddess" appears to be central to their beliefs.*

I learned this on my first visit, though, even now, I have trouble deciding what it means. Is Essomuai a goddess or a philosophy? Some legends include her, like their creation myth, but she isn't actively worshipped. They treat her more like the sun or the rain, something around them. As I mentioned in Creatures of the Continent, these beliefs are intimately tied to how they view the abilities of Shapewalkers and their connection to the magical realm.

She turned the page and found another ink etching, this one of a giant building. There was no way to judge its scale, but based on the large wooden doors, it looked to be at least ten stories tall. It was made of white stone and crowned with bell towers at least twice the size of the cottage. The center held a huge stained glass window in the shape of a flower. It had ten petals, each one ending in a different symbol, and in the middle were those overlapping triangles from the cover. The caption read: *The Temple of Essomuai.*

She stared at the picture for a long time, her fingers tracing the puffy clouds floating above the towers. What an incredible treasure. Why had Nela never mentioned it? She'd often laughed at her granddaughter's little obsession with architecture. She must have known Sumi would never stop pestering her to visit Anushai. She eagerly turned the page, reading on:

I made this etching during my first visit to Anushai. I was so overwhelmed, I forced my guides to stop on the spot and let me sketch it. I have still never seen a landmark to rival it anywhere on Wellonai. The temple is in honor of Essomuai, though the word temple is perhaps not accurate enough a translation. In my thirty years of visits, I have never found a priest or priestess there. It appears to belong to the public itself. Thus, there was no one within to answer my questions, and the visiting public appeared keen to escape my questions.

The interior is completely open, save for a large fountain at the center.

There are no pews, and despite visiting at many different times of day, it appeared that there were no organized services. There is a bell tower in each corner, the ropes simply hanging down within the building. I saw many Anushai ring the bells, but when I asked them why, many simply said, 'to ring the bell is to hear the toll.'

To call the fountain large does not do it justice. It is some fifteen paces wide, and built to match the symbol of the Shapewalkers with sections of marble and obsidian that end in a crystal bloom. The water flows on its own, and I believe now that the site was chosen due to some natural spring. There are four channels dug into the floor, and as the water overflows, it runs along those channels into various parts of the city.

Some people bring flowers, setting them into one of the fountain's petals and letting them flow into the city. When asked how they chose, some mentioned one of the ten royal houses, though I saw no markings to indicate them. I have still never been granted an audience, but it is rumored that a similar fountain sits in the imperial palace. I hope to do further research on the house system, as it appears there is a fascinating history behind their model of governance.

Sumi stroked her chin, thinking back to *The Borimol Plains*. There had been a lot of drama in the stories about the main heroine trying to marry a duke from another house. She had never really stopped to think about the significance of that. Hopefully she could find out more. She turned to the last section of the chapter:

There is an inscription in the fountain, so carefully laid into the stone, that at first, I hadn't noticed it. It is a poem of sorts, perhaps better stated as a meditation on Essomuai. The poem is broken into ten lines, each part in a different black or white quadrant of the pool. A scholarly friend who helped me translate it was adamant she was no expert in Essomuai, but our discussion left me under the vague impression that the temple had been built, not to worship this mysterious force, but to summon it.

Below is my transcription of the poem. It does not appear to "rhyme" in either language, but it certainly has a cadence to it in the high form of Anushai. Note too that modern interpretations of this poem often interchange Essomuai for the Anushai for 'we' (essom), but here I have used the original reading:

You belong to us, and we to you. You are the flower, Essomuai is the field.
Why do you doubt that you were planted with purpose? Essomuai is the prism, but yours is the light.
If your color would not be, neither would the field.

Shine truly in your own color, and you touch Essomuai.
If even one traveler should pass, let your color make them smile.
You may never finish the work, but neither may you abandon your
season.
No flower would wilt, because another has blossomed.
None would choose not to love, because others have loved before.
Essomuai is the field, but you are the flower. We belong to you, and
you to us.

Sumi looked up into the darkness of the library, breathing in slowly.
This was the prayer of her people. The wisdom she needed must be in
these short, sacred lines. There was so much she was desperate to know.
Why had she been given these powers? And who could she possibly be
without them? But even with all those doubts swirling in her mind, just
reading the poem made her feel less alone.

Suddenly, the words that Nela had spoken when she was thirteen rang
out in her mind: "There is strength to be with others, but not if you
cannot be you. You cannot be rose in bouquet without own color, little
flower." Lines from the poem bubbled up to her, this time in Nela's
voice, all of it connecting.

You are the flower, Essomuai is the field.
Shine truly in your own color, and you touch Essomuai.

A peace came over her. No matter what she was, she was Nela's
granddaughter. She was Mr. Furttenhur's shopkeeper, Mr. Tellemuir's
customer. She was Berillai and she was Anushai. These were her words
too. She read them through once more, and then turned the page, finding
another version of the poem.

For those who are both curious and linguistically inclined, I have
included the original in Anushai:

Teya toma essom, et essom toma teya. Teya siom heyal, Essomuai siom
saldal.
Welshema hulyal welshem, yonen jungun jayal.
Essomuai siom leyon, guyang siom teyal.
Guyan buyel siom, buyel siom saldal.
Gonyeol kelnang jelshul, fanshum bulneng beyol.
Guyang teyal guyan, Essomuai teya moyal.
Rul guyom saldal, guyang meyon shial.
Heyal buyem kewel, enel heyam kaiyal.
Lun renall buyel, welshem enem renall.
Essomuai siom saldan, Heyal siom Teya. Essom toma teya, et teya
toma essom.

"Nela," Sumi said, closing her eyes, "wherever you are, I hope you hear this prayer. And Essomuai…if you're real, I hope you hear me too." She held up the book and slowly read the words aloud in her people's tongue. Her pronunciation had never been perfect, but as she went, her cadence seemed to match the words. She started out whispering them, but as each line followed the next, they almost pulled the words from her lips. By the time she reached the end, her voice had almost risen to a shout: "Essom toma teya, et teya toma essom."

She felt a lightness in her chest as the last words left her lips, not like the butterflies of her earlier transformations, but something more solid somehow. She felt almost weightless, like she might even change her shape. The moment passed, and she was still just Sumi, sitting on the floor, but she was still changed somehow. The weight on her heart was gone, and she began to laugh, giggles rushing past her hand as she clapped it over her mouth, the lightness desperate to escape from her chest.

She knew now what Nela meant by strength. Strength wasn't doing everything perfectly, and strength wasn't forcing yourself to fit into someone else's shoes. It was being yourself, truly and fully, and then being brave enough to be part of the whole. You had to trust that you were enough, and that every day you lived was another chance to share your color.

Nela's power hadn't been her unstoppable will, but her vision to bring so many people together. She had seen the color in each person, and knew how they'd make her vision a reality. It didn't matter that she had been terrible at sewing, because Ms. Uppelhar was a retired tailor. She didn't need a farm when she could write letters to farmers, asking them to give what they could. And it didn't matter now that Sumi was a mousey shopkeeper. She was enough. If even one color was missing, you couldn't have a field.

She stood, a new energy seeming to lift her. It didn't matter if she never used her magic again. Her powers were nothing if she was just going to use them as another way to hide herself. There had to be people in the city just as lonely as her, and they needed her color too. She could be their umbrella or their trolley token, but she had to be their Sumi first.

She needed to find her place amongst her people, the part of the field where her flower would shine the brightest. Even if it took a lifetime, and even if she could only do one small thing a day, it didn't matter. Another line from the poem bubbled up: 'You may never finish the work, but neither may you abandon your season.' Her ancestors had gotten her to this point, and she was finally ready for what came next.

She returned the book to the shelf and marched out of the darkness
with her lantern held high. She felt like she had swum to the bottom of
a cave and emerged with a treasure in hand. She ran down the steps and
waved to the Master Librarian as she returned her lantern and rushed
back out to the street. There was still a slice of daylight left on the
horizon, and a plan was already forming in her mind.

20

Do you think your storms can shake us Alomus? Here beneath the earth by the heart of the true god? No wind can reach us in him no thunder in our ears. Here, in our power, we are truly free.

-Excerpt from the Poems of Boran Stonekeeper

—:—

Parimu tried again to tie his uniform tie, his face so close to the mirror that his breath fogged the glass. He scowled, yanking it out of its knot. He squeezed his temples, letting out a long sigh. That made the fifteenth failed attempt.

"Just do it how you've always done it," he said to himself. "The Queen has better things to think about than your damned tie!"

That thought, however, made him smile. He still couldn't believe he'd be meeting Queen Welaya. He would be stepping into a sacred temple, a mere mortal whose breath wasn't worthy of the halls he'd be passing through. His whole life had been in service of a crown he assumed he'd never lay eyes on. That had always been enough for him, of course, but to think that a blacksmith's son would stand before the throne…

"Keep your wits about you man," he said to himself, taking a deep breath, "this is no time to lose your head."

He re-tied the tie and put his jacket back on, refusing to fuss with it any longer. He stepped over to his desk and picked up the picture of his father, rubbing his thumb along the edge of the frame. It had cost him dearly to have it commissioned, but on a day like this, he couldn't imagine not having a piece of his father with him.

"I won't forget my roots, I promise you, pa," he said in a reverent whisper, carefully placing the photograph back on the desk. As he left, locking the office door, images of his father's shop came bubbling into his mind. His father had been the only blacksmith in Emillon, and they were busy enough that he helped out before and after school. He could still picture him closing the forge at the end of the day, reaching for his whiskey bottle.

"We did our bit today, son," he would always say, stroking his long beard as he took one carefully measured pull on the bottle. "Every fool wants to be the captain, but there's more to sailing a ship than waves."

Would he have been proud of his son?

He reached the exit of the police office and turned up the hill. The summons had told him to use the Peerage entrance instead of the front gates. He had never been to the palace before, obviously, but it seemed sensible for security's sake. The letter had been waiting for him that morning after another long night of searching. He had decided to sleep at home, but unfortunately, that had meant taking the trolley on the way to work, the blasted contraption bursting with people.

All of that had left him in a sour mood as he climbed Fort Street towards the office. Ever since the lines went in, the city seemed to be leeching outward, gobbling up towns and villages as all that "technology" smothered them in chaos and commotion. He would never abandon Berill, but the kingdom certainly did try a man's patience.

As he passed the front desk, Nichols was there again, holding out a letter on crisp, cream-colored parchment, the royal seal on the front. He hadn't had the usual smug look on his face — they both knew what the letter was at a glance. He had taken it silently, staring at the letter in his hands. He wasn't sure how long he stood there, but he had finally snapped out of his trance, thanking Nichols as he rushed to his office. The letter had called for him to arrive at the palace by four, and the whole day had been spent in a frantic flash of preparation.

He breathed a sigh of relief as he turned into the Lournoy District, the quiet streets giving him a moment of peace. Still, as he looked up at the gilded mansions, he couldn't help but feel a weight on his heart. This wasn't what he wanted for Berill either. The rich, sequestered in their modern castles, were no closer to Berillai ideals than the people below. They had simply cut themselves off from the ruckus. What he truly longed for was a return to his youth, when people had lived by the old ways.

Emillon had been a proper village, at least two day's journey from the city by horse. It had started as a fishing outpost some two hundred years earlier, his grandfather — also a blacksmith — moving there to supply the fishermen with hooks. It had felt like the Anterissage, when the Berillai still lived on the Isles of Dawn. There were no trains then, and everyone had worked together to survive. Now, the Berillai were strangers to each other, nothing but a breeding ground for monsters.

He shook his head. He needed to focus on the present! With the Queen's help, he actually had a chance of ridding the world of those creatures. That would at least be a start to getting things back to how they were meant to be. He turned onto the drawbridge at the Peerage, stopping for just a moment to look up at the great stone keep, a shiver going up his spine.

As he approached the entrance, a pair of guards checked his summons before waving him through where another pair of guards waited for him. As the door closed with a heavy metallic clang, he blinked in the darkness, adjusting to the torch light. The building had never been renovated, and the arrow slits on the sides were the only source of natural light.

"Ah, Mr. Parimu", a voice said, "you've arrived."

He took his summons back from the guards and turned to find a chamberlain in fine livery standing before him, flanked by yet another pair of guards. According to the letter, this was the man who would take him to the palace.

"Sir Gerrette," Parimu said, performing a simple quarter bow from the waist.

"Welcome to the Peerage," he said, smiling as Parimu returned to standing. "Please, come with me into the anteroom. If you don't mind, my men will check you for weapons now."

"Not at all," Parimu said, "I left everything at headquarters, as you instructed." He followed the three men into the front hall. The ceiling held an ornate chandelier filled with dozens of candles, making it far brighter than the entryway. He looked to his right, and his breath came up short as he saw the doors to the voting hall. It looked like a cathedral, but one where men worshipped the law. There were dozens of wooden benches all leading down to a central dais where the arguments were made.

He snapped back to attention as the guards stepped up to frisk him. They efficiently ran their hands up and down his arms and legs, skipping no place where a weapon could be hidden. Parimu was a tall man, but the guards were easily a head taller than him and twice as wide. He could tell they were using restraint in their search, but the implication of their presence was clear: If you were not who you said you were, you could be dispatched quickly and efficiently. Once they were done, the men stepped silently behind the chamberlain.

"Very well," Gerrette said, nodding. "Now, one final formality. I have been informed of your passphrase that you have on file with the crown.

As you know, this information is never to be used with anyone other than captains and palace officials. Please whisper it to me so only I can hear it."

He had never had to use the phrase before, but he would never forget it as long as he lived. It was the deepest secret a navy man could hold. You made it up the day you enlisted, ensuring it was something only you would know. For him, that meant it was buried deep in his past. He stepped on the plush carpet, speaking directly into the chamberlain's ear.

"Jalicyne is the most beautiful girl in Emillon," he whispered, his heart breaking just a bit as he said the words out loud for the first time in fifteen years.

The chamberlain stepped back, nodding, his face a cheerful mask.

"Wonderful," he said, "thank you kindly. Most romantic, I might add."

Parimu's face flushed. He felt completely exposed revealing such a personal thing to a stranger, palace official or not. He bit his lip, nodding once in reply.

"Very well," the chamberlain said, "please follow me, Mr. Parimu."

Sir Gerrette strode across the floor, away from the voting hall and towards an archway in the northwest corner of the room. It led to a long hallway that crossed under the palace walls. Instead of torches, the hallway was lit with speaking stones, the carpet changing from the green and grey of the Peerage to the silver and navy of the royal house.

As his eyes adjusted to the blue light, he noticed a silver glint on the walls. His jaw dropped, and he almost stopped following behind the guards. Those were the Sea Blades, the personal swords of the founders of Berill. He gasped in spite of himself, the chamberlain laughing.

"Magnificent, aren't they?" he asked, continuing down the hallway at a fast pace, making it clear he'd had seen their majesty a thousand times. "They're here to remind the Peers of the oaths their forefathers swore to the crown."

"Incredible," Parimu whispered. Beneath each sword was a tiny silver plaque with the name of the bearer. Halfway down the hall, he saw Laeryia's bad, almost gasping again. Legend had it they had all been cast from Umilai's Heart, the mythical ore deposit that had made them the strongest blades in the world. Laeryia's sword, though, was even more imposing than the others. It was almost as tall as he was, and its wide hilt was inlaid with sapphires. On the pommel, there were dozens of notches that held what looked like bones.

"And the bones?" Parimu asked as they passed the sword.

"A nice reminder to our enemies who pass through on their diplomatic missions," Sir Gerrette said, the smile never leaving his face. "You know the Berillai saying: 'steel for friends, bone for foes'. I believe those are from the final campaign of the Mesop Wars."

He wasn't even in the palace yet and it already felt like stepping into the history books. They stopped by one last set of guards, their escorts showing their tattoos before they passed into a well-lit guardhouse. It was still cloudy out, but after the dim of the Peerage, the light pouring in the windows seemed incredibly bright. The doors opened onto a winding path, the palace looming in the distance.

His eyes were wide as they followed the path, his head turning in all directions. He probably looked like a rube, staring like that, but he couldn't resist. From the serenity of the palace gardens, the city felt thousands of miles away, like a distant moon. It was so peaceful, he could even hear the wind as it blew through the pines lining the perimeter.

The path they were on cut through the pristine gravel of the grounds, meeting with others that wrapped all the way around the palace. Perfectly cut bushes lined the walkway, rivaling the balustrades in their neat precision. How tasteful it all was! Palaces on the Continent were probably filled with frills and delicate things, but not Berill. Not only did the pines perfectly capture their practicality, but it was a good reminder of the brutal winters their ancestors had survived on the Isles.

As they finally reached the back entrance, his heart pounded, and he realized he was holding his breath. He let it out slowly, stepping carefully on the plush silver rug. It wouldn't do to appear before the Queen mooning like a child! He tried to keep his eyes straight ahead as they passed through the stunning hallways, the walls filled with windows that glowed in the light. This was no fortress, it was a monument to their people's victory. His chest swelled with pride as he took in the oil paintings of past monarchs that lined the walls, the fearless leaders who had made it all possible.

Finally, they came to a beautifully lacquered door, the wood carved in an intricate battle scene with men on horseback. His pulse seemed to jump again. This would be the Queen's private dining hall...the summons saying she would meet him during tea. As they approached the door, the guards stepped up to either side, putting their backs to the walls and standing at attention. Gerrette knocked twice on the door and stepped back.

"Remember the proper etiquette," he said to Parimu, "stop walking when I do, and kneel with your head bent. You may rise when Her Majesty tells you to do so."

Parimu nodded; he knew the protocol well. He had never thought he would have the honor of using it with the Queen, but every navy man knew how to greet those of rank. The Queen's brothers had once toured a port he was stationed in, and every single man had knelt in the snow rather than dishonor the princes.

The door opened and a butler's face appeared. In contrast to the colorful livery of the chamberlain, he wore a plain black suit and a grim expression. He said nothing, simply staring out at them.

"Director of Reality, Queen's Detective, Relsenair Parimu," Gerrette said matter-of-factly. He was surprised the man knew his full title... The butler nodded once and disappeared back into the hall. Through the door, he heard the man announce his him before swinging the door open.

The chamberlain stepped through with a quick step, and Parimu followed. Despite it being the 'private' dining room of the Queen, it held a dark mahogany table some forty feet long with room for fifty or more. In the center of the room was a roaring fire in a hearth as wide as his house. And at the end of the table, in a pool of sunlight, sat the Queen. He tried to avoid looking at her directly, focusing on keeping his steps sharp as they passed the rows of upholstered chairs. When they were ten feet away, both men halted, kneeling down.

"My Queen," Gerrette said, which Parimu echoed in as clear a voice as he could, forcing the words past the tightness in his throat.

"Please rise," the Queen said in a smooth, even voice, "your Queen is both pleased and honored to receive her loyal subjects."

They rose, and for the first time, he beheld Her Majesty, Queen Welaya. She was *beautiful*. Her hair sat in loose curls that flowed down her shoulders, and her head was topped with a silver crown brimming with sapphires. She wore a navy blue gown covered in silver moons of all different phases. He had expected her to be youthful, only in her thirties, but it was her penetrating gaze that surprised him.

She appeared to be between courses; a table servant just leaving with a dish as they approached. Behind her, two guards stood with their hands on their swords. For a moment, she said nothing, smiling slightly as she appraised him. He nervously smiled back. He hadn't expected her to look at him, much less smile. After a moment, she turned, breaking the spell as she reached to her side and held up a folded piece of parchment.

"I received your letter, Mr. Parimu," she said, "and I was most interested in your proposition." She returned it to the table, her smile fading to a pensive look. "Tell me, why do you hunt the Shapewalkers when the rest of the kingdom would sooner forget them?"

He took a breath, afraid his voice would shake. In his office that morning, he had written out what he wanted to say over and over again.

He had no idea how to speak to royalty, but he had decided to speak the truth all the same.

"Your Majesty," he said in a voice that was thankfully clear, "I swore my oath under your father, King Talmun. He was a great king, and while his passing is already more than ten years gone, I wanted to offer my sincerest condolences."

The Queen tilted her head in acknowledgment. There was no sign that he was to stop speaking, so he continued. "I swore that I would stop at nothing to protect his kingdom from Shapewalkers. That kingdom is now yours, but the threat is not gone, and no amount of modern conveniences will eliminate it. The Continent grows smaller by the day, but the trains we think speed us away from the past, simply make travel easier for our enemies. But the crown is wise, and I believe you remain vigilant, even if others forget. That is what gives me the strength to fight on."

He swallowed as he finished, his throat feeling like it had a stone in it. At least he had gotten through his speech without stuttering... To his surprise, the Queen began to chuckle.

"It is very rare that the crown is referred to as wise in this day and age, Mr. Parimu," she said, taking a sip from a chalice on the table. "Most think me a fool because of my age. They believe that a young queen may be manipulated to their gain. But they forget this crown has survived for over eight centuries. I rely on the wisdom of generations of House Berill. Do you know why the crown is silver and sapphire, Detective?"

He cleared his throat. "I do not, my Queen," he said. "We use silver in the hunt of Shapewalkers, of course, and I've heard it said that silver holds the truth."

"Very good," the Queen said, smiling. "The legends say the Heart of Umilai was encased in a vein of silver. It was the message to King Rummon that he was to conquer this land. He put the steel in his sword and the silver in his armor, which terrified his enemies. Not because it glowed brightly but because it made a mirror. When King Laeryia forged this crown, he put silver in it so we could see ourselves as clearly, showing our weakness before our enemies find it for us."

She picked up the sapphire necklace resting on her chest and held it up. The stone spun on its silver chain, and the Queen let it flash in the light. It was the deepest blue he had ever seen.

"Sapphire is to remind us of the sea," the Queen said, "so that we never forget where we came from. The Continent is weak and corrupt, but our people were forged from the strongest steel. Though we descend from similar men, the peers seem to have forgotten this lesson. They have been seduced by the riches of the Continent. Those riches are ours to claim, but they must never come at the cost of our strength."

Parimu found himself nodding along to her speech. His mouth had fallen open and his heart beat had quickened. This was truly the voice of a queen, the type of leadership that men would rightly die to follow.

"My Queen," he said in a whisper that felt like a prayer, "tell me how I may serve."

"You have designed the plan for your own service, Mr. Parimu," the Queen said, the smile returning to her lips. "I simply needed to judge your sincerity. I have a great many enemies, Detective, men who would sell the crown itself if they could profit by it. They wish to see me fail, but I will not allow them to control this kingdom. They may own the railways, but they do not own the land they sit upon."

She held up his letter again.

"You said there is another Shapewalker, which you aim to capture on Alomidiar. It sickens me to think one of those...things roaming the beach among my citizens." She gripped the edge of the table, taking a deep breath. "I will grant you the full brigade of troops you requested. They will come from my own guard so the Peers cannot tell you how to use them. The festival gives us the perfect cover. I will make an announcement today that you have been ordered to maintain stability at the beach."

His mouth fell open. Growing jaded after so many years of begging for scraps at the RPS, he thought he might receive a fraction of his request. In truth, he hadn't even really believed in his own gamble until the Queen had sent her summons.

"Thank you, your Majesty," he said, stammering. "I will...use these resources to your honor."

A knock came on the door and the butler moved to answer the next guest. Their time was up. The chamberlain bowed and Parimu followed suit. As he stared down into the carpet on one knee he thought he felt a tear welling up in his eye. Before they could rise, the Queen spoke again.

"I believe you will serve well, Mr. Parimu. But do not fail me. My enemies are many and their teeth are sharp. The Peers do not like me to meddle, but I will have this Shapewalker's head, even if I have to use my Thorns. Go in courage and serve the crown."

The Sterling Thorns... He gulped. There was no-one more secret, serving directly at the Queen's discretion. He actually knew almost nothing of them beyond their fearsome reputation. If he failed and they had to be called upon... He bowed again and turned from the Queen, following the chamberlain out of the room. He couldn't fail now, no matter what it cost him.

21

"To what will you dedicate your breaths, daughter? Like the plants, drinking in the sun, pushing every ounce of their being into life, you also have a choice. To grow, to feed, to become more than the seed you were when you began."

-Excerpt from The Borimol Plains
—:—

Sumi stood in the hallway of a teahouse on the east side of Berill, readying herself for the next phase of her plan. She took a deep breath, the smell of flowers rushing into her nose. Her arms were laden with blossoms, a stack that stretched from her hips to her shoulders. She stood in front of a closed door, and could hear muffled voices coming through from the other side. Nela's women's group was having their weekly meeting, and she was going to crash it.

She had marched straight from the library to Mr. Furttenhur's shop, where she had discarded another large stack of old flowers in the wood box the day before. She had dug them out, and then, barely able to see over the pile of blossoms, carried them up to the tea shop. She had always found these women intimidating — they all had Nela's matronly power to some degree — but now she was calm, her resolve finally stronger than her fear. She pushed the door open with her knee, finally feeling like a knight again, storming an enemy castle.

As she burst into the room, the conversation stopped. All the women turned to stare at her, though they probably couldn't make out her face behind a jungle's worth of vegetation. She moved to the side table and laid down her giant bouquet before turning back to the group. Before they could interject, she raised herself up and pushed through the little speech she had prepared.

"Hi everyone. I've really missed working with you all, and we always

179

have extra flowers at the shop and, well — I thought maybe I could help you take them on your rounds when they're available."

She took a deep breath, her lungs begging for air after speaking more words than she probably had in a month. The women stared at her for another agonizing second before Mrs. Perrino, the new leader of the group, jumped out of her seat and came to Sumi, wrapping an arm around her.

"Well, that would be just wonderful, Sumi," she said, smiling and turning to the other women as she nodded. "Right ladies? We were just discussing how sad it is that Alomidiar is tomorrow and so many of our families have no decorations."

Finally, the other women snapped out of their trances, nodding and humming in agreement. Soon they were all up out of their seats and ushering Sumi to an open chair, pouring her tea and passing her biscuits. She dove into the flow of their conversation, providing details of the kinds of flowers she had brought as the women planned their routes for the evening. And strangely, after her adventures, she was a much more knowledgable participant than she'd ever been before. She knew the name of every street they mentioned, and even had a few suggestions for what order the stops should go in.

It felt like a missing piece had finally slipped into place. Without her magic, she was still only one Sumi, but if she could be part of something, she could be so much more, too. She had always envied these women and the field of flowers they had made themselves into, doing things she thought impossible. But now, for the first time, she knew she was part of that field, too. Even if all she had done was dive into the trash and retrieve some flowers, she could still help these women spread joy throughout the city.

———

Half an hour later, Sumi was stepping out of the teahouse with Mrs. Perrino, a smaller stack of flowers in her arms. Mrs. Perrino shouldered a large bag full of treats, the group having baked extra for the holiday. As they made the rounds, they'd pass them out to each family so they could enjoy the festival without worrying about how to afford something extra.

The pair set out into the city, starting in Mrs. Berkin's neighborhood before heading west towards the warehouse district. It felt so similar to her adventures as a Shapewalker, and yet, completely different. She felt a familiar rush of joy as she placed the sweets into the children's hands, relishing the excitement in their eyes. But this time, she didn't have to run away after she helped them, she got to celebrate with them.

Mrs. Perrino introduced her to each family, and she shook hands with mothers, fathers, aunties and sisters. Each of them looked her in the eye and smiled. They were seeing her eyes and her face, not the surface of an umbrella or the shining edge of a coin. She also couldn't fly away on the wind or sneak off into the night; she wasn't only seeing now, but being seen.

After a few hours, they had finished their rounds, and Sumi walked Mrs. Perrino back to her house on Rekip Terrace. She lived in a pretty little cottage, not unlike her own, though in slightly better repair. The shutters on the windows were painted a deep blue, and the walls had been freshly whitewashed. As the older woman unlocked her front door, she asked Sumi to wait a moment while she slipped inside.

A moment later, Mrs. Perrino came back out with a final bag of sweets, slipping it into Sumi's hand. She tried to protest, but the older woman closed her hand firmly around it.

"I want you to have a special day tomorrow too, dear," she said, smiling. "I was so happy to see you tonight. We really were so afraid to impose after Essie passed. But to have you join us on your own... The flowers were such a nice thought. I hope you'll join us again soon."

Sumi nodded and smiled, blinking to hold back tears as Mrs. Perrino squeezed her arm and disappeared into the house. She walked out of the garden, turning towards her own terrace. As she reached the end of Rekip, she paused for a moment to look out at the water. The clouds had blown into the sea during their tour of the city, and she found a brilliant full moon hanging over the bay. She walked on, the moon following alongside her as it rippled on the waves. She pulled out one of the spiced caramels from the bag and held it up.

"Cheers," she said to the moon before popping the candy in her mouth. "I always thought you looked lonely up there." But the moon wasn't alone at all. It had the water to hug, and the stars to dance with. It even had her to walk beside. She just hadn't thought to look for all those companions hiding in plain sight.

"None of us are as alone as we think, are we?" she asked the moon. She spun in a circle in the moonlight, laughing as the fog of her breath streamed into the sky. She had been dreading going through the holiday without Nela, but now, she couldn't wait to go to the beach the next day. Just like the moon, the entire city would be with her on Alomidiar. She was still a part of this place, and she would enjoy every minute that her flower brightened this field.

The next evening, Erso stood on a small bluff in the dunes at the end of the beach, looking out over the sand as it teemed with festival goers. He shielded his eyes with a gloved hand, trying to find something, anything, to guide him to the other Shapewalker. He growled, punching his palm with his fist. He had been circling the festival since the gates opened two hours earlier, but there was still no sign of her.

At least he knew for sure now it was the woman from the trolley yard. A week earlier, he had run out of the police station to chase down another ripple. With Aelibis dead, he'd known it would be the other. He had transformed into an owl again, surging over the rooftops, his lungs burning as he pushed forward with every fiber of his being. For once, luck had been on his side, and he reached the source of the ripple just as the police were swarming a maze of alleyways on the west side of the city.

There hadn't been much time. As soon as he came over the last rooftop, he saw that same beautiful woman running for her life down the alley and away from the police. He had banked hard, curving his flightpath to match up with her, watching her turn again and again as she struggled to escape. She made a final left, and his heart sank as he realized it was a dead end. The police whistles were blaring in the dark, growing closer with every step.

"Transform!" he had shouted at her in his mind. Without hesitating, he had dropped to the ground, transforming back into his human form as he ran down the alley in the opposite direction. He went straight for a group of trash cans and started kicking them over. He heard the police shouting in his direction, and he ran down the alley, trying to lead them away from her.

Just as he reached the end of the alley, a tidal wave of police had surged through the brick walls. Some shouted in his direction, giving chase. He turned the corner and instantly turned into a rat, disappearing as he climbed a drain pipe. He had scurried across the rooftop in her direction, hoping he could get her out of the dead end somehow. But just then, he heard more shouts, and a fire hawk shot out of the alleyway and into the night.

In the week since, she hadn't made a peep. He had wanted to follow her, but she had disappeared in the darkness like a shooting star, gone in an eye blink. He had spent every day scouring the city, but still hadn't seen a thing. In his endless searching, though, he finally had a realization: The first time he saw her, she hadn't been the man with one leg— she had been his trolley token. He shook his head in disbelief. That was one of the most sincere things he'd ever seen a Shapewalker do. He couldn't let Parimu have this one, no matter what.

There was another thing that had occurred to him. Before Aelibis died, she had been so hard to track he had thought she might know what she was doing. But after that night in the alley, it was clear she was a novice. There was no way she could suppress her ripples if she let the police get right on top of her like that. And if she didn't know how to hide, she wouldn't stay free forever. Even a fool like Parimu would know what she was if she walked right in front of him.

That was why he was here, the wind whipping at his face and his shoes full of miserable Berillai sand. The rage from Aelibis still burned inside him, and there was no telling what he'd do if he failed again. It was little consolation, but Aelibis at least knew the risks of being a thief. If he let this woman die the same way, he wasn't sure he would ever recover. The chess board had narrowed to this point. Parimu was going to try and use the festival to capture her, and Erso had to stop him.

The police headquarters had been flooded with gossip about that cursed fellerhurn all week. In a surprising coup, Parimu had gotten the Queen's aid, and had been clomping around the city with a whole mess of royal guards in tow. He was using some excuse about 'maintaining order' at Alomidiar, but it was clear what he was really about. He aimed to kill the other Shapewalker, and he was going to dig through the sand looking for her if he had to. His only chance would be to find her first.

The woman was clearly smart enough not to transform now, but that left both men in an unfortunate position. He was positive his senses were more finely tuned than Parimu's, but they would both have to be basically right on top of her if they were going to sense her keyhole in this crowd. At least he still remembered her face, but that would be even harder to find with the whole city jammed into one place.

He let out a sigh and slid back down the sandy slope into the chaos of the festival. He would have to find her, or this time he'd really rather it was him on the end of the noose.

———

Sumi looked out at the festival, a smile on her face. The sun was nearly down, and the main festivities would begin any minute. There were dozens of bonfires set up along the beach, their red flames making a brilliant contrast with the slate grey of the sea. It took her back to her childhood, that day on the beach celebrating with the orphans. Maybe one day the women's group could bring the children here to see the whole city lit up…

The best part was, she could try to arrange that herself, now that she was working with the women's group again. Her heart still felt full from making the rounds with Mrs. Perrino. Only a day earlier, the city had seemed so distant. But now, it felt like it was something she could grasp in her hands. Seeing all the happy families wandering about no longer filled her with jealousy. Instead, it only perfected the spirit of the holiday.

It was fitting to reunite with the place she loved so much on a day like Alomidiar, when the city felt most truly itself, everyone coming together. And in some ways, celebrating like their ancestors, all the Berillai myths somehow seemed true. Like they really had been dropped on the beaches by Umilai, crashing on the shores of the Isles as sea foam as they grew into human beings. Though how all of that fit in with Essomuai was something she still hadn't puzzled out...

Still, the legend about Alomus — and the holiday that came out of it — was even stranger. While Umidiar was about thanking Umilai for the bounty of life, Alomidiar was about defying the other god. If she remembered right, Alomus was the god of the sky, and the two were brothers, their mother, Velloni, creating the earth. But they were always jealous of each other, especially when Umilai created his own people.

The people of the Continent were supposed to be Alomus' children, right? He had been stuck in the sky, though, so he'd rained them down like seeds, letting them grow in Velloni's soil. It was odd to think of now, actually, knowing she was a Shapewalker, but the myths said something about their magic coming from Velloni — even if the Berillai claimed they lacked the strength of the sea.

At any rate, making his own children hadn't been enough, and Alomus had tried to destroy the Berillai, creating the first winter and covering the Isles in snow. In the story, Umilai had tried to reach his people, but the beaches were frozen over with ice. His rage had shaken the earth, pushing up the speaking stones, their blue light filled with the ocean itself. Through them, Umilai told his people of Alomus' betrayal, filling their hearts with fire.

Every tree but the pines were dead, so the islanders cut them down to make boats. Their sheep were dying, so they sheared them and sewed the wool into sails. Even the rocks cracked from the cold, so they stole the ore to make their swords. Umilai sent a great wave to carry their ships to the Continent, where they rained devastation on the coast, filling their boats with treasure and leaving the Continent to burn. That part seemed a bit gruesome, to be honest, but that was the purpose of the bonfires. They believed the smoke from their pillaging had choked Alomus, bringing spring back to the Isles.

Winters had entered their normal cycle then, and now, on Alomidiar, they burned giant pyres to send smoke into the sky as their ancestors had. Many were just large bonfires, but in the center of the beach, the palace would always build one giant sculpture. It was placed in front of Umilai as an offering, and the Queen always lit it herself. That's when the festival always began in earnest, full of dancing, laughter, and — most importantly — food. The hearty squid pies and sausage rolls were some of the best food all year.

She walked along the beach, chuckling at the story as she wove through the crowd. There were people everywhere, standing arm to arm in their thick winter coats, laughing and talking. She did her best to absorb all that joy, but it was almost too much to contain. She finally made her way to the central square to take in the main sculpture. An honor guard of palace soldiers ringed the area for the Queen's arrival, but she could still see the shape of the pyre as it rose into the air.

"Wow," she mouthed, leaning her head back. This year's sculpture was in the shape of a massive cresting whale, its back crashing from the surf. It was easily twenty feet high, and the base was carved with roiling raves. The planks were a pale color, since they always used freshly cut pine, and the inside would be filled with the branches of the felled trees, the smell of the needles filling the air.

She headed back up the beach to find a better vantage point, but as she crossed the sand, she paused, spotting a little boy wandering alone in the crowd. She turned in a circle, searching for his family, but she only saw knots of revelers. He looked like he'd been crying...was he lost? She hesitated for a moment; was it really her place to step in? But suddenly, Essomuai's poem floated up in her mind, filling her with strength. If she didn't help this boy, who would?

She rushed over to him, leaning down to his level.

"Hi there," she said in a soft voice, "do you need help?"

He turned to Sumi, his eyes red from where he'd been scratching them with his sleeve. At first there was hope on his face, but he slumped as he realized she was just another stranger.

"No, I'm alright, ma'am," he said, shaking his head and sniffling, "I'm just looking for my mother. I know she's here — somewhere."

She knelt down in the sand and gripped his shoulder. He wasn't a tiny child, but he wasn't old enough to be fending for himself, either.

"It's alright," she said tenderly, "let's just find her together, okay? My name's Sumi, I can help you."

He eyed her for a moment, but nodded.

"I'm Heikal," he said. Sumi took his hand, squeezing it in hers as she stood up and started to scout around.

"What does your mother look like?" she asked. "Do you remember what she was wearing?"

He continued to rub his eyes with his free hand as he looked out at the crowd, thinking.

"A blue dress," he finally said, "and...her brown coat."

"Okay," she said, nodding, "and what color hair does she have?"

"Sort of light and curly, like mine," he said, twirling a finger in his hair. She nodded, turning back to the crowd. That wasn't much to go on, but hopefully his parents weren't far. Though, with how crowded the festival was, who knew how far a child could wander...

She walked them in a slow circle, pulling Heikal along with her. There were a handful of women around them, but none of them matched his description. More importantly, none of them seemed to be frantically searching for their children. She stopped, taking a deep breath. There were thousands of people on the beach, and she couldn't see much better than Heikal with everyone standing shoulder to shoulder. If they kept wandering around, they'd risk going in circles opposite his parents. She needed to find a central location where they might look...

She stood up on her tiptoes, craning her neck to see over the crowd. Every three blocks or so, she could see electric lights sticking up above the festival grounds. Those would be police boxes... The RPS had them on street corners throughout the city, but they had put up dozens more along the beach for the festival. If she were a parent, that's probably the first place she'd go.

She gulped, thinking back to the officer in the alley, but she squared her shoulders. *This little boy needs me,* she thought. *Besides, what are the odds the same officer would be at that exact box?* It wasn't like she was walking around as a fire hawk. He couldn't recognize her if she didn't transform...right?

She leaned over and tapped Heikal on the shoulder, pointing to the light poles above the crowd.

"Let's go that way," she said, "if your parents are trying to find you, they'll see the lights too. The police can help us find them." He nodded, so she began marching them in that direction, weaving through the crowd as she clutched his small hand.

As they approached the street, the crowd thickened with people trying to enter the festival. Heikal had been growing slower as they walked, the ordeal taking its toll. She didn't want to risk losing him in the crowd, so she stopped and picked him up under the elbows, pulling him to her chest. He wasn't terribly big for his age, and she had carried plenty of children volunteering with Nela over the years. He rested his head on her shoulder, squeezing his arms tightly around her back. She smiled sadly, patting him on the head as she started forward again.

She trudged ahead, her breathing picking up as she fought to push across the sand with the extra weight. But she kept putting one foot in front of the other, and finally, they reached the police box. It was a tiny one-room hut that seemed no larger than the employee room at the flower shop. It had been made of wooden planks that would be easy to disassemble, though it seemed sturdy. Inside, she could see a desk and an electric light hanging above a telegraph machine.

There were two policemen in front of the box, standing in their uniforms and looking out over the beach. One was older, with a grey beard. The older one smoked a pipe, while the younger one warmed his hands over a fire they had built in a large metal drum. She didn't recognize either of them from the alleyway, so she set her jaw and walked up to the other side of the fire. The older one noticed her first, placing his pipe down on the windowsill of the police box and coming around to greet them.

"Evening ma'am," he said, tipping his uniform cap, "how can we help?"

She began to explain as the older man stood listening. Once she told him that Heikal was lost, he started taking notes, nodding as she described where she found him. When he had all the details, he ripped the page from the notebook and handed it to the younger officer, asking him to begin telegraphing the other boxes. She let out a long breath as the officers went to work, relief flooding her mind. Nothing bad had happened, and they'd find his parents soon. She turned to face the sea, holding Heikal as she slowly rubbed the back of his head.

She heard what sounded like more officers coming around the back of the police box. As she focused to hear what they were saying, her blood ran cold. She recognized one of those voices... She turned her head just in time to see the policeman from the alleyway coming around the front with a group of royal guards behind him. She whipped back towards the sea and away from the men, using every ounce of her strength not to bolt.

He never saw you, she thought, *he wouldn't know you from anyone else on the street. Act calm, act calm, act calm.* She began to fidget, but stayed where she was. She wasn't about to abandon Heikal, and there wasn't much she could do at this point without calling more attention to herself. It would be better to calmly finish this business with the policemen and walk away, disappearing into the crowd.

She listened with her back turned as the policeman from the alleyway talked with the other officers. It sounded like they were discussing some kind of search.

"Well, we're sure to find them eventually," he said. "I'll take the guards for another pass, but blow your whistles if anything pops up."

How high up was this officer to be commanding palace guards? Now she'd really done it, poking a giant! Their search could be to find her for all she knew! She took a deep breath, clinging to Heikal for ballast as she stared at the water.

"Miss," the original officer with the beard called, coming out of the hut and waving her over. She turned, eager to have the ordeal over with. She walked over to the fire where the officer stood. She kept her eyes on him as he spoke, trying to keep her face in profile from the other policeman. He explained their call system and that she was to wait there with Heikal by the fire until his parents could be notified. She nodded, turning away, but just then, everything fell apart. It happened like a cannon shot, exploding in the blink of an eye.

Heikal had been playing with the buttons of her collar, sighing sleepily in her arms. She saw a flash of metal, and looked down, realizing he had pulled her pendant out of her blouse on its long chain. He was turning it, letting the light of the police box flash off its emerald center. She gasped, shoving it back under her shirt, but as she looked up, she locked eyes with the policeman at the edge of the circle. His eyes were wide, eager and hawk like as they stared at her. She started to turn, to run, to do anything but stand there, when the policeman blew his whistle.

"Arrest them!" he shouted. The police box became a flurry of commotion. Palace guards were suddenly everywhere, kicking up sand and swarming around them. Arms pulled her and Heikal apart, wrenching her shoulders back as manacles were slapped on her wrists. She cried out, drawing the attention of the crowds, but no-one came to save her. She heard Heikal somewhere behind her, yelling out for his mother.

Two guards dragged her between them, her feet kicking across the sand. As they came around the side of the police box, she whipped her head around, seeing a large group of police carriages lined up on the street. The guards dragged her to the rear of one and wrenched open the door. She had one last glimpse of the beach. The Queen had lit the sculpture of the whale, and the flames were rising as the crowd cheered. A bag was thrown over her head, and she was rammed into the carriage, everything swallowed by darkness.

22

One day, you too may find quiet at the bottom of a cave, when you feel only the silence of the ancient earth, even the air gone to you. And it is then, and only then, that you will know your strength.
-Excerpt from the Poems of Boran Stonekeeper
—:—

Sumi tried to track the turns of the police carriage as she waited in darkness, her heart pounding. After the first two twists, though, she lost track. At least the frequent turns meant they were taking them somewhere other than the gallows — that would have been a short trip. If it was only her in trouble, she probably would have rather gone straight to the noose, just to have it over with, but it wasn't only her... *Heikal*. The last thing she'd seen was that poor little boy being dragged to the other carriage.

She made a promise to herself: if these were going to be her last hours alive, she'd spend them getting Heikal out of this.

Finally, the carriage jolted to a stop. She couldn't see anything through the bag over her head, but she heard the carriage door wrench open. She was grabbed by the shoulders and pulled down, the air wheezing from her lungs as she hit the hard stone beneath her. Men grabbed her again from both sides, their hands like vices on her arms. She tripped once or twice as they frog marched her over the uneven pavement, but they kept her upright, forcing her forward until her feet were under her again.

She tried to listen to everything around her, straining her ears for some sign of Heikal, but all she could hear was her own breathing. Ahead of her, she heard the sound of a metal door opening.

"Stairs ahead," one of the men said in a rough voice as they approached. As soon as he said it, she stepped in front of her and found

189

only air. Her foot landed hard on the first step down, but again, the officers kept her moving. Halfway down, the door slammed shut behind them and she heard another one opening ahead. They turned down a hallway, the heels of her boots clicking against brick. Finally, they stopped, and she heard a key grinding in a lock.

They marched her forward, spinning her around before one of the guards told her to sit. She did so, finding a hard wooden bench beneath her. The manacles were removed from her hands, and then the bag was ripped off her head. She blinked, adjusting to the dim light as she found herself in a jail cell, torches glowing on the brick walls. One of the guards pulled out a silver band and clamped it around her neck.

"What is that?" she asked, clutching at the metal as it squeezed against her throat.

"Quiet," one of them said as they walked out of the cell. "The detective will be here soon to deal with you."

They slammed the cell door and left, their footsteps trailing off down the hallway. As soon as she could no longer hear them, she was on her feet, pressing her face up against the bars.

"Heikal," she hissed in as loud a whisper as she could risk, but no one answered. She called out again…still nothing.

Where could they have taken him? She started pacing, but then stopped, eyeing the bars. They were close together, but could she escape through them? Probably too tight for Amis, but maybe as a trolley token… She stepped back and closed her eyes, clenching her fists. She pictured the token, going through the memory in her head, but she didn't feel the lightness bubbling up. There was a weight to her chest, like the ice had reformed over her heart, only twice as thick. She reached the end of the memory and poked one eye open…nothing.

She grabbed at the silver band around her throat; could this thing be keeping her from transforming? Her pulse thudded in her neck as it pushed past the tight collar. Maybe it was just fear holding her back? She closed her eyes to try again when she heard the door re-opening down the hall, followed by the click of footsteps. She snapped her eyes open and silently stepped back to the bench, sitting just in time for the officer from the alley to appear in front of her cell.

"My name is Detective Parimu," he said. "I can't promise you anything, but if you answer my questions, I may be able to make things easier on you." He stood with his hands behind his back, sizing her up for a moment. "Tell me," he finally continued, "what were you doing at the police box? What was your plan?"

Sumi cocked her head.

"Plan..." she repeated, confused. "What plan?"

He slammed his fist against the bars of the cell.

"Your plan!" he shouted. "It's one of the biggest holidays of the year, the Queen herself was present for the lighting ceremony. I thought maybe I'd find you stealing things, but to find you at the police box with another of your kind... How many others are there and what was set to happen today? Why did you come to Berill? I want the truth!"

She shook her head, the gears of her mind grinding. She knew being caught with the symbol was bad, but this felt...bigger than that.

"This is my home," she said, "I was just there for the festival. I'm...I'm Berillai."

The detective laughed, a dark sound, more like a scoff. "Your accent is good," he said, "I'll give you that, but you're from the Continent if you can use their magic. No matter. Tell me about your accomplice, what was the point of him transforming into a child?"

Her eyes widened.

"No!" she cried out, stammering as she spoke in a rush. "He's just a boy, please. He was lost and I wanted to get him to his parents, that's all. He shouldn't be mixed up in this."

"Mixed up in what?" he asked eagerly. "You admit there was a plot?"

She closed her eyes and set her jaw. Whatever happened next, she had to get Heikal out. She opened her eyes, speaking slowly and deliberately.

"No. There is no plot. You saw my necklace — I admit, I am what you think I am. But I really just found the boy while he was looking for his parents. Do what you want with me, but let him go, please."

Her throat caught at the end, her heartbeat drumming into her temples as she imagined Heikal being hung next to her in the gallows, all because she foolishly dragged him around with her.

The detective shook his head, rubbing his forehead and sighing.

"Well, of course you'd deny it. You...things make it so no one can know head from tail of anything. Tell me something else, then, is this your real body?"

She nodded. She'd give him anything he asked if it got Heikal released.

"Well, I'll take that as true for now," he said. "The silver should have done its job." He looked away for a moment, muttering under his breath. "The collar may be too small for the boy, though..." His gaze shot back to her. "No matter if you're lying, we have other methods if needed."

"Why would I be lying?" she asked. "Why would I let him pull out my necklace if he was my accomplice? He's just a boy!" Her voice cracked at the end, tears rolling down her cheeks.

The detective raised a hand, silencing her. Then he began to pace outside her cell, almost as if he were talking to himself. "This could all be part of your plan. Your kind spend so much time in other peoples' skin you become quite good actors as well — I've seen it all before." He finally stopped, turning back towards her with a look of disdain. "Save your fake tears, we'll know the truth soon enough. You creatures are a blight on this city, and I'll be damned if I let you destroy it. I won't have this kingdom ravaged by some shapewalking menace who only wants —"

"You're wrong!" she shouted, standing from the cot before she realized what she was doing. She glared at the detective, his eyes widening for a second in surprise. "I'm not like that at all," she continued, "these are my people, too. This has been my home my entire life, and I would never ever do anything to hurt it." She stood there, surprised at herself, her chest heaving and her fists clenched.

The detective let out a long sigh, breaking his eyes away and staring out into space, his arms folded.

"If you really have lived here your whole life," he said in a quiet voice, "then you know how broken this place is. The people have no sense of belonging. The factories are full of strangers and the Continent is forcing their ways on us. The people are like sheep surrounded by wolves."

He turned back to her, his face fixed in anger again.

"I can't do much, but at least I can protect them from monsters like you. You claim to be a citizen of this kingdom? If that's true, did anyone else know what you are? Or did you hide it, knowing it was a shameful, evil thing?"

She sat back on the bench, staring at the floor as a deep sadness washed over her.

"No," she said, barely above a whisper. "No one knows what I am. Probably no one even knows who I am. But I didn't hide my powers because I thought they were evil. I thought I had to be something special before I could let people know me, but I was wrong." She took a deep breath, speaking in Anushai, *"Guyan buyel siom, buyel siom saldal."*

"Your curses won't save you here," the detective snapped. "Your magic doesn't work with that collar on."

Sumi looked up at him defiantly.

"It isn't magic," she said. "It's the poem of Essomuai: *If your color would not be, neither would be the field.*" She stood, feeling a strength come back to her legs. She raised herself up as she faced the detective. She had fought for this treasure, and she wasn't going to hide it now. Even if she died, she'd die speaking the truth.

"I feel your pain," she said, approaching the bars. He backed away, watching her warily. "I know what it's like to be alone in this city, but we won't build community by being less of ourselves, by picking out who belongs and who doesn't. If we can't be who we are, how can we be anything to anyone else? I belong here just as much as you, detective, and just as much as that innocent boy. This is our home, yours *and* mine. If you love this place like you say, then remember that and let him go."

She looked him in the eyes, only a foot between them as she poured her heart out. His eyes were wide again. He opened his mouth to reply, but suddenly the heavy clang of the door sounded at the end of the hall. He spun, turning towards the doorway as footsteps approached. Another officer walked up, his face hidden as his white-gloved hand snapped a crisp salute.

"Sir," the newcomer said, "royal messenger here for you, said the guards at the beach need you immediately."

"What is it?" the detective asked, his hands clenching.

"Don't rightly know, sir," the policeman said, "they're keeping it all hush hush. Bit above my pay grade, but it sounded urgent. Told me to find you right away."

"Okay," the detective said, nodding. "I'll go now, but stay here and keep guard. Watch this prisoner like your life depends on it. If anything happens, I'll have your badge, and you'll be lucky if you escape with your life, understand?"

"Of course, sir," the policeman said calmly. The detective nodded and raced off, his shoes slapping quickly against the floor.

Sumi stepped back, sitting on the bench again. She felt slightly dizzy after her outburst. She tried to catch her breath, preparing for another attempt. She'd need to try to get this new officer to release Heikal before the detective returned. As he stepped over and put his back to the bars of her cell, he began to whistle. Her head snapped up, her eyes narrowing as she recognized the song. He was whistling 'Mad Jaim', the song about the shapeshifting merman.

The hallway door slammed shut again, and the policeman stopped whistling as he turned his face towards her, winking. He had a waxed mustache and a smile on his face. He seemed familiar somehow. She gasped, pushing back into the wall behind her.

"You!" she cried out, pointing. "The man from the trolley station... Have you been following me for the police this whole time?"

He turned all the way around to face her and held up a hand.

"Easy," he said, "I'm a friend." He moved closer to the bars of her cell. "I don't work for him — I'm just like you. This should make things more comfortable." He stepped back and closed his eyes. He started to glow, and not even a second later, he was standing in front of her, the same man, but wearing the suit and bowler hat from the trolley yard.

"Now," he said, "let's get you out of here. Put your back against the bars and I'll get that collar off you." She stood hesitantly and stepped over. He spun his finger in the air and she turned around. She didn't know what he did, but the collar clicked, falling to the ground. She took a deep breath and rubbed her neck, grateful to be able to breathe normally again.

The man stepped over to the cell door and squatted down, sticking his face in the key hole and eyeing it carefully.

"I'm going to change into the key for this cell," he said. "Unlock it and take the key with you. Go left down the corridor and you'll be at the back door to the jail. Stick me in the lock there and I'll let you out." He stopped looking in the key hole and looked up at her, brows lifted, waiting to see that she understood. She nodded quickly. "Good, now be quick about it. Our friend Parimu tends to be a bit...overzealous."

There was another soft glow, and as the air shifted, a soft humming in her ears. She blinked, and the man was gone. She scrambled off the cot and ran to the bars, finding a key on the ground just as he had said. She shook her head to clear away the shock and knelt on the ground, reaching through the bars and snatching up the key. She fumbled with it slightly, but got it in the door and turned it, the lock clicking. She shoved the door open and grabbed the key, slipping it into her pocket.

She looked down the hall the way he had described, but didn't see anyone in the remaining cells. She took the key from her pocket and held it up in front of her face.

"I'm sorry," she said, "but I have to look for the boy they brought with me. I can't leave him."

She wasn't sure what kind of response to expect from a key, but she suddenly felt a warm aura coming from it that seemed like approval. She slipped it back into her pocket and ran in the other direction. There was a metal door ahead of her and another stretch of hallway to her right. She took the turn, and ran past another group of cells. Some of them were occupied, the grizzled men staring as she passed, but she didn't see Heikal.

She reached the end of the hall and took another right before stopping to listen. She heard the sound of sniffling and jogged down two more cells, finding Heikal sitting on a cell bench crying, his faced buried in his hands and his shoulders shaking. He had one of the silver collars around his neck, though it hung loose on him.

"Heikal!" she whispered loudly.

The boy looked up, his eyes wide and red.

"Sumi!" he cried out, running up to her. "I want to go home. He kept asking me how old I am, I don't understand."

She nodded, patting his hands as they clutched the bars of the cell.

"Don't worry," she said. "It's just a big mistake, we're going home." She shoved the key into the lock and prayed it would work. Nothing happened for a few seconds, her hands tight on the bars. But then, there was a flash of light inside the lock, and she turned the key with a click, yanking the door open.

She dropped it back in her pocket as Heikal ran out and jumped into her arms. She scooped him up and sprinted down the hallway. She heard a yell from the direction of her cell and tried to run faster, desperate to escape. They reached the end of the hall, another door blocking their way. She pulled on it, but it didn't budge. She heard the policeman's shoes coming up the hall. There wouldn't be time to do the trick with the key again. She looked to her left and saw a wooden door, different from the others she had passed. She opened it and found a broom closet full of mops and buckets.

She clutched Heikal to her chest and stepped carefully over the buckets before closing the door behind her. She eased back into the mops and stood tensely, holding Heikal close. He was shaking, so she hugged him tighter. As her eyes adjusted to the dark, she finally noticed a key hole in the closet door, light filtering in from the hallway. With one hand, she pulled the key out of her pocket and held it by her mouth, whispering to it.

"Can you jam the door?" she asked.

She felt the warm aura again and leaned forward, sticking the key in the other side of the lock just as the detective slammed around the corner.

"No, no, no!" he yelled as he reached Heikal's empty cell. She felt the boy tense again and held him tight, covering his mouth with her hand. He was still shaking, but he didn't cry out. She took in a deep breath and held it as the footsteps approached the end of the hall.

The detective pulled on the iron door first, but found it locked. He rattled it once or twice before cursing and stamping his foot. She shut her eyes, praying for a miracle. The detective turned, his breath coming through the door. She heard his hand on the knob, but as he tried to turn it, the lock jammed. He shook it a few more times before finally letting go and running back the other way. She let out her breath, panting as her lungs burned.

195

"Okay," she whispered to Heikal, "let's get out of here, quickly now." She stepped forward carefully, terrified she'd kick a bucket. She returned the key to her pocket and eased the door open just a crack. There was no sound in the hallway beyond. She opened it wider, putting Heikal on the ground.

She silently closed the closet before putting the key in the other door. After a short wait and another glow of light, they were through, another set of stairs up ahead, leading to the back exit the other Shapewalker had described. They ran through the last corridor, Heikal frantically pumping his legs as he clung to Sumi's hand.

She emerged into the back lot of the jail, grateful for the cold air as sweat started to bead on her forehead, her heart still fluttering like a trapped bird. She blinked in the dark before marching them forward, terrified to stay even a moment longer. She forced herself to walk slowly, her heart racing. The station yard was quiet, only a few horses attached to their carriages, but there was no-one in sight. Luckily, the back gate was open, and in a matter of moments, they were outside the station walls.

She looked around, fairly certain of where they were. It looked like the top of the warehouse district, north of Wembly. There were rows of squat brick buildings with long loading bays. She walked a few more blocks before pulling Heikal around a corner, ducking into the shadow of a warehouse as she took him by the shoulder.

"Why don't we get you home?" she asked. "Where do you live?"

He nodded slowly, his eyes still wide, but he said nothing.

"What is it?" she asked.

"Won't he find me again?" Heikal asked, looking back towards the station.

"No, I don't think so," she said, rubbing his shoulder. "I'm so sorry, Heikal. He just mistook you for somebody else. Once we get you home, he'll forget all about you. If you see him again, just stay out of sight, alright?"

The boy nodded again, his face still tense, but he finally told her he lived in Artridge Gardens. That was across the city from, straight down Laeryia Boulevard... It was deathly quiet between the warehouses, but it was sure to be more crowded by the beach. The festival crowds could hide them, but they would also be risking the palace guards. The trolleys ran for free on festival days, maybe they could slip through that way?

But first they'd have to get the collar off Heikal. She looked over her shoulder before turning him around. It took her a full minute to find the hidden clasp on the collar and another minute before it opened with a click. She never would have gotten hers off on her own… She quietly set it down before taking Heikal's hand and hurrying down the street. They'd figure out the trolley when they got there; for now, they just needed to keep moving.

The click of her boots felt deafening on the cobble stones, every noise bouncing off the warehouses in the dark. She looked over her shoulder every few seconds, but eventually, they followed the slope until she could smell the salt in the air from the docks, her heart leaping as she heard the familiar chime of the trolley bell.

They jogged down the last block to Laeryia Boulevard, the darkness giving way to hundreds of street lamps that beat back the night. Although, it was hard to know whether to be glad to leave the darkness behind or scared to lose its protection… The blaze of the pyre still lit the sky by the beach, and even by the docks, there were dozens of people milling about.

They marched up to the trolley station, watching the trolley approach, its electric lights giving off a dull yellow glow. As she watched it, though, she noticed a dark shadow by the conductor. The only people permitted to stand by the conductors were…the police. She gasped, yanking Heikal back into the shadow of the nearest building.

Heikal clutched her hand tightly, his nails digging into her palm. She stood in the shadow breathing hard, her mind racing. Were the police watching for them on the trolleys or was it just for the festival? They couldn't just stay in the warehouse district forever… They needed something else, a carriage, anything. They just had to get out of there and hope they hadn't already been seen.

She pulled on Heikal's hand and got them back to the edge of the street, staying out of the light of the street lamps. She looked down at him.

"We're going to cross the street," she said. "We have to be quick, but don't run, okay? Just act natural, like I'm your mother."

He nodded, and they crossed the street, her back tall and her shoulders straight like someone with nothing to hide. They stepped off the curb and cut straight across. Finally, the trolley caught up with them, and she eyed it from the corner of her eye. She walked with Heikal on her left, hopefully hiding him from view.

"Look straight ahead," she whispered out of the side of her mouth. The trolley lingered for a moment at the station, but after a few people hopped on, it continued along its route. She breathed a sigh of relief, squeezing Heikal's hand.

"Well done," she said, "they didn't notice us."

They left the warehouse district behind, the crowds growing thicker. She didn't know where to look, turning her neck in all directions. After a few more blocks, they finally found a carriage. The driver was sitting on the box in front, likely waiting for the festival to end. The rear of the carriage was covered, perfect for hiding them.

"We're going to take a carriage," she said, hurrying to the end of the block. She reached for her purse and froze. She didn't have her purse! The guards must have pulled it off her. She closed her eyes, pinching the bridge of her nose. She could ask the key to change into a coin, but how would she get him back?

Suddenly, an idea struck. A very foolish idea, but if there was a time to take risks, it was now. She took Heikal, dragging him towards the closest alley.

"Aren't we getting in the carriage?" he asked, looking back at it longingly.

"We will," she said, "I just have to do something first." She pulled him behind a nearby dumpster. "Just close your eyes until I say so, and no questions when you open them."

If anyone would see her it would have to be Heikal. They couldn't risk walking all the way across town, and for her plan to work, they couldn't look as different as they did. She closed her eyes and pictured Nela, the same smiling face she'd first transformed into. She reached out for that strange stillness she had found in the alley when the police were chasing her. She was free, for now, anyway, and that cursed collar was off her neck. And most importantly, Heikal needed her.

"Essomuai," she whispered, "if you're there, please help us now."

She focused on her memory with Nela, but she imagined Heikal there too, all three of them together in the garden of the cottage. It was a memory and it wasn't. She pictured herself merging with Nela, the two of them becoming one to get this little boy home. She felt a lightness enter her heart, but there weren't bubbles, and no explosive pop. There was just a glow, a shift in the air, and suddenly, she had transformed. She looked down, finding Heikal a little taller, the hand that held his leathery and wrinkled.

"Come now," she whispered, "quickly, and like I said, no questions."

He opened his eyes and looked up, drawing in a sharp breath.

"Are you?" he started to ask.

"No questions!" she said, but smiled at him warmly and winked. "Hurry now, and let me do the talking."

She walked up to the carriage. She couldn't see his face, but the driver

198

had a top hat and a thick beard. She cleared her throat as she approached to get his attention.

"Evening, ma'am," the driver said, turning towards them and tipping his hat.

"Hello," Sumi said, smiling with her most charming, toothy grandmother smile. "Would you mind doing us a favor since it's a holiday?"

"Well," the man said, laughing, "hard to deny a request like that — it's bad luck. I'll certainly do what I can!"

She rubbed Heikal's head fondly.

"This is my grandson. His mother's taken ill, and he ran all the way to my house to fetch me. I've no coin, I'm just an old pensioned widow…but perhaps you wouldn't mind taking us to Artridge Gardens? His father will certainly pay you what you're owed when we arrive."

The cabby turned on his box to face them. He looked her up and down, eyeing them both carefully. No-one in Berill liked dealing with strangers, but cabbies least of all. If anyone could sniff out a ruse, it was a night driver. She held her breath and returned his gaze, trying to maintain her sweet smile.

"Well," he said, his smile returning, "can't rightly have you walking the streets at night. Lots of fun at Alomidiar, but lots of rough characters, too. I'm happy to help."

He jumped off the driver's box and turned to open the carriage door for them. But as he grabbed the handle, he paused, meeting her eyes.

"Times are a bit tough," he whispered, "you're sure the boy's father can cover it?"

She felt the key in her pocket, another warm glow entering her mind.

"Yes, I promise," she said. "He's a good man with good work; I'm positive he can."

"Right then," the driver said, the easy smile lighting up his face again, "you and your boy hop in here, it's much warmer than up top. I'll have you to Artridge Gardens in a jiff."

Once they were safely in the cab, the horse clopping down the boulevard, Sumi leaned back, putting her arm around Heikal and tousling his hair.

"You did brilliantly," she whispered to him. He smiled, but kept glancing at her out of the side of his eye. Eventually, he couldn't contain his curiosity any longer.

"Is this why the police took you?" he asked.

She nodded.

"I'm sorry," she said again. "I didn't mean to get you mixed up in this.

Some people don't like my kind, but I promise I'm a good one."

"I agree," he said, smiling. "You're not scary like in the stories."

She chuckled. At least he didn't think she was a monster. She never would have forgiven herself if he had come to any harm, but all was well now. They were safe in the carriage and he was almost home.

"Just remember," she said, patting his head, "this is our secret, alright?" He nodded firmly, crossing his heart.

She leaned back and closed her eyes. As the adrenaline started to wear off, it took every ounce of strength she had not to fall asleep in the gently rocking coach. She forced her eyes open, worried she'd lose her form. Heikal had been looking out the window, but he turned back towards her.

"What do I tell my mother?" he asked.

"Just tell her you got lost after the festival." she said. "Trust me, she'll be happy you're home safe."

Heikal sighed.

"You don't know my mother. Still," he said, smiling again, "I guess it'll be worth the adventure."

As they passed the beach, she looked out her window to see what remained of the festival. The whale was completely gone, small trails of smoke lifting off the dais. The other bonfires were still raging, but people were starting to emerge from the beach to return home.

That might be the last Alomidiar she ever saw. She still didn't know where she'd go now that the detective had seen her face. Surely the police would realize their mistake with Heikal — hopefully, they'd just assume the evil Shapewalker had kidnapped the child…But it wasn't as if she could simply walk around the city after this. For the moment, though, she could only feel relief.

After riding for another half hour or so, they finally reached the outskirts of Artridge Gardens, the cab driver knocking on the roof. She climbed out slowly, not feeling Nela's age, but trying to act it anyway. After helping Heikal down, she bowed repeatedly in thanks, promising to send her son-in-law out with the money. Then, they left the driver on the side of the street, disappearing into the maze of apartments.

Artridge Gardens was dense but clean, the brick flats stretching up in every direction. There were almost no streetlights in the area, but Heikal seemed to know the way, and after a few minutes of seemingly endless turns, he pointed to his door. He turned to face her, rocking back and forth on the balls of his feet, staring at the cobblestones.

"Well, goodbye, Sumi," he finally said. He turned to go, but then ran back, burying his face in her skirts and giving her a tight hug. "Thank you for getting me home."

"Of course," she said, holding the back of his head, "I'm just sorry I got you into this mess. You look out for yourself, alright?"

He nodded into the fabric of her skirt, and she felt a small stream of tears wetting the folds of cloth. He turned and ran to the door, not letting her see him cry. She watched him duck into the building before leaving herself, wandering back down the narrow street. She felt her strength slipping, and ducked into an alley, the light flashing as she returned to her true form.

She slumped down against the wall, catching her breath for a moment. Finally, she mustered the strength to push herself back to her feet. Then she dug in her skirt pocket and took out the key, tossing it to the ground. As soon as it struck the cobblestones, there was a dull glow, the man was standing before her again in his suit and bowler hat.

He smiled at her, removing his hat and giving her a little bow.

"Thank you kindly," he said, "it was getting a bit stuffy in there."

"Sorry," she said, biting her lip, "longer than I thought."

"No trouble at all," he said, waving a gloved hand. "There's worse places to be on a cold night." He stretched, looking up at the crack of starlight showing through the top of the alley.

She stood there watching him, taking him in for the first time since their escape. He was wearing a fanciful tweed jacket and carried a cane with a gleaming brass top. It could be the transformation, but he seemed far too high class to be lurking around the jail. He ran a hand through his hair, and let out a sigh before putting his hat back on. He looked back down at her and smiled.

"Who are you?" she finally asked.

"Ah, sorry," he said, nodding. "I'm Erso, Erso Milak'erat. Time was a bit of the essence back there in the jail, no time for introductions and all that. He offered her a hand, which she hesitantly shook. "And you are?"

"Sumi Elerair," she said, suddenly all too aware of her shabby dress.

"Pleasure to meet you," he said. "You were great back there; I still can't believe we got out." He chuckled. "Though, I'm afraid if we don't pay your poor cabby soon, he'll come looking for you. Let's get him taken care of, then I can buy you a drink and we can talk."

He beckoned for her to follow and turned out of the alley. She followed him in a daze, listening to the click of his shoes on the cobblestones as he sped ahead. She wasn't sure how he knew the way since he had been in her pocket, but he wound his way back and forth until they were at the entrance again. He nodded his head towards the shadows and she slipped out of sight as he went over to talk to the carriage driver. Apparently satisfied, the cabby flicked his whip, heading back the way they'd come.

"Well, that's settled," Erso said as he came back around the corner. "Paid him double what he was owed and asked him to be quiet about it. Seemed to work well enough for him."

She nodded, giving him a nervous smile. She had been able to maintain a mask of strength when she had Heikal to worry about, but now she felt like a leaf being swept down a river, unsure whether to paddle or just be pulled along.

"Thank you for paying the cabby," she managed to say, "the detective took my purse and everything in it." Her eyes popped wide and she gasped, realizing what else was in the purse. "My key too! He'll be able to figure out where I live won't he?"

Erso squeezed her shoulder, the gesture surprisingly soothing.

"Don't worry about that yet. It'll take him longer than you think. Though, I reckon you'll want to clear out of town for a while. Why don't we save that for after a drink, eh? It's best not to think on an empty stomach, only breeds panic."

He motioned for her to follow and headed away from the beach. After a few twists and turns, they finally stopped at a bar. Light glowed from inside and it had a large painted sign out front with a mug of ale and a loaf of bread. Over the door the name read 'The Grainer'. Erso poked his head in and disappeared, returning after a moment to wave her in.

"Friend of mine is working tonight," he said, "he'll make sure we aren't bothered."

She looked up and down the street before nodding and following him inside, eager to be out of sight.

23

She already felt free. No matter what he said, no matter what she did next, she had changed. Something inside her had finally blossomed, a seed pushing towards the light. And in that moment of possibility, there was everything.

-Excerpt from The Borimol Plains

—:—

The inside of the pub was cozy and quiet. There was a long bar by the door, lined with casks, and rows of booths along the sides of the room, leading to a roaring fire. There were only a few people — a couple sitting alone on stools by the bartender and a few others in booths. As Sumi's eyes swept through the room, the bartender nodded at her. Erso led her to a booth in back, offering her the side facing away from the door.

He went back to the bar and returned with two mugs and a tray of pretzels. He settled into his side of the booth and took a drink, raising his eyebrows over the mug. She had a million questions floating in her mind, but just as she opened her mouth, her stomach rumbled loudly.

"What did I tell you?" he said. "Never think on an empty stomach."

How did he do that? He was so…soothing for a stranger. Ignoring the flush on her face, she grabbed one of the pretzels and took a bite, her eyes widening.

"These are incredible," she said between mouthfuls as she swallowed it down with what turned out to be spiced ale. She was speaking with her mouth full like a wild animal, but he was right about the empty stomach thing. Now that she was sitting by the fire with some food in her, she felt almost human again.

"I always heard the first meal out of prison was the best," he said with a wink, picking up a pretzel for himself. "It's the flour that makes them so good, pure Amoriai golden grain. My friend who owns this place,

203

he's from out east; we knew each other back in the day. When he moved here — for gods know what reason — he started shipping in the grain." He rolled his hand through the air in a circle as he took a sip of his ale. "Anyway, it's much better than the stuff you lot have here; climate's all wrong for wheat."

She took another sip of her ale. The spices were perfect, like Alomidiar in liquid form. She wasn't exactly used to drinking, but it did seem to calm her nerves.

"You're from Amoriai, then?" she asked.

"You could say that," he said, twirling his mustache and staring up at the ceiling, "though I don't really feel like I'm from anywhere now. More of a wanderer these days."

"My grandmother was from Anushai," she said. "Have you ever gone north in your travels?"

Erso popped another piece of pretzel in his mouth.

"Many times," he said, grinning, "pretzels there are about as bad as they are here, unfortunately. Much better way of life, though — not a problem to be a Shapewalker there. Was the woman you turned into your grandmother?"

"You could see that?" she asked.

"More or less," he said, shaking his hand. "I assume you know what it's like to be a thing instead of a person?"

"Ah, right," she said, thinking back to her time as a trolley token. "What about when I touched the key, how did you do that?"

"I was hoping you could sense those," he said with a smile. He took two more of the pretzels and lined them up next to each other. "We're all connected in a way, people like us. We tap into the same energy when we transform, and we can communicate just a bit through that energy." He reached for a salt and pepper shaker on the table, putting them on either end of the pretzel line. "Not sure if your grandmother ever told you anything about all this, but the Anushai call our power Essomuai."

She nodded. She didn't mention praying to the goddess, but if she had learned anything, it was that.

"Well, in Amoriai," he said, "we call it Mu'lalat. We think of it more like a hallway. We turn into different things more or less by walking down that hallway and going through the right door. I can signal you in the same way along those pathways. I've never got anything as clear as words through, but it's better than nothing."

She stared at the pretzels, nodding as the gears of her mind ground together. Mu'lalat and Essomuai. Learning about this magic felt like a house with hundreds of rooms, each door opening another layer of something she hadn't even begun to understand. Was the energy that traveled through Mu'lalat how he found her in the jail?

"Oh goodness!" she said, springing out of her seat. "I still haven't thanked you properly." She bowed three times in quick succession, as deeply as she could. He got out of his own seat, gently lowering her back into the booth.

"Really that isn't necessary," he said, smiling. "You being alive right now is a pretty good reward."

"Well, I still can't thank you enough," she said, holding his eyes so he knew how much she meant it. "I'm just a shopkeeper, but if there's anything I can do for you, please let me do it. It was a very brave thing you did."

"All in a day's work, I suppose," he said, taking a long sip of his ale and sighing.

"You do this often, then?" she asked. "You're like some kind of Shapewalking knight!"

A cloud seemed to come over him as he scoffed. He looked away, setting his jaw as he shook his head. But the moment passed, and he looked back at her with a softer expression.

"If only that were true," he said. "I'm no hero. The heroes I've known are mostly gone, cut down by people like Parimu. There's people that hunt us in almost every kingdom now. I do what I can, or try to anyway. I wander from place to place and see if any ripples appear. Basically, my job is trying to train new Shapewalkers before they get themselves killed."

"That's noble work," she said.

"Just a second," he said, finishing his ale as he stood to get another. He looked at her with a raised eyebrow to see if she wanted more, but she waved him off. A moment later he was back on his bench with a fresh mug.

"Anyway, there's really nothing noble about it," he said, picking up where they left off. "It's mostly that I don't like staying in one place too long. But at least I can get an animal out of a trap once in a while, you know? Keeping our kind alive is the only way to stick it to 'em, even if some of us are too hard headed to stay out of the noose."

He took another long drink.

"Honestly," he continued, "I can't let you get too carried away praising me. I've lost as much as I've won, and I know I can be a coward. I've cut and run plenty of times when things got too hot. I guess that's why I've survived this long. But you're something special, and for once, that meant me doing the right thing."

"There's nothing special about me," she said, cursing the ale for making her more flushed than usual, "I promise you."

"You really are something," he said, chuckling, "you don't even know enough about the world to know how special you are."

She cocked an eyebrow at him.

"Are you sure you didn't bust the wrong girl out of jail?"

"Believe me," he said, "I got the right cell. I mostly save burly pirate types who try to punch me."

He put his palms together, pointing his finger tips at her.

"Look," he said, "I've trained maybe a dozen or so of our kind. And believe me, I'm the last to judge, but to a tee, everyone I found was using their powers for something greedy. Sometimes it's just to survive or it's some kind of hustle, but not you. The first day I followed you, you know what you did? You helped a guy with one leg. It was the darnedest thing I'd ever seen. Shot off one hell of a ripple though — sensed you a mile away."

She shook her head; it had never occurred to her that he had witnessed all that. But she tried to set all that stuff about being special aside as a more pressing question came to mind.

"Those…ripples," she asked, "is that how you found me? Could you sense me through the… Mu'lalat?"

"That," he said, raising a finger, "is probably the most important part of our discussion." He took another pretzel and broke off a piece. He held it in his palm and showed her. "There's ways to hide it, but if you don't know any better, transforming sets off a massive flare to anyone who can touch Mu'lalat, especially new Shapewalkers like yourself." He took his piece of pretzel and dropped it into his ale with a splash. "Especially when you're relying on memories, it's like dropping a cannonball in a puddle."

She thought back to her training, nodding her head. Especially the first time she used a memory, there had always been that feeling of forcing her way through some barrier. She stared down into her ale, her throat tightening with shame.

"I thought I was being so careful," she said, "using alleys, moving around at night. But every time I transformed, I was bringing them straight to me."

"Don't blame yourself," he said, smiling sympathetically. "There's a lot to learn about these powers, and there isn't anywhere to learn it in a place like Berill. Trust me, don't start beating yourself up for what they do to us, or you'll never stop. Just because the detective wants you dead doesn't mean you deserve it."

She thought of that night in the alley, the detective's face coming around the corner, his cry as she escaped.

"If the detective wants our kind dead, how does he track us? How can he see those ripples?"

"I think our friend is not so different from us as he'd like to believe," Erso said with a smirk. "I suppose he probably doesn't know, or at least won't admit it to himself. I'm not positive how developed his powers are. For example, sitting across from you right now, I can tell what you are with no transformation. There's an energy to you, a kind of hum in the air. We call those keyholes. Still, I'd have to be close to you to tell. So in that regard, Parimu and I were in the same boat these last few weeks, both waiting for you to transform."

He sighed, squeezing his forehead.

"I'm just sorry I didn't come for you sooner." His hands that had been casually resting on the table made tight fists. "There was another Shapewalker I was trying to help, but I failed. I kept putting you off, thinking I could save him, but it almost meant losing you in the process."

"The hanging?" she asked in a quiet voice, suddenly feeling cold. He nodded solemnly. "I'm sorry about your friend," she said. "I was there that day; it was horrible."

"Thank you," he said. "I couldn't really call him a friend, though, just another lost soul."

They both fell silent for a moment, and Erso stared across the booth into nothing, his eyes glowing in the lamplight. She hadn't noticed before, but they were like gemstones, a deep brown splashed with flecks of gold.

He finally shook his head, smiling as the jovial mask returned to his face.

"Anyway," he said, "it doesn't matter now. We got you free. So tell me what else you were doing with your powers. I bet a good person like you helped a bunch of old ladies, too, eh?"

She laughed, waving her hands in front of her.

"I guess you got my number. But really, I'm not as great as you think. I didn't do much of anything. If you're looking for a saint, you should've met my grandmother. She could do anything for anyone."

He put up a hand, cutting her off.

"I've met enough kind people to know that most of them are humble, too. It's okay. I know it's strange to receive compliments, but you don't have to wriggle out of them. In this case, the bill fits."

She was about to protest again, but swallowed her rebuttal, nodding as her cheeks burned again. He took out his pocket watch and fiddled with it.

"This is a twisted world," he said, "and most of the kind people I've met… Well, they weren't given enough power to get the vultures off their back. But then I met you, and for the first time in my short, miserable life, I saw someone who had the power and the heart to do some good with it. And if I let you hang after I'd seen that…well, then I'd really be just as worthless as I feared."

"I don't think you're worthless," she said, smiling. She took a drink of her ale and sat for a while thinking, wanting to say so many things, but not knowing where to begin. She realized how good it felt just to sit with someone like her. It was alright if they were all scared and broken like she was. Maybe it was because he had saved her life, but it felt like she knew him already. And for the first time in her life, it gave her the courage to speak from the heart.

"I spent so long drifting through life," she said, "like a tiny boat. First in my grandmother's wake, and then on my own, back and forth on the same track every day, nothing ever changing. I saw all these wonderful people around me. And I wanted to help them, to be a part of their world, do even a fraction of what came naturally to my grandmother. But I knew there was nothing special about me, so how could I do any of those things? And finally I got this power, and I thought, 'Wow, here's my chance, I can finally do something for someone.'"

She took a breath and finished her ale before continuing, the words pouring out of her.

"And it didn't turn out how I thought; I was lonelier than ever. It made me so happy to help these people, it really did. But of course, I had to help them and disappear. I couldn't be a part of their lives, not with a secret like this. But only recently, I realized I was wrong. I am enough. I don't know how it relates with Mu'lalat, but I realized in Essomuai, we're all part of this…light. I think it's the light that shines when we transform, made up of every color in the world. And it showed me that my color mattered, too, and so does yours. We can't go through life so alone. The magic's not enough if we only shape ourselves; we have to shape each other too."

She finally stopped and looked at him, terrified he'd run away, scared off by her outburst. But he didn't. He scratched his chin, absorbing what she said. And then, he smiled.

"I like that," he said. "I've felt that way plenty of times myself, running from place to place, not knowing a soul. Most of the people I've ever had in my life were snatched away by chance, or worse. Most of the time, it makes me feel safer, because at least if I'm on the move, I'm free. It quiets that voice in my head, needling me to run, to move on before I lose more than I already have."

He chuckled, a sad sound. The type of laugh you make when you don't know what else to do.

"But what am I free for?" he asked. "It feels good to save a hapless kid once in a while, but it never lasts. It changes nothing. We're still hunted and hated, and worst of all, we're alone. Sometimes…life feels like this giant bonfire. We burn as bright as we can, and when our light runs out, our job is done. I've found a lot of peace in that, but sometimes I think, I'm only one small twig. How brightly can I burn on my own, you know?"

He nodded, looking into her eyes.

"You're someone who'd be special even without these powers. And you made me realize if I could save you, maybe I'd deserve to stop being so alone. And if I died trying, well, at least I'd have burned a little brighter."

She nodded. She couldn't have possibly said it better herself. They had to burn together to make their fire brighter. They sat in silence, staring at there drinks, but it wasn't awkward, and she didn't feel her usual need to fill it.

Finally, Erso drained his ale and pulled out his watch, looking at the time.

"We'd better get moving," he said. "But first, I'd like to make you an offer. It's time for me to leave. It's gotten a bit too hot in this city, and the detective has seen both our faces. Why don't you come with me? I can train you. We'll start from the beginning, and in a month or two, I'm sure you'll be better than most. We can even see Anushai if you want — maybe you've still got a relative or two there. Once you're ready, the world is your oyster. You can come back here, move on, whatever you like. But for now, I say we see what we can make with two lights in this dark world."

He stopped, catching his breath, his eyes glued to hers.

"What do you say?" he asked. "Want to come with me?"

In the blink of an eye, a thousand images flashed in her mind: the cottage where she'd lived her entire life, the view from their garden overlooking the bay, Amis scratching at the door. She thought of all the places she knew better than herself: the flower shop, the beach, the trolley, all the little things that made up a place and a life. She thought of Mrs. Perrino and the women's circle, and the families she had shared flowers with only days before. This was her home, and there was so much she still wanted to do here. It felt like she had just discovered the secret of Essomuai, and she still wanted to live it out...

But everything had changed, too. Of course, she couldn't stay. She wouldn't only be risking herself, but everyone who knew her. But she didn't have to just run away either. This was a chance for her to harness her powers, to use them safely. She swore it to herself — she *would* return. She had come too far, and learned too much. These people deserved her color and her love. But if she could train... Maybe she could be a part of that community again as her whole self, Shapewalker and all.

She took a deep breath and let it out, looking back at Erso. His eyes were searching, wide and hopeful. She finally nodded, smiling.

"Yes," she said, "I'd love to."

Erso smiled, standing from the booth. He grabbed the mugs in one hand and reached out with the other to help her up. The journey stretching before her seemed long and hard, but it was a start. She took his hand and stood, stepping out of the booth and into the rest of her life.

THE END OF BOOK ONE